THE
13ᴛ𝔥
BLACK
CANDLE

BOB GOODWIN

The 13th Black Candle

© Bob Goodwin 2015

2nd Edition - 2022

ISBN (Paperback) - 978-0-6456850-0-8
Cover design by Spiffing Covers

www.spiffingcovers.com

Bob Goodwin AUSTRALIA

In memory of

William Henry Goodwin (Harry)
13/10/1914 – 01/06/2015

A creative artist
A distinguished gentleman
And my Dad

Chapter 1

Tuesday - June 3rd 1986

11.55 p.m.

Simon Stacey looked beyond his car headlights and into the darkness as he drove along the quiet country road. Being one kilometre from his home, he could normally spot the location by the external night-lights; but tonight, there was just blackness. One minute later he turned onto his property and headed down the driveway.

'Shit!' He braked sharply to avoid hitting a metal jerry can. The car skidded a metre or so on some loose gravel before coming to a halt. After a quick scan of the area, Simon got out and retrieved the can. He shook it. It was empty. 'Huh, weird. Who's been in my shed?' He shrugged his shoulders and placed the can off to the side of the driveway before continuing towards the house.

'Alison, the bloody security lights. They need to stay on!' he muttered.

As the headlights of the Mercedes illuminated the rear of the house, a man, wearing only a pair of shorts, darted across in front of the car.

'What the fuck?!'

The man stopped in his tracks, turned, and raised a pistol. But then, as if suddenly changing his mind, he lowered the weapon and ran.

Simon instinctively put his foot on the accelerator. With the car almost upon him, the man had little choice; either scale the high pool fence to his left or become one with the driveway. He tossed the gun over the fence, then with outstretched hands, grabbed the top rail and swung his legs high. The vault itself was a medal winner; the landing, however, was a disgrace. He plunged chest-first into the grassed area surrounding the swimming pool. Simon slammed on the brakes. Before his winded adversary regained his feet, Simon was out of the car, through the pool gate, and had the pistol in hand.

'Who the hell are you? And what in God's name are you doing on my property?' Simon was trembling. He held the weapon uneasily with both hands, but its general aim towards the stranger's head kept him from running off a second time. Clutching at his chest, the man slowly straightened himself up.

'Mr Stacey, it seems you have me in an awkward position. You don't really want to use that gun, do you? It would be very foolish.' He took two steps backward off the grass and onto the tiles that encircled the pool.

'Don't move! I may not be a good shot, but from this distance I'll do you some serious damage. That's a promise. How do you know my name? Who are you? If you've harmed my family, I swear I'll kill you!'

'I can assure you, Mr Stacey. No harm has come to your family.' The man slowly lifted his arms from his chest and displayed two open hands, as if to reinforce his sincerity. 'My name is Romoli.'

'Keep talking and keep living.'

'Your wife signed a contract a long time ago. You might say I have come to see that she honours the agreement.' Romoli glanced at his watch.

'What's the hurry, dickhead? You're not going anywhere until I'm good and ready!' Simon's voice became louder and impatient. 'I don't like this. I'm not hearing what I want to hear. You got any ID? Empty your pockets. Now!'

'Don't panic,' Romoli replied softly, while turning his two pockets inside out. A handkerchief, a few silver coins, and some newspaper clippings fell to the ground.

'That's it?'

'Hey, I travel light. Sorry.'

'Move to the side.' Romoli took a couple of steps sideways. Simon knelt and picked up the pieces of newspaper, at the same time keeping a close eye on his captive. He held them toward his car headlights and scanned the headlines.

MAN DISEMBOWELLED BY DRUGGED YOUTHS

WOMAN SLAIN IN RITUAL KILLING

LIVE HUMAN SACRIFICES BY BIZARRE CULT

COURT TOLD: CHILDREN TARGETED BY SATANISTS

WITCHCRAFT SECRET SOCIETIES WIDESPREAD.

Among some jottings in pencil at the top of each clipping was a date, clearly written in red biro. None were more than two years old. Down the side of one piece of paper was a short list of what appeared to be phone numbers.

Simon had seen enough. He now had a very good idea what this oddball was on about. As he shoved the pieces of paper into his pocket, his expression changed. His eyes narrowed, his teeth clenched, and his head moved slowly from side to side.

'She made a commitment,' said Romoli very matter-of-factly. 'I needed the articles to help remind her of our continuing work. She signed her name in front of many people. She signed it in blood.'

'You bastard! You deadshit, deviant bastard! She's finished with all that Satanist crap. I helped her over it. That's ancient history.'

'Ancient history? No. Continuing history? Yes,' nodded Romoli. 'And our future will therefore be assured. And just to put the record straight, we are not Satanists.'

'An arsehole by any other name would still smell like shit,' retorted Simon.

'We are the Order of the 13th Black Candle.'

'Yeah, as I just said.'

Romoli glanced at his watch once more. He smiled and extended his arms to the sky. 'Dear Lord, Prince of Darkness and Ruler of the Universe, accept this offering from your loyal servants.'

'Shut up!' Simon glanced nervously back at the house. It remained shrouded in darkness. Everything was still. Romoli continued his prayer.

'Hail Satan, accept our souls. Hail Satan, accept our gift.'

'I'm warning you! If you've harmed my family I swear I'll blow your fucking brains out!' Stacey straightened his arms to steady his quivering aim. 'I'll shoot! I swear I'll shoot!' His finger tightened on the trigger. There was a tremendous flash of light, followed almost instantly by a thunderous explosion. Simon felt his body being pushed forward by the force of the blast. The gun discharged. Romoli flew backwards into the pool. Stacey fell forward onto the tile work.

The man's body was face up in the water, slightly below the surface. Golds, yellows, and reds flashed over the pool from the explosion. Romoli's eyes and mouth were wide open. Bobbing up a few centimetres, his face protruded from the rippled pool surface, then slowly sank. A stream of small bubbles ran from his mouth. An enveloping cloud of redness, emanating from the back of his head, closed over him, and he disappeared.

Chapter 2

The First Interview

It came as some surprise to Simon that he was permitted to freely leave the Alderley Police Complex after an exhausting three hours of interviews with numerous police officers and detectives. He had endeavoured to be as cooperative as possible, without disclosing more than was absolutely necessary. The investigators were very sympathetic to the loss of his family, allowing him several opportunities to take a break and compose himself. They wanted to know all the details of where he was and who he was with when his Samford Valley home burnt to the ground. They focused at length on anyone who may have had reason enough to commit such a dreadful act. Simon gave them a few names of individuals he had crossed swords with over the last few years, knowing full well that they were all dead ends.

While they did take his fingerprints *for the record*, and to assist in eliminating him from their line of enquires, it did seem strange that nothing had been said about a body in the pool or a weapon being found at the scene. And there was no reference to the empty jerry can he'd left lying on the ground.

Detective Marshall had provided him with some general details about the arson. An accelerant had been used; probably petrol. They were still investigating how ignition had taken place. The fire was virtually an instantaneous explosion throughout many rooms of the house. Any occupants had no chance of survival. Two bodies had been found, an adult and a child, and were awaiting formal identification.

Simon walked slowly to his parked Mercedes-Benz W126. He stood near the driver's door, staring out across the busy South Pine Road but not seeing anything. There was a lot to think through. And the numbness he was feeling was not helping. He stood motionless for a full two minutes before opening the car door.

'You okay there, Mr Stacey?' came a call from behind him. He turned. It was Detective Marshall. Marshall was a tall, slender man with a weathered complexion. He had seemed compassionate, thoughtful, and knowledgeable. *For a cop*, Simon thought he was not too bad.

'Yeah. I'm okay. Just needing a few deep breaths before I go.'

'You sure you're okay to drive? I can get one of the boys to drive you if you wish.'

'Very kind, but I can manage. Thanks.' Simon raised his hand and nodded. The detective replied likewise.

Sitting in the car, he managed to decide on three things. Right now, he needed to see his best friend, Adrian Devlin. He needed rest, and tomorrow he needed to go back to his property to see the damage, take a look around, and convince himself that the nightmare was real.

Chapter 3

Narangba

Simon completely missed the highway turnoff to Adrian's Narangba flat and had to double back at the next exit. He briefly told himself off, then forgave himself the error as he drove the extra ten kilometres before pulling up in Main Street outside a block of six brick veneer flats.

The area was on the outskirts of Brisbane, about forty kilometres from the middle of town. As a place to live, Simon didn't mind it; it still had some rural appeal and some good-sized acreage properties. At the same time, it was handy to the station and a few shops. But the best thing about Narangba was that this was where his lifetime friend Adrian lived, and for the time being, this was also the place he would be calling home.

There was one parking space for each flat underneath the building. Number two was vacant, but Simon decided to park on the street anyway; it seemed the courteous thing to do. He slipped on his jacket when he felt the cool air against his skin. Looking down at himself, he would normally have felt a little embarrassed at his untidy appearance, as his jacket, shirt, and pants were all creased and dirty. As he had told Detective Marshall, he'd had an argument and a bit of a fight last night at a poker game with his friends. Teddy Duncan had a bit too much to drink and didn't like losing, but liked it even less when Simon went to leave. That's when the fight started. But right now, he needed to lie down. Sleep deprivation was taking its toll. Later, when Adrian turned up they could talk, share a drink or two, and try to get their heads around the whole bloody mess. Simon climbed the fourteen stairs, lifted a small plant pot, grabbed the key, and let himself in.

*   *   *

Five hours later, Simon Stacey woke himself up screaming. He breathed heavily for a few moments while he slowly regained orientation to his whereabouts. It was dark, but the room was partially illuminated by the street lights. He took a moment, sitting on the side of the bed, then plodded through to the bathroom. He flicked the light on and splashed copious amounts of water over his face.

He studied his dripping image in the mirror. Still wearing the same clothes. Still untidy.

'You look like a fucking hobo, Stacey. Get your shit together!' From his pocket, he removed the newspaper clippings he'd obtained from Romoli. He wandered to the kitchen area and placed them on the table under a bottle of Johnnie Walker. Back in the bathroom, he stripped off and took a long shower.

*   *   *

Simon didn't bother to dress; he wandered into the kitchen-dining area just wrapped in a towel. Adrian had not arrived home. This was not completely unexpected, as he had left the poker night earlier than everyone else with some hope of getting lucky with Angela. Maybe the passion and lust were still running rampant. The only way Adrian could know about Alison and Robbie was if he had heard about the Samford Valley fire and deaths on the news via radio or television, and if that was the case, he would definitely be here right now.

Simon moved the phone from the bench top to the table, poured a big glass of Johnnie Walker, and looked through the phone numbers scribbled down the side of one of the newspaper clippings. There were two that he knew immediately; his own, and the Bodytone Fitness Club. The other three were unfamiliar, so he rang them one at a time and hung up after each call. Strangely, one of the numbers was the Alderley Police Station. Another was Ward 21, the psychiatric ward at the hospital. The final one he called several times but it just went unanswered.

Chapter 4

The Bodytone Club

Apart from a handful of new recruits trying to hide in the back row, the room was alive with synchronised activity, and the third aerobics session of the morning was well underway. The four large black boxes were visibly vibrating with Peter Gabriel's "Big Time." Despite the hard work of the ceiling fans, all faces were beading sweat. Full wall mirrors at either end reflected a multi-coloured plethora of leotards, and enough footwear to bring a smile to the face of any Nike shareholder. A solitary performer shouted out commands from the slightly raised platform area.

'And one - and two - and three - and other - arm - and two - and three - and four'. The counting and staggered speech continued monotonously, never missing a beat. 'And - don't - forget - to breathe - and one - and two...'

Charles Madden, the fitness club manager, had been standing near the door watching the aerobics show for the last two songs. Deborah, wearing glistening sky-blue leotards, moved alongside him.

'Why is it necessary to remind people to breathe?' muttered Charlie. 'A perfectly normal automatic bodily function. I really wonder what happens to these people when they go to sleep at night. Perhaps they have a cassette playing under the pillow. Now breathe. In two three four and out two three four.'

'Charlie, it's important. It helps you keep rhythm, allows your body to work more efficiently, and stops you getting exhausted too quickly,' replied the slender brunette standing at his side.

'You've been an aerobics instructor too long, Deb. The brainwashing seems to be working.'

'Maybe you should try it, Charlie. What have you got to lose except that lower back problem and a couple of kilos?'

'The last thing I want to do is bust my backside learning how to count and breathe, and my weight is exactly right for my height.

Thanks all the same.' Charlie was amused with Deborah's attempt. It was not the first. Several of the regular staff had been trying for the past few months to convert him to their fitness religion.

'It would be good for you. You know, a healthier lifestyle and all that.'

'What are you suggesting? That I'm not healthy? Not fit?'

'I'd have to see you work out to know that for sure.'

'Well, that event seems most unlikely.'

'That's a shame,' she replied coyly.

'Hmm…I best be on my way. My morning rounds await.' He held his farewell glance a little longer than he normally would have for a polite good-bye. Deborah smiled.

Charlie Madden generally made two strolls a day through all areas of the prestigious club, greeting and chatting with members and staff, checking on any repairs, and looking for new ideas. The appointment of a part-time medical practitioner, a part-time physiotherapist, together with the development of the social club, were three such ideas that had proved most popular. These innovations were all financed by the wealthy club owner, Simon Stacey. Membership had increased fifty percent in the few short months since these developments had come to fruition. The social club, more affectionately known as Pluto's Den, boasted a games room, a quiet lounge, covered outside barbecue area, restaurant, and a small but well used night club. The two bars within allowed members to replace those kilojoules they had worked so hard at removing in the gym, pool, sauna, squash courts, and aerobics classes.

Chapter 5

The Ruins

It was a challenging start to the day after a little too much Johnnie Walker the previous evening, but Simon had somehow found his way, as planned, to his property. Now, here he was, surrounded by the charred remains of a once beautiful home.

He lowered his head, sighed heavily, and tried desperately to hold back another emotional outburst. The attempt caused a choking ache in the back of his throat and a stabbing pain over the bridge of his nose. He pushed his thumb and forefinger hard into the corner of each eye in an attempt to suppress the feeling. It may have been better to allow his grief, anger, and confusion to run full rein and discharge itself completely. However, this trauma would demand a long passage of time, and would not simply be satisfied by one massive catharsis. Besides, there were reasons why he needed some control. He couldn't get swallowed up by this; not yet.

Past and recent events weighed heavily on his mind. Things that he had long forgotten now welled up like an eerie fountain of muddled happenings. The sensation pushed back against his fingers. A knot at the base of his sternum grew tight. He wanted control, discipline, and reasoning; later the grief.

'Later, please later,' he pleaded, as he pressed harder with his fingers. He kicked a small piece of charcoal and forced himself to raise his head and survey the burnt-out shell that was once his home. His breathing was forced in short, controlled grunts. It seemed to help. To prevent a total meltdown, he tried to focus on his property and on the surrounding landscape of low rolling hills.

He looked across the Samford Valley. It was a cool and cloudless winter morning. A few houses could be seen in the distance, with any closer locals being well hidden behind native tress and gullies. It was a picture fit for an artist's brush and one that belied the tragedy that had occurred only 32 hours earlier.

Simon's home had been a stand-out in the local community, with five bedrooms, three bathrooms, a study, sunken lounge with adjoining bar and entertainment area, and of course, his pride and joy, the library. It was only twenty kilometres from Brisbane City, where he had spent the previous five years. But from a lifestyle point of view it had seemed so much further. Now, after his dream's destruction, he failed to comprehend both his feelings and commitment towards its completion in the first place.

Simon stepped gingerly through the soggy black mush and angled himself carefully under some flimsy charcoal framework that somehow had remained standing. The recliner rocker was in an upright position, with the mesh of exposed springs supported by the remains of the burnt wooden frame. Hundreds of books were spread amongst the rubble; some of the larger ones he recognised as long-standing favourites. All, however, both large and small, were damaged beyond any hope of repair.

For Simon, the library had occupied many of his recreational hours. He could picture the room. Two of the library walls had been exclusively devoted for exhibition of his family photographs. The old brown and white print he had painstakingly restored depicted the stern, bearded face of his grandfather, and was the first in the family tree series that staggered across one wall. The lower-most image was of his son, Robbie; a fine shot indeed, which captured the innocent, excited gleam in his eyes and that unforgettable cheeky smile which always preceded a high-pitched chuckle. The picture had sprung to life, and Simon could see his son toddling towards him. There was the smile, soon followed by the chuckle. Quickly the volume and intensity of the laughter gathered an unusual, disturbing dimension. Louder and louder it became. Something was wrong. The chuckle had altered. It was no longer a chuckle. His son was now screaming. The flames gathered behind the child as if in anticipation. They sprang forward and enveloped him. In a flash, Robbie was gone.

Simon opened his eyes, then closed them as tightly as he possibly could, moisture oozed between his lashes. The tortured image of his son wanted to return, but he somehow found the strength to suppress it.

Crouched and nestled amongst burnt, water-soaked books and broken glass, Simon shook his head slowly and ventured another look. He attempted to identify some of his possessions. Why he even wanted to, he was not sure. It was something to do, and having something to do seemed to help, if only for a few seconds at a time. To his left, he noticed a large pile of burnt paper. The top pieces disintegrated as he pushed at them with his fountain pen. He carefully slid the pen into the middle of the stack and tipped it to one side. A small, undamaged section of a photograph revealed itself. It showed the face of Alison. She was wearing a blue, floppy towelling hat. Simon recognised the picture instantly. She had just thrown some manure his way after he had surprised her with the camera as she tended the roses. Tears welled in his eyes, and two drops fell in quick succession onto a charred piece of wood and disappeared like water into a sponge. Another terrifying image was forming in his mind.

'Hey, Stacey!' came a commanding shout. Simon welcomed it at first. 'I told you not to disturb anything.' It was the policeman guarding the scene of the tragedy. The two had argued only minutes earlier, with Simon finally being permitted a few minutes to look through the ruins. Forensic investigators had spent all day yesterday examining the scene and taking evidence. The area was still surrounded with blue and white police crime scene tape.

'Just a small bit of a photo. No harm done.'

'If you touch anything else you'll have to leave. Looking only! Is that clear? The forensic guys will be back here later. They will kick my arse.'

'Okay, okay. I get the message, all right!' snapped Simon, catching himself by surprise with his sudden change into irritability.

He stood and meandered through the rubble, coming to another halt in the remains of the lounge. He moved slowly toward the fireplace. With images of Alison dancing through his mind, he cupped his face in his hands. A warm stream of tears now flowed uncontrollably down his cheeks. Simon was wearing a grey, pin-striped suit which he had intentionally left at Adrian's flat. It was possibly not the best thing to wear given the state of the area in which he now stood, but there was little other choice, with pretty much everything else having gone up in smoke. He sat down on the cracked brick surround of the fireplace. Simon always prided himself on his appearance, no matter what the occasion. It was his trademark, a sign of confidence and success.

He tried to focus his vision and attention on a winding trail of ants that had carefully plotted a dry course through the black sludge. In ant terms this must have been like Hiroshima, thought Simon, yet here they are organised and already going about their business of cleaning up and starting afresh. Lucky ants.

Startled by the sound of a car pulling up sharply on some loose pebbles in the circular driveway, Simon quickly rose to his feet and reached for his handkerchief. He wiped his face, not realising that his right hand was partly covered with the black ash that coated the brickwork where he had been sitting.

'Mr Stacey!' a voice shouted, as a car door opened. Simon hesitated. The voice was very familiar, and one he knew he should recognise immediately, but the name somehow eluded him.

'Yes, I'm in here,' his voice wavered. 'Just a moment.' Looking down at his red silk tie, he cursed as he noticed that, not only was it wet from his tears, it also bore a large, sooty smudge.

'Shit. Shit. Shit,' Simon muttered as he removed the tie and stuffed it in his hip pocket. Proceeding through what used to be a set of sliding glass doors, his eyes met those of Inspector John Cochran. How could he not have recognised that husky sergeant major voice? 'Yes, Inspector. I'm guessing you have some more questions for me?'

'I'm sorry, Mr Stacey, maybe just a couple. And if you could remove yourself from the crime scene it would be greatly appreciated.' The inspector glanced over at the policeman on guard duty and shook his head. Simon took a few careful steps forward and lifted the tape over his head. 'Thank you. Look, I know this must be difficult for you,' continued the inspector. 'But it would be a great help to our investigations if we could have a chat.'

Simon was surprised by Cochran's manner. He had addressed him as *mister* and used the word *sorry* in the same sentence. The fat man's sensitivity was verging on the impressive.

'What's puzzling you, Inspector? You're unusually restrained and oddly polite this morning.' Stacey was demanding self-control. He and Cochran had some history and they did not get on. *Seize the moment*, he told himself. Such directive self-talk seemed foreign; his responses normally flowed freely. His brain was struggling for sharp, cutting responses. 'Hey, I know, you old devil,' continued Simon. 'I'll bet you got lucky last night. And I'm guessing it must have been with your elocution teacher? Good score.' It was a slightly provocative remark, but wasn't terribly impressive. Simon knew he could have done better, but given the present circumstances it was the best he could muster. Still, it would irritate the crap out of lard arse, and once again it was something to be doing, and provided a brief respite from the torment.

The policeman had clenched his fists. He pressed his lips and teeth tightly together, then made a concerted effort to relax them before responding.

'Stacey, now I accept that you're very upset, but we both want answers, don't we? I know you've already been very helpful and that you've spent several hours at the station, but there are a few things that have come to light that quite honestly leave me a little perplexed.' There was a firmer tone in his voice, but the air of concern and the attempt at empathy still prevailed.

Simon stood in front of Cochran, trying hard to look into the fat man's eyes. Direct eye contact had served him well in his dealings with difficult acquaintances in the past. With Cochran, it was different. His podgy face made it seem you were staring at his eyelids rather than his eyes. Simon pondered for a moment on the close resemblance to a walrus; just a few long whiskers under that flattened nose, and SeaWorld would be signing him up.

'Dropped the *mister* already, have we? Shame. It wasn't really you though, was it?' The man was a hopeless case, thought Stacey, couldn't even hold a pretence together for five minutes. 'So, you'd like to know what's going on.' Simon paused. That knot in his gut tightened. His temples pulsed in pain. Any sense of control was plummeting headlong into the ground. 'Well let me tell you, Inspector. This is my house, my new house. This is my life's achievement. You know what I really created here, don't you? I created an elaborate coffin. A crematorium. Notice how I've cleverly installed open skylights throughout the building and developed a wonderful, charred, rustic appearance, so authentic you can even smell it. Quite novel, don't you think? I must say though; the carpets are a bitter disappointment. Scotch-guarded to the max, and the damned water has got into them like a fucking sponge. And what about —'

'Stacey!' bellowed the six-foot policeman. 'Shut up!'

'Please, please let me continue, Inspector. My family. Alison, my wife, and my son, Robbie; my little boy; only a little boy, Inspector; nearly two. Nearly two years old...' Simon's speech faltered and stopped. The tight knot spread quickly to his stomach and like a wave into his throat. His mouth watered uncontrollably. He dropped to his knees, vomited at Cochran's feet, then sobbed loudly for what seemed like an eternity for both men. Reaching into his pocket, he removed what he thought was his handkerchief and began loudly blowing his nose into his red tie.

'Fuck, look at me. What a mess. If you ever run out of hankies, Cochran, let me know. I'll lend you a silk tie.' Stacey continued wiping his face regardless. He thought for a moment of wiping the regurgitated specks from Cochran's shoes, but then changed his mind.

Simon slowly forced himself into an upright position and exchanged his tie for his handkerchief.

'Sorry, Inspector,' he said, wiping his face roughly and spreading more soot across his nose. His own words caught him by surprise. Now both men had used that word. He forgave himself the indiscretion.

'You have no need to apologise, Stacey,' replied Cochran. 'We do need to talk again, and you need to clean yourself up. Be at the Alderley Police Station by 1.00 p.m.' Not waiting for a response, he pushed his bulky frame through the open car door and dropped heavily onto the seat. The suspension groaned as if to complain at the insult of the one hundred and thirty kilograms. The engine sparked into a throaty rhythm and jerked as the gear stick found its notch. 'Be there, Stacey!' he said firmly. 'And don't tamper with anything around here.'

The white Ford Falcon XF sedan looped around the driveway and was quickly out of view. Simon thought about the gun and the jerry can, both covered with his fingerprints. If they had found either, Cochran would have just taken him in immediately. It seemed that someone had done him a favour. But who? And why?

He looked to the side of his private roadway, at the large rectangular plot of carefully turned soil. Several rather bare-looking sticks protruded from the earth. Alison had a passion for roses. She had spent much of last weekend tending her garden. Many other plots had been planned, and she had meticulously marked them all with sticks, string, and coloured ribbon. To the right of the garden was the oval-shaped swimming pool and spa, both covered in a fine, black-and-grey speckled film. Simon stared at the coated water, imagining it to be a thick, oily quagmire. A place where you would slowly descend into the murky depths and be captured and tortured for eternity. A soft, cool breeze reached his cheeks. A chill penetrated his spine and goose pimples spread from his neck to his limbs. On the pool, a slow wave ran under the carpet of mire.

The garden beyond the swimming enclosure was a picture, with two pergolas and some strategically placed garden furniture. A cobblestone path wound its way through the thick grass carpet, finishing at a large, aluminium garden shed that was carefully tucked away behind a cluster of native trees and shrubs. The goose pimples were receding. Robbie had been so fascinated with the garden, spending so much time running, playing, and rolling on the cool grass. Hide and seek had taken on a whole new dimension since moving from the city. The goose bumps were gone.

With the stale smell of wet charcoal lingering in his nostrils, Simon hung his head, turned, and slowly made his way along the driveway to the entrance where the solitary policeman stood on guard.

Chapter 6

Second Interview

After thirty minutes of driving he arrived back at Adrian's Narangba flat. Simon pondered for a moment on how he had arrived at his trusty friend's dwelling in what only seemed to be a matter of minutes. He thought back and had no memory of passing the Samford Valley Dairy, had completely missed the deserted sawmill at Eaton's Crossing, and surprisingly had not the slightest recollection of even turning onto the highway.

Back inside the flat there was still no sign of Adrian. Simon placed a call to his Bodytone Club. He spoke to Wendy, the receptionist, and enquired about Angela, one of the personal trainers.

'She has called in quite ill, Simon. She said she would be away for a few days,' recalled Wendy.

'Can you give me her phone number please?' Simon wrote down the number as she spoke. 'Thanks for that, Wendy. Now I need to ask you, have you heard about the fire and the deaths out at Samford?'

'I heard about that on the news. They didn't give out any names. I hope it wasn't anybody you knew.'

'Are you sitting down?' Simon proceeded to give her the details. He asked her to inform Charlie Madden, and to also let him know that he would be dropping around in the late afternoon.

At the kitchen table, he picked up the newspaper clipping with the list of phone numbers. He checked them off against Angela's number that Wendy had just given him. There it was, on the list, third from the top.

'Fuck me!' He dialled the number and waited. It rang out. 'Shit, Adrian. What the hell is going on? I need you.'

The two men had shared so much and had always been there for one another when the chips were down. The bond they had formed from school days was still as strong as ever. Simon could recall numerous occasions when he and Adrian had teamed up to do battle against some of the school's hardheads and overlords. They had certainly copped some hidings, especially in the beginning, but their track record of memorable victories had improved markedly when they realised their strength lay with their guile and cunning rather than their modest physical attributes.

Simon glanced at his watch: 11.45 a.m. He sat motionless for a few seconds then checked his watch again, having already forgotten the time. He went to pour himself a drink but changed his mind.

'Move your arse, Stacey. Inspector Cochran awaits,' he muttered to himself as he moved to the bathroom. After noticing his charcoal-smeared appearance in the mirror, he was pleased to feel the steady stream of soothing, warm water running over his face. The old, thinning towel was only sufficient to render him half-dry. On entering the bedroom, a further dilemma — no clothes. His legacy from the fire was one suit now in need of dry cleaning, and yesterday's dirty clothes. He threw the towel to the floor and marched to the second bedroom. Simon rummaged through Adrian's drawers and removed a creased and faded pair of blue denim jeans. Turning to the plastic laundry basket, precariously balanced on a chair near the end of the bed, Simon delved amongst the assortment of items. After rejecting two T-shirts he lifted a pink floral blouse.

'Angela? Huh, the plot thickens.' The sleeve of a white shirt caught his eye, he pulled it free. Well, it was almost white, and it did have most of its buttons. It would have to do. Simon spent a few minutes searching for an iron. This proved fruitless, and just served to cause irritation.

'Jesus, Stacey, get your shit together.' His legs had slipped into the denim before he realised he wasn't wearing underwear. He continued cursing himself and shook his head in disbelief of his faltering style. Taking a little extra care with the zipper he was soon dressed, out of the flat, and on his way to see Cochran.

He briefly surveyed the block of flats and the few nearby houses before turning the ignition. While Narangba itself was a nice enough place, Simon wasn't particularly impressed with the edge of suburbia; to him it was a sign of a steady deterioration in living conditions right through to the noisy metropolis. His rural living desires developed as a child on an avocado farm with his parents until the age of six. A succession of extraordinary weather conditions had led to multiple crop failures and the family moved to town. The city had its purposes, but over the years, incentives such as wealth, success, and beautiful women had been strong enough to override his preference for country living.

Soon enough he was back at the Alderley Police Complex. He entered the front parking area and took the only vacant spot in the *Reserved Police Only* space alongside Cochran's vehicle. The building was large, with various police activities being distributed throughout many offices over the two-storey structure. Simon entered the reception area of the ground floor.

The first thing noticeable on entering was an offensive odour of stale, sweaty feet. He looked around to locate the source of the smell. The desk sergeant was typing away awkwardly with two fingers at a computer keyboard behind the counter, refusing in any way to acknowledge Simon's presence. Simon continued his surveillance. He spotted the problem. In the far corner, a pair of joggers sat propped up on a low wooden stool in front of a bar heater.

A large dot matrix printer kicked into action then stopped. The sergeant walked slowly to the other side of the room, grabbed a new roll of printer paper, then returned and fed it into the machine. He jabbed with annoyance at a few buttons. The machine came back to life. Simon had decided he would neither say a word nor rap his knuckles on the bench. He placed his hand over his nose and waited. The game continued for some time until the sergeant spoke.

'You know anything about computers?' he snapped.

'Just enough to get me into trouble.'

'Huh, what's the good of ya? Down the hall, second on the left. He's expecting you. And you're late.'

With some relief Simon proceeded down the corridor. Behind him came the sound of spray from a pressure can. He smiled, brushed at a couple of creases in his shirt with his hand, and then knocked three times on the door.

'It's open. Come in.'

'Good morning again, Inspector,' said Simon, trying to sound relaxed.

'It's afternoon, and secondly, you're thirty-three minutes late ...' Cochran paused as he looked up. 'And where did you get those clothes? It's just not you, Stacey.'

'They're not mine, they belong to a friend who is helping me out.' Simon looked about the room. 'I must say, this office is pretty ordinary. A bit of a step down from your inner-city room with a view.'

It was in that Brisbane City office where the two men had met three years earlier. Stacey's apartment had been ransacked. Nothing was missing, but the place was a mess. Glassware and bottles smashed, books and documents ripped, and blood smeared over windows and mirrors. A heated argument had erupted after Simon repeatedly insisted he couldn't help with any enquires. Their second encounter was more recent; Stacey's car, another Mercedes, had been stolen. Investigations failed to discover any trace of the vehicle. In both cases, no one was apprehended.

'This office is just fine, Stacey. Can I offer you a cup of tea or coffee?'

'You are really trying hard, aren't you? It's good to see a man who recognises his own shortcomings and tries to change them,' said Stacey. Cochran forced a grin but said nothing. 'Do you have any freshly squeezed orange juice?'

'No.'

'That is a shame. I'll have nothing then.'

'As you wish. Now, we have some rather disturbing results of our preliminary enquiries. Please sit down.' Simon carefully slid out a rickety wooden chair and sat down. The inspector shuffled a few sheets of paper as if collecting his thoughts.

'The fire was, of course, deliberately lit, and this is a homicide investigation. Traces of several incendiary devices have been found at the scene. I believe Detective Marshall gave you some details. For what it's worth, Stacey, suffering for anyone inside would have been minimal.'

Simon was silent. How do other people know that suffering was minimal; that they all died instantly; that there was no pain? How can those who are alive tell others what dying is like? Maybe seconds seem like hours and suffering is unbearable. Maybe you have to feel the fire singeing the cilia from the depths of your lungs. Maybe you have to watch your own flesh burning and falling from your bones.

'There's more, I'm afraid. A third body was found late yesterday morning. A man aged probably thirty-five to forty. One point eight metres tall, that's about five foot eleven. Weight estimated at eighty kilos. He was discovered in your back yard behind the garden shed. He had a single gunshot wound to the head and he was naked. Any ideas on this guy?'

Simon's brow was now resting on the edge of the desk. His hands grasped the laminated surface on either side of his head, as if to prevent his falling to the floor.

'Stacey, if you're going to throw up again can you use the basin in preference to my shoes?'

'That sounds more like the John Cochran we all know and love,' mumbled Simon. 'I'm not going to do an encore. But I might just decide to die right here. There's another body? Jesus!'

'What about this bloke behind the shed then? Do you know who he might have been?' said Cochran.

'I think it might have been the milkman.'

'Shit, Stacey, it's time for some straight answers. This is not just another break and enter like at your damned flat. It's murder. It's now triple murder! This guy was shot in the head and guess what? His tongue had been cut out of his head. So, don't fuck me around here!' The inspector was overheating. The two men's complexions were at stark contrast. Stacey pale and ready to pass out, and Cochran on the verge of exploding.

'It was an apartment or a home unit, not a flat. And I honestly have no idea who that bloke is, or was. His tongue cut out? What sort of deal is that? Some mafia thing? Fuck me.'

'Was there anyone else besides your wife and son staying at the property?'

'No. There was no one else there when I left the house at seven o'clock on Tuesday night. I don't know anyone who hates me enough to do such a thing. Why didn't they get out of the house? There must have been noises. They should have heard something. They should have got out. There were so many exits. Windows, doors. They should have got out!' Simon found his speech was racing as he tried to keep pace with his thoughts.

'I believe the arsonist planned it so that no one would escape with their life. We are still waiting on final results of the autopsies, but despite the state of the bodies, we have confirmation that one was your wife and another was most likely your son — according to weight, age, height, etcetera. As for the other body, we have no leads.'

'I really want to help. Don't you think I want to nail the murdering sons of bitches?' Simon's voice faltered as a solitary tear ran down his cheek.

'There are a couple of questions I must ask that I know you're not going to like.'

'Okay, Inspector, go on then, don't be shy.'

'You told the detective yesterday that you were with that Duncan fellow, playing cards, at the time of the fire.'

'Yes, I was,' replied Simon cautiously.

'I'll need his full name and address to confirm that.'

'You think I had something to do with this! Are you crazy? This is totally absurd.'

'At this stage I don't know what to think. I have to check out all the angles. Isn't it true that you stand to collect five million dollars from your wife's life insurance policy?'

'That policy is nearly three years old. It covered both our lives. I don't need the money, anyway.'

'Isn't it true that you altered the policy six months ago and doubled the payout?'

'You arsehole, Cochran! That's enough. Are you charging me?'

'No, I'm not. But if you hinder investigations, I'll ...'

'Well thank you very much and good-bye.' Simon promptly stood up and made for the door.

'That name and address, Stacey!'

'Twenty-One Kingsview Terrace! Teddy Duncan!' shouted Stacey. He wrenched the door open, hesitated briefly, then looked back at the inspector. 'Those fat cells have infiltrated your brain, Cochran. Your synapses have been replaced by cellulite.' He slammed the door and left.

After taking few deep breaths, Cochran sifted through his paperwork, examining the reverse side of each page. He flipped over the second-last sheet and found what he was searching for. There it was; *Edward Duncan - 21 Kingsview Tce. - Deceased — time of death estimated at 0400 hrs. on Wednesday 4th June — (approx. 4 hours after Stacey's house fire).*

Chapter 7

Familiar Friends

Upon completion of the afternoon rounds, Charlie Madden entered the foyer and reception area. His office was located behind the reception desk where Deborah stood chatting with Wendy, the receptionist, and two other fitness enthusiasts. Charlie smiled.

'Hey, Charlie,' she said brightly. 'Excuse me for a moment guys,' she said to her companions before stepping across in front of Charlie Madden.

'Hey there, Deb. Always nice to see you. What's up?'

'How are you?' She placed her hands on his shoulders. 'That news about Simon. I know you were probably closer to him and Alison than most people here.'

'It has shaken me up. I do worry for Simon more than anything. He's a strong guy but this…' he paused and swallowed, 'I don't know how someone could ever recover. It's just too hard.' Charlie dropped his head, stepped away from Deb, and turned away. The small group had all stopped chatting and watched with Deborah as Charlie scurried into his office with his head lowered.

'I'm just going to see if he's okay,' mouthed Deb softly to her friends. They all nodded. She followed him into the office and closed the door.

Charlie was sitting with his elbows on the desk, resting his head in his hands. As Deborah entered he immediately grabbed a pen and paper.

'You know, Deb, I've got a couple of great ideas. I have been thinking about the night club area. It's a bit too small, but if we open the side wall towards the barbecue we can double the floor space as well as… as well as allow easier access to…' Deborah squatted down next to him and grabbed him in her arms and squeezed.

'You are a good man, Charlie Madden.' She kissed him on the cheek.

'Sorry,' he squeaked.

'You have nothing to be sorry about.' She turned his head to face her. 'Showing you have feelings is a good thing.' Deb kissed him on the mouth. Lightly at first, then more passionately as he responded.

'Wow,' said Charlie when they finally broke. Their faces were still close.

'I think we should sleep together,' said Deborah.

'Really!'

'Oh, do you think that's a bad idea?'

'Oh, yes… I mean no. I mean of course. Yes, yes. It's probably the best idea I've ever heard in my life.'

'I have been told you can cook.'

'I do okay. You should come over for dinner.'

'Yes, I should.'

A sharp rap on the door disturbed the conversation.

'Hey, Charlie, you got a minute?' Came a loud voice through the door.

"It's Simon!' declared Deb.

Charlie blotted his face with a tissue and settled himself back at the desk. Deborah took only a moment to turn the door handle slightly to release the lock and sit opposite Madden.

'The door's open. Come on in,' said Charlie. He took some deep breaths and began drawing on a blank sheet of paper. As the door opened, Deb took the initiative.

'That sounds like a good idea, Charlie. How do you think it will work out cost wise?'

'Ah! Simon. It's good to see you.' Charlie stood and moved to the side of the desk. Deborah gave Simon a consoling hug and a kiss on the cheek. Apart from his serious expression, Stacey looked a million dollars. He'd felt compelled to do some shopping after seeing Cochran, and had notched up a bill for five grand to restock some of his wardrobe. He was very smartly attired in a white wool sports coat, navy blue tie, and blue pin-striped business shirt.

'We're all so sorry to hear about Alison and Robbie,' said Deb. 'It's horrible. How are you managing? Is there anything we can do?'

Simon returned the kiss, shook hands with Charlie, then dropped into the soft single recliner lounge to the side of the doorway.

'Thanks, Deb. I'm just managing to cope and that's all. If you don't mind I'm trying to focus on the practicalities for the time being — to keep me from losing my mind. But it's comforting to know I have such good friends.'

'If there's anything we can do, you know we are always here for you,' said Charlie. 'You have no need to worry yourself about this end of things. Everything is just fine. Business is booming.'

'I know I can rely on you both, as I can on everyone here. I just thought I'd better put you all in the picture before you read it in the papers tomorrow morning.' Simon paused and swallowed heavily before continuing. Deborah sat down.

'It's been confirmed that the fire was deliberately lit. So, you see, it's murder. My family has been murdered. And so was someone else; an unidentified man's body was found as well. Now, I believe that whoever orchestrated this tragedy has some master plan. I have no idea at this stage what that might be or who is involved, but it does mean that you all need to be a little careful.' Stacey was concentrating on his words, trying to keep his emotions under control. He looked up at his two friends. Deborah and Charlie were stunned.

'What the hell are the police doing about it?' asked Charlie after an extended silence. He began a slow pace around the office.

'They don't tell me much. They just ask lots of questions. Apparently, they have very few leads at the moment.'

'Why do we need to be careful here? Is there some sort of threat?'

'No. There is no threat, Charlie. It's just me being careful. When someone targets your family, and blows up your house, it makes sense to take a little extra care. Wouldn't you agree?

'Sure. Of course.'

'You need to tell everyone to keep their eyes open. If they see anything unusual or anyone... Charlie, can you sit down please?' Simon was both surprised and a little irritated by Madden's behaviour.

'Sorry, just thinking, that's all. I think better when I'm walking.' He returned to his desk chair.

'Now let's get this clear; I don't want anyone else getting hurt. I don't think anything is going to happen here at the club, but I'm not prepared to take any chances. I've hired a security guard. His name is Oscar Schliemann. He's a big German guy who knows his business. You can expect him tomorrow morning. As far as security matters are concerned he is to have full control. He will be doing a little quiet research for me as well, so tell him anything he wants to know. No secrets whatsoever.'

Deborah sat quietly. Her dark-brown eyes glistened as the first tear ran down the side of her nose. While she found the whole scenario very upsetting, it was the soulless act of Robbie's fiery murder that cut the deepest.

'And what if we see something then?' asked Charlie, fidgeting with his pen.

'Tell Schliemann, he'll know what to do. That's what he's getting paid for. And one more thing; let's not start a panic here. Use those staff management skills of yours, Charlie. I'm counting on you. We don't want to scare off our members, do we? It's business as usual.'

'Okay, sure. I'll chat with the others this afternoon. Where will you be in case I need to contact you?'

'I'm staying at Adrian Devlin's place. I think you already have his details.'

'Yes, I do.'

Simon stood and moved over to Deborah.

'Are you okay, Deb? I'm sorry about all this, but we'll have it sorted out within a couple of weeks.'

'I'll be just fine, thanks, Simon. You take care now. It's nice having you around.' Deborah blotted the tears from her cheeks.

'Right then! I'll be in touch. Sorry I have to rush, but as you might appreciate there are a few matters I still need to attend to. Are there any other questions?'

'Probably lots, but I'm lost for words at the moment,' replied Charlie.

'Well, you know where to reach me. Leave a message on the answering machine if you need to.'

Stacey reached across the desk. Madden stood, and the two men shook hands firmly.

'Thanks, my friend,' added Simon. Charlie nodded and escorted Simon to the main entrance. On returning to the office he found Deborah still sitting quietly, but looking much more composed. He squatted beside her chair.

'You okay?'

'Yeah,' she sniffed. 'I'll be fine. What sort of a world is it, Charlie, when a family can't be safe in their own home?'

'You hear about this sort of thing, read it in the papers, then, suddenly it's all so real, and so very close. It's frightening. Makes you realise how vulnerable we all are. I don't mind telling you, Deb, it makes me a little nervous.'

They both pondered quietly for a moment. Charlie felt a hint of guilt for not being able to devote his thoughts completely to Simon's cruel ordeal.

'Deb, about before?'

'Oh, that. It's nothing. I'm fine, really. Just got a little upset with all that talk. It's so sad.'

'No, no, I don't mean that. I mean before that.'

'Oh, that! I guess I was a little forward, wasn't I!'

'I'm not complaining.' She laughed lightly at his remark. It helped dry up her tears.

'I've been trying to get your attention for a while. I wasn't just sitting on your lap at the night club the other night for the benefit of the photographer.'

'I guess I've been a bit preoccupied,' said Charlie, with a slight flush in his cheeks. 'Sorry.' Deb put her finger over his lips.

'No more sorrys. Just dinner. At your place.'

'What about this evening?' Charlie wasted no time with his response.

'I'd love to, but I've promised to babysit three kids for friends. Worse still, I'll be going to spend a couple of days with my parents. They live out of town and I'm driving up there tomorrow after work. I haven't seen them for ages. Mum's been a bit unwell. But I'm free on Monday evening.'

'Monday, eh! Seems an awfully long time away. I'll just check my diary.' Charlie grabbed the book off the desk and opened it. 'Yes, it looks like I have some room in my schedule.'

'Best pencil me in then.'

Chapter 8

The Briefing

The idle chatter quickly subsided as Cochran marched through the open door to the debriefing room and took up his position in front of the large whiteboard. He threw some notes and photographs on the table. The four men took up their pens and notebooks.

'Close the door, Johnson!' barked Cochran. The young woman was already standing in anticipation of the predictable instruction that drew a brief glance and smile from her four male colleagues.

'I'm assuming that you've all read, and committed to memory, the reports already on file in this case.' Cochran took hold of a fistful of papers. He raised a few clipped sheets in the air.

'The autopsy reports on the fire victims.' He dropped his arm, slapping the papers onto the desk, repeating the procedure with each document.

'Autopsy report on one Edward Duncan; forensic investigation of house-fire — incomplete; ballistics report on bullet fired at unknown male, together with his autopsy; some brief notes of mine on Simon Stacey, as yet — most incomplete! Any of you not familiar with any aspect of these reports will be, before you leave this room this afternoon. Now, I'm looking for some inspiration. Come on, Johnson, inspire me.'

'Sir, it seems that Stacey had a lot to gain financially from the fire. He has no alibi since Duncan is dead. I wonder at the possibility of the unknown male being his wife's lover.' Cathy Johnson tried to sound firm and confident while pressing her pen heavily into her notebook. It was only her second week with the Criminal Investigation Branch, although it seemed much longer. Cochran hadn't given her a moment's peace.

'Shit, Johnson, I said I was looking for inspiration, not desperation! His alibi may yet be sound. What about neighbours? Telephone calls? What about passers-by? What about other people at

Duncan's place that night? Someone else may well be able to place him at Duncan's house at the time of the fire and the shooting. So, don't tell me he's got no alibi, at least not yet. It seems you're assuming that whoever lit the fire killed our John Doe and removed his tongue. Don't assume anything, Johnson. Don't even assume you'll be a real cop one day!'

Cochran's harsh approach to Cathy Johnson was deliberate. He used the same manner with any new detective. It was his make 'em or break 'em style, and everybody knew it, even Johnson. Despite her knowledge of the fearless fat leader, it did little to lessen the impact of his blunt and often rude remarks. She hung her head for a moment and muttered under her breath.

'Lard arse, son of a bitch.'

'Something else to say, Johnson? Please share it with us all!' roared Cochran. He spread his arms wide to the group, beckoning, almost daring the young constable to repeat herself. Cathy stood. She could feel her heart pounding in her mouth. It was obvious to everyone that she was deeply embarrassed. She had come to the CIB with a reputation of being confident, determined, and resourceful. When she started in the branch, Cochran had read those very words back to her from her file and then laughed in her face. She was convinced that she had qualified for special attention purely on the grounds of her gender. He had beaten her back at every turn, making her look like a bumbling fool. Now here she was again in a no-win situation. Perhaps it would be that her desired police career as a detective would be nothing more than a pipe dream, but the least she could do was salvage some of her dignity. She brought herself to attention and looked straight at Cochran.

'I called you a lard arse son of a bitch, sir!' She placed her pen and notebook in the breast pocket of her navy-blue jacket, turned, and made for the exit.

'You leave this room and you'll be sitting behind a desk for the rest of your working life. Now sit back down. After all, that's the most thoughtful remark you've uttered in two weeks.' Cochran paused momentarily. Cathy Johnson removed her hand from the doorknob and returned to her seat in disbelief.

'Now, Briggs. Can you inspire me?' The inspector continued as if nothing had happened. Detective Noel Briggs was caught a little by surprise. He um'ed and ah'ed momentarily before collecting his thoughts.

'Sir, we need to gather more information about Stacey, and about Duncan. If Stacey wasn't at the fire, and if he wasn't at Duncan's at the time of Duncan's death, then where was he between the hours of midnight and four in the morning? What about possible enemies of the Stacey family? It seems more than coincidence that Duncan died on the same night and —'

'Hang on, Briggs, hang on. What's this coincidence crap? Duncan was murdered. Don't you read reports? Sure, he died of alcohol poisoning, but he also had bruising to his lips and gums. And he had traces of scotch in his lungs. If he had been drinking from that bottle all night there would have been more than two sets of his prints on it, now wouldn't there?'

'Yes, sir. I hadn't yet read the full report, sir,' said Briggs.

'What have you been doing for the last two hours, Briggs, playing pocket billiards?' It was obvious the inspector was becoming irritated. His characteristic colouring was a sign that the raging bull, always lying just below the surface, was about to charge forth.

'Sorry, sir, I had a dental appointment,' replied Briggs, with little concern for his own welfare.

'Ah yes. A dental appointment. I see.' Cochran spoke softly at first. He twisted his fist hard into the palm of his other hand. 'We're gathered here for our first official briefing into a multiple homicide investigation while you're reclining in a pneumatic chair, no doubt chatting up the dental nurse! I hope he drilled out all the crap between your ears and replaced it with something useful. With a head like yours, anaesthetic wouldn't have been necessary, would it, Briggs?' The raging bull had emerged.

'It was not my regular dentist, sir. His name is Mr Morgan. Howard Morg —'

'Shut up, Briggs, otherwise you'll need to make a return visit!' bellowed Cochran.

'Begging your pardon, sir, but Howard Morgan is a friend of Stacey's. He was playing cards with Stacey and Duncan last Tuesday night. On the night of the fire.' Briggs sat back in his chair and brushed his nose with his hand. The room fell quiet.

'Are you trying to make me look like an arsehole, Briggs?' Cochran glared about the room. Only Cathy Johnson, now well primed with confidence and delighted to be a witness to a rare turn of events, made eye contact. 'Well it seems from the expressions around this room that you've succeeded. As usual, Briggs, you're treading a fine line. It would be beneficial to your health and your future with CIB to exercise a little more caution in your approach. And if you or anyone else distracts us from our prime objective by stupid horseplay they'll be out on their ear with my boot so far up their arse that they'll need a shoehorn to clear their throat.' The inspector stretched his fingers, interlocked them and cracked all his knuckles. The bull had been caged, at least for the moment. 'Go on, tell us your dental story, and make it interesting.'

'Morgan says that Adrian Devlin left early for some hot date. Everyone else apart from Stacey left at eleven. They had been playing poker, and Stacey had cleaned everyone out except Duncan. They had all been drinking beer, Duncan more than the rest. He was well-known for his drinking habits, hence his nickname — Drunken Duncan.' The senior constable flicked over to the next page in his notebook and cheerfully continued. 'Morgan claims Duncan had verbally abused Stacey several times because he kept winning, but this was nothing unusual. There was a single phone call that night. It was for Stacey, at ten o'clock. Morgan has no idea who from or what it was about.'

'And what about Stacey's state of mind before and after the call?'

'Calm and relaxed the whole time, as always.'

'Briggs, maybe you can tell me why they were playing cards on a Tuesday night?'

'Yes, I can, sir,' said the detective, with a smile. 'It was Howard Morgan's fortieth birthday. There was to be a small celebration, but as was often the case when these guys get together, someone brought out the cards.'

'Hmm. Anything else?'

'Just one thing, sir. Will the department cover my dental bill?'

'Don't push your luck, detective. And seeing as you've started the ball rolling, you can pay a visit to Stacey's fitness club and talk to some more of his friends there. Let's be clear, Briggs. Everything is to be by the book. And by the way, use your head to think, and not any other part of your anatomy. Am I being heard?

'Yes, sir. By the book, sir,' nodded Briggs.

'Dempsey and Hogan, you'll both be —'

There was a sharp rap on the door. The desk sergeant immediately entered, delivered a piece of typed paper to Cochran, and left without saying a word.

'Thank you, Sergeant,' said Cochran slowly, after the door had already shut. He paced slowly back and forth across the wooden floor, head down, reading the double-spaced type.

'An update from forensics on the incendiary devices used,' said Cochran. 'It seems that there were at least six light bulb incendiaries. Marshall, you've been in the bomb squad. Tell us all about these devices.'

'Yes, sir,' replied the detective sitting in the back row. 'Usually a high wattage light bulb is used. A small hole is drilled in the metal base and a volatile flammable liquid is introduced via a syringe or eyedropper. The light bulb is then placed in a suitable socket. The liquid sits in the bulb until the light is turned on, and a fiery explosion usually follows. The main problems with this type of device are, firstly, it is quite time consuming to prepare, and secondly, the perpetrator needs access to the targeted premises to install the light bulb.'

'Thank you, Marshall.'

'Just one thing, sir,' asked Johnson. 'Why install so many? Why not target one or two key switches?'

'A fair point, constable. A timer switch was set in the main fuse box.' Cochran tapped the piece of paper with his index finger. 'Switch the power off. Install the bulbs. Turn all appropriate light switches to the on position. Pour flammable fluid over the floor and furnishings. Place the timing device in the fuse box. Power comes on and bingo, all bulbs explode, house burns down in minutes. No one gets out. And I'm sure that's why there were so many explosive bulbs used. No one was going to escape, and the house, with any evidence it may contain, would be totally destroyed.'

'Ingeniously deadly,' added Marshall. 'Sounds professional. Six simultaneous explosions. Six balls of instant fire; burning glass razors flying in all directions; spot fires throughout the house, but only for a second. Then the soaked floor and furniture erupts. The air explodes, and the interior of the house becomes a furnace. You would think that Stacey's wife would be disturbed if someone was changing six light bulbs and lacing the place with petrol, unless —' Marshall hesitated as he collected his thoughts. 'Unless it was someone she knew. Someone who had ready access to the house. Someone like…her husband. Why would she get out of bed at midnight to check up on her own husband?'

'Or her lover?' said Cathy Johnson excitedly, thinking back to her earlier remarks, and deciding they were worth some consideration after all.

'It is also possible that she couldn't wake up,' added Cochran. 'While forensics have excluded all common type drugs, they may yet come up with something. At this stage, however, Simon Stacey knows more than he is revealing. He needs to come forth with some answers pretty smartly. Now, as I was about to say before, Dempsey and Hogan, you two are going to tail Stacey, starting tonight. He will not fart without one of you knowing about it. Briggs, you can extend your enquiries to friends, family, neighbours, and contacts of Edward Duncan. Marshall, you're going to do some research on Stacey. Parents, schooling, employment, the lot. I want his life history, and I especially want to know about his wife. I want to know how he made his fortune, and who he stepped on to get there. I'll be interviewing Stacey again. Johnson, you'll be coming with me for the time being. All tasks are effective immediately.'

Cochran turned, removed some transparent tape from his pocket, and began securing several gruesome photographs to the whiteboard. The first two showed two bodies burned beyond recognition. One of a child with arms outstretched as if beckoning for help at that last desperate moment. The other of a woman was barely recognisable. All that could be made out was the rough shape of a head and a torso. A large cracked charcoal beam lay across where her legs once were. The next two pictures were of the unknown naked man, whose body was pale, with mottled blue patches over all areas. The entry site of the bullet in his forehead was a small, perfectly round hole. The exit point, shown in the next photo, showed the true extent of the damage — a large, pulpy red cavity the size of a golf ball. Cochran tore off another piece of tape and placed the fourth victim beneath the rest. Edward Duncan's body was also pale, with obvious swelling and bruising to the lips. His cheeks, chin, and chest were decorated with a greenish-yellow sludge; the half-digested remains of the evening's meal.

Cochran gestured to the whiteboard with his meaty fist.

'This gives you some idea of the animals we're dealing with. We've already got four murders, so take care. Whoever did this will kill again without a second thought. So, no heroics. Call for backup. Everyone will keep Desk Sergeant Carter informed of their whereabouts at all times. If there are no further questions, let's get amongst it.' The stern-faced inspector waited a few moments. The room was in silence.

Chapter 9

Surveillance

'What makes you think Stacey will be at Devlin's flat, sir?' asked Cathy. Her words broke the prolonged silence. Both had been deep in thought since driving away from the police station. Cathy was spending equal time thinking about both Cochran's attitude problem and the investigation.

'You know, Johnson, I was really looking forward to my wife's roast and Yorkshire pudding tonight. I haven't eaten since lunch. Lashings of rich, brown gravy. More than enough for the main meal so you can mop up the remainder with a few slices of bread and butter. Beautiful. Then the lemon delicious, with ice cream and caramel sauce,' said Cochran, licking his lips.

'Caramel sauce with lemon delicious? Sounds sickly, sir.' Cathy looked the inspector up and down. *No wonder you're such a fat turd*, she thought.

'It's the gravy and the sauce that make the meal, Johnson, and I don't know if Stacey will be home or not. I'm presuming that someone will be there. If not Stacey, then Devlin. If neither, we wait. There's no need to look at me like that, either. You should watch the road when I'm driving. Good food not only feeds the body, Johnson, it feeds the brain. And I think you're undernourished.'

Cathy Johnson's gaze was still fixed on Cochran. It was the second time today he'd left her feeling dumbfounded. The rude remark, while somewhat irritating, was par for the course, but the baffling thing was that not only did he have an acute sense of hearing, but he seemed to have ESP as well.

Big John continued to drive at his usual leisurely speed. A few minutes later they turned into Main Street and pulled up behind Stacey's vehicle as the sun disappeared behind the distant D'Aguilar Range.

'Guess the man's home, Johnson. Let's go and have a chat, eh?'

Cathy felt unsure of herself. While she'd had some partial involvement in a couple of other homicide investigations, there had been nothing of this magnitude. This would be the first case she hoped to see through from beginning to end.

As Cochran alighted, the soft vinyl seat sucked in air, as if breathing a sigh of relief.

'Move it, Johnson. You didn't just come for the drive, or the pleasure of my company, as enjoyable as I know that must be.'

'Yes, sir,' replied Cathy promptly. The inspector's words jolted her into action. Quickly out of the car, she glanced to her coat pocket and nervously reached for her notebook. In her haste to appear enthusiastic, she overlooked the cement curbing. Her feet failed to maintain momentum with her body, and she fell face first on the damp, grassy footpath. Her first reaction was to look up to see if Cochran had noticed. He was walking towards the flats. From her position, an image of the back end of Jabba the Hutt flicked into her mind. She shook her head, found her footing, and scrambled to her feet, then set off in pursuit of her leader. She felt like an embarrassed young schoolgirl tagging along behind the headmaster.

Cochran slapped on the door with an open hand. After a few seconds the fluorescent tube above the door flickered into life. The thin white curtains behind a glass panel in the middle of the door shifted slightly to one side, sufficiently enough for the inspector to make out Stacey's profile.

Simon slid the newly installed bolt to open, then uncoupled the chain lock, and finally opened the door.

'Good evening, Inspector. I wondered when you'd be paying me a visit. Care for a game of cards?' Stacey couldn't help himself. Cochran's presence just seemed to bring out the worst of his sarcastic predisposition. 'Do come in.' Simon caught sight of Cathy Johnson. She was standing on the steps, a few paces behind Cochran. 'Oh, I see you've brought your girlfriend. It promises to be a good night for everyone then, doesn't it?'

'Heaven forbid!' said Johnson automatically. Bright-pink colouring immediately warmed her face. She could feel her ears almost glowing. The inspector's head turned slowly to look at her. He pursed his lips and breathed heavily through his nostrils, but said nothing.

'Sorry, sir,' said Cathy. She felt she should say more, but decided one foot at a time was probably enough.

'Come on in,' said Simon. 'Make yourself at home. Have a seat.' The two entered the lounge and sat on the red vinyl divan. 'Anyone for coffee? Or perhaps you'd like something stronger?'

'Nice of you to offer, Stacey. No thanks,' Cochran replied politely. 'I'd like to get to the point straight away. To be quite frank, you're in serious shit.'

'Really? Tell me something I don't know.'

'Where were you between midnight Tuesday and 4.00 a.m. Wednesday morning?'

'I was at Duncan's place. We had a card night on. I thought you knew that already. Tell me, Inspector, was Teddy murdered?'

'What makes you think that?'

'It was reported in the paper that he died from alcohol poisoning. It stated there was an empty bottle of scotch next to his body. Teddy was never a big scotch drinker. Maybe once or twice a year. Was he murdered? He was a friend of mine. I think I deserve an answer.'

'Yes, he was, and not a pretty sight, either. And whoever did it was either very clever or very stupid. Anyone with half a brain could have worked out he was murdered. It's all very mysterious, and we know that everyone except you left at eleven. When did you leave?'

'About two I think. I'm not really sure.'

'What if I told you that your friend Teddy died at one thirty?'

'Then I left at one,' replied Simon promptly.

'Jesus, Stacey! I'll have you on a charge if you don't give some straight answers!' shouted Cochran, as he jumped to his feet. Cathy Johnson sat in quiet amazement at Stacey's defiant arrogance.

'Look, I don't know what time I left.' Simon was up from his chair and pacing back and forth. 'I'd had a few drinks. But I do know that Teddy Duncan was very much alive when I did. Dead people don't throw rocks at your car when you drive away.'

'Go on.'

'We had an argument. The other boys had just left. We sat and had a couple of beers, then Teddy spent some time showing his photographs. It was his hobby, and mine, so I was quite interested. He had some rather nice shots, too. When I suggested I should go home, Ted said he'd like a few more hands of poker. I wasn't keen, but Teddy was getting a little irritable, which was a little unusual. He was usually a pleasant drunk. Anyway, I decided to go along with him. It was silly of me, I suppose, because he was in no frame of mind to win, and losing would only make him worse. I decided it would be easiest for both of us if I beat him convincingly and quickly.'

'Pretty damn sure of yourself, aren't you?'

'Always be sure of your opposition. Know them better than they know themselves.'

'Yeah, okay, poker genius. What happened next?'

'I cleaned him out in just a few more hands. Then off he goes to get even more money. I told him we have rules with friends — only a limited amount. It's all supposed to be friendly and fun. But he comes back with this wad of cash. I got up and walked out. That's when he crash tackled me in the driveway. So, I pretended I would play some more. I sat back at the table and when he went to get us both another drink I bolted. The last I see of him is in my rear-view mirror, shouting and throwing rocks at my car. And that's the story.'

'Hmmm, was there a phone call during the evening?' asked Cochran

'You've done your homework! Nice one. Yes, there was a call.'

'Well, what was it about? Who was it?'

'It was Charlie Madden, my club manager. He said he had a brain wave for enlarging the night club area at Bodytone. He's like that when he gets an idea in his head. Anytime of the day or night.'

'You don't have one of those new mobile phone gadgets, do you?'

'At around three grand each! That's a joke, right?' said Simon. 'No, I don't have the need for one. He called me on Teddy's home phone.'

'How did he know where you were?'

'Didn't ask him. He probably rang my place first. He's a resourceful character. Anyway, he would know all my regular contacts. Very thoughtful and persistent, that's why I like him. That's why I hired him.'

'He's probably a cunning bastard like you, no doubt,' said Cochran without sounding too objectionable. 'You never returned to Duncan's house later that morning?'

'No, I did not. I did not kill my friend, for Christ's sake!'

'Stacey, do you own a firearm?'

'I did own a single-barrel shotgun. You probably found it in the ashes of my house. You're barking up the wrong tree, Cochran.' Simon couldn't sit still. He found himself standing up and pacing nervously for the third time since the police had arrived. The bent metal framed dining chair rocked back and forth every time he stood. He remembered Charlie Madden once again, and how his behaviour had caused him irritation back at the club. Now he was doing the same. It felt strange. Disguising anxiety, even fear, had never been difficult before. Perhaps events were taking their toll. Pictures of the sinister swimming pool filled his mind. Being drawn in. No strength to fight or resist. A filthy pit of despair that would control him forever.

'Where is Adrian Devlin?' asked Cathy Johnson. Her soft voice was a pleasant change to the harshness of her colleague. Simon fixed his attention on her voice as he dragged himself back to the present. He locked his eyes onto the delightful policewoman.

'Inspector, it was rather remiss of you not to introduce me to your charming companion.'

'Simon Stacey, meet Constable Cathy Johnson. Now answer the bloody question, formalities are over.'

'Cathy, I don't know where Adrian is. He was at the poker night. He left early, and I haven't seen him since. I suspect he's out with a girl called Angela, getting his bones jumped.' Stacey maintained eye contact with Johnson and settled himself back into his rickety chair.

'Angela?'

'She's a part-time personal trainer at Bodytone. Angela Philpot.'

'Thank you, Mr Stacey,' continued Cathy most politely. 'I realise it may be difficult for you, but I do need to ask you some rather sensitive but very important questions about your wife.'

'Please go ahead, Cathy,' said Simon, trying to sound equally polite. John Cochran raised his eyebrows and rolled his eyes.

'Did you have any reason to suspect that she may have been having an affair?'

'Alison and I were very happy. I'm sure she wasn't seeing anyone else. I'm sure I would have known. I guess that's a typical response of most men about their wives, isn't it? But I'm positive it's a correct one. Do you have a husband, Cathy?' At the mention of Alison's name, that sickening knot in his chest returned. He needed to focus on something else to maintain control. The young policewoman seemed fair game.

'Was Alison expecting any visitors on the night she died?' The inquiry went unanswered. Simon thought for a moment that he could detect a slight quiver in her voice. He decided there would be two possible reasons for this. Either she was inexperienced in her work and a little tentative and apprehensive, or there was an interesting connection developing between the two of them. He opted for the latter. It certainly was the most preferable distraction and the easiest to work with. Somehow, though, it also seemed wrong, but he pursued it regardless.

'No. No visitors, Cathy. At least not when I left for Teddy's place. How is it for women in the force these days?'

'What about enemies, Mr Stacey? Johnson ignored his remark.

'Enemies? Sure, I've stepped on a few toes over the years,' admitted Simon. 'A few rough and tumble card games here and there, but nothing to deserve such retribution.' He focused back on the constable. 'I'm sure with your good looks and such wonderful charm you could handle most of the lads back there at the station.'

'One more thing, Mr Stacey. Can you tell me where you went to when you left Edward Duncan's house? I believe it was nearly five in the morning before you were sighted at the scene of the fire.'

'Feel free to call me Simon, Miss Johnson. It is Miss, isn't it?'

'Yes, it is Miss, Mr Stacey. And let's be quite clear. You have no chance of manipulating your way into either my head or my vagina. Now, do I need to repeat the question?' Cathy remained softly spoken, with an obvious forced smile.

'You have no need to repeat anything.' Simon immediately felt somewhat deflated and subdued. Yet another blunder. Another symptom of his inevitable slide towards personal incompetence. 'I didn't go anywhere in particular, just drove around. I had a few things to think over.' Stacey realised he had said the wrong thing. Johnson had thrown him off guard.

'What things?' asked Cochran. Simon stalled. He had no immediate reply. He sat and shrugged his shoulders. He was annoyed at his floundering behaviour. Screaming and shouting somehow seemed the appropriate thing to be doing. Totally out of character; but then so was everything else he seemed to be doing at present. Restraint was fortunately exercised and the outburst was internalised to a mental barrage of self-abuse.

'What things did you have to think over? I want an answer, damn it!'

'Nothing important. Nothing that concerns your investigations.' Simon was disappointed at his answer. There was no way Cochran was going to let it rest at that.

'I'll be the judge of that. Now what unimportant things kept you out driving half the night, instead of going home to your loving wife?' demanded Cochran.

'I have nothing further to say. I wish to speak to my lawyer, and I want you to leave now.' Despite his floundering efforts, Simon was clear on a couple of points. There was no way he was about to confess to shooting some guy in the head. And he was not about to give them any more reasons to think he was in some way responsible for the arson and death of his own family. Sooner or later they may well find the gun and the jerry can, and then his life would be over.

'Stacey, let's sort this out right now!' shouted the inspector. 'You got something to hide?'

'I have nothing further to say. I wish to speak to my lawyer, and I want you to leave now.'

'Did anyone see you out driving? Did you stop anywhere?' asked Cathy.

'I have nothing further to say. I wish —'

'C'mon, Johnson, it's the broken record routine. The shop's closed. Let's go.' Cochran walked to the front door. Cathy quickly followed suit. 'We'll be back, Stacey, tonight, with a warrant to turn this place inside out.' Cochran slammed the door closed. The vibration was too much for the outside light, which promptly extinguished itself.

Walking towards his car, Cochran glanced around the street. The vehicle he was looking for was parked in the shadows, on the opposite side of the road to his own.

'It's Dempsey and Hogan. About bloody time, too!' grunted Cochran. He crossed the quiet street, with Cathy Johnson hot on his heels. 'Where the hell have you two been? You should have been here before me!'

'We stopped off on the way to buy something to eat, sir,' explained Dempsey, while trying to swallow a mouthful of hot chips and sauce.

'Did you, Dempsey? Well I'm not impressed, not impressed at all. In fact, I'm bloody angry. Would you care to appease my anger, Dempsey?' asked Cochran, leaning through the open car window.

'Certainly, sir. If I can,' said Dempsey tentatively, rather unsure of what was to follow.

'Thank you very much, Detective,' said Cochran, taking hold of the packet of chips, which was still three-quarters full. 'Now, you two, I've told Stacey I'm coming back tonight with a search warrant. It just might be enough to provoke him into doing something stupid, so be alert.'

'Are you really getting a warrant, sir?' asked Dempsey.

'What do you think? Of course I am, you goose! That is, after I get something substantial to eat. Thanks again for the chips.' Cochran left the two men to their task and proceeded to his own vehicle. 'Back to the car, Johnson. Mind out for the curbing this time, won't you?'

*   *   *

Simon watched through the bedroom window as Cochran drove away. Overall, he considered the police had been rather slow in getting their act together. He lifted a recording device to his mouth and once more started pacing.

'Adrian, where the hell are you? If you're out screwing Angela I hope the wait was worth it. You need to be careful, her phone number has somehow ended up on a list of people I don't trust. I have to tell you that I'm in trouble, really big trouble.' Simon pressed the pause button on the handheld recorder. There was much to say, but words needed to be selected carefully. Deep in thought, he continued his slow walk back and forth.

Headlights from a car turning into the driveway caught his attention. The light beamed through the thin curtains and moved across the wall of the darkened room. He moved back to the window. The car looked like the yellow Holden Commodore from flat four. As the vehicle entered the driveway the headlights illuminated the outlines of two persons sitting in a parked car underneath the broken street light. He wasn't sure how long Cochran might be, or who else may decide to pay him a visit. He knew he had to hurry. He released the pause button.

'It's Thursday night. Good old Inspector Cochran seems to be gathering a case against me. If you read tomorrow's paper, you'll see why. Yes, he suspects me of being involved in the murder of my own family. Teddy Duncan is dead. Murdered. Once again, I seem to be prime suspect. In fact, I think I'm the only suspect. It might seem hard to believe, but I think Alison was being pursued by those bastards from that so-called sex club from years ago, and I don't even think she was aware of it. That seems to be the cause of all this bloody horrible mess. Apart from me, others might be in danger. Who exactly, I am not sure. You need to be careful. Don't trust anyone. Angela included. I have a plan, both to buy myself some time, and hopefully to find some answers...'

*   *   *

Richard Dempsey looked over at his partner. Gerry Hogan had just demolished another slice of pizza. There were two pieces left.

'Gerry, how about sharing that pizza with your mate?'

'Get out! This is my dinner. It's not my fault you gave yours away to guts-ache,' snapped Hogan.

'I didn't give it away. It was stolen!'

'Stolen, eh! Better report it to the cops then.' The penultimate piece of supreme was beginning to disappear.

'Listen, I did you a big favour. If I hadn't insisted on driving, it would have been a case of stolen pizza, not chips,' Dempsey retorted.

'You know, that's the saddest thing I've heard all day. But, I'm a reasonable man. How about you go for first walk, and take this last slice with you to keep you warm?'

'Why the hell not?' Richard Dempsey wasted no time in getting his hands on the lukewarm food. 'I'm off then. I'll be round the back of the flats. See you in a while.' Hogan's mouth was too full to respond verbally, so he raised his hand in an affirmative salute.

The two men had time to exchange positions four times before Cochran and Johnson returned with the warrant. The inspector wasted little time in leaving his vehicle and checking with Hogan on developments during his absence. John Cochran was rarely in a hurry. But when the situation required more immediate action, he was equal to the task. During his police career, he had seen numerous examples of faulty judgements, made under pressure. The teenage girl perched precariously on the Story Bridge railing was a tragic case in point. He had been talking to her for twenty minutes, she was just beginning to reconsider her options, when an overzealous patrol car came hurtling across the bridge, siren blaring. As it screeched to a halt with doors opening, the young lady lunged forward and ended her life on the rocky escarpment below.

'Hogan, how long have his lights been off?' asked Cochran.

'Five minutes after you left, sir.'

'And you haven't heard a sound since?'

'No, sir, but he's definitely in there,' replied Hogan, nodding his head, trying to reassure the inspector.

'I'm sure he is, but what the hell is he up to? C'mon, there's no time to waste. I have the warrant. Let's go.' A hint of urgency had crept into Cochran's voice.

*   *   *

Simon's eyes opened. He had trouble focusing. The spinning room prompted memories of the octopus ride at the Brisbane Ekka, which, despite Alison's reassurance, made him sick time and time again. But this was worse. It was like there was a drive belt attached to his brain, spinning it around inside his skull. He was lying on the divan near the door. He could hear voices, and felt a sense of impending doom. *Got to get out, got to get out, danger,* he thought. The door seemed light-years away rather than just two metres. He attempted to stand, but somehow found himself lying on the floor, looking at the ceiling. He closed his eyes, but the merry-go-round continued. His limbs felt like jelly. Edging across the floor, he felt for the door, then stretched and stood as he reached for the doorknob.

As part of his earlier plan he had deliberately left the door unlocked. With the support of the windowsill and the doorknob, he managed to achieve a near standing position. The latch turned with the weight of his hand. Suddenly the door swung open, depriving Simon of one of his major means of support. With one hand still on the windowsill, he took one step forward. His knees began to buckle. He swung around the doorframe. Everything went black as he plunged headlong down the stairs.

'Oh hell!' shouted Cochran, but there was no way for his bulky frame to escape the human projectile. Simon's head hit Cochran squarely in the chest, sending him backward down fourteen steps. Hogan clung tenaciously to the railing, and narrowly avoided joining the twosome in a heap on the ground.

Cochran groaned in agony, 'Get this bastard off me for Christ's sake. Ooh, my God, I think my back's broken.'

Johnson and Dempsey dragged Stacey off his unwilling safety net, and lay him on his side.

'Hogan, call an ambulance!' shouted Cathy Johnson, quickly responding to the situation. 'Sir, I think it's best you stay where you are until the ambulance arrives.'

'You're a great fucking comfort, Johnson. Shit! Fuck you, Stacey!' bellowed Cochran. 'Any other words of wisdom?'

'I would suggest that in your present position you should remember the saying: *Don't bite off the hand that feeds you.*' Cathy removed her jacket, folded it over and placed it under Cochran's head.

'Is that a threat, Johnson?'

'Damn right! Now, can you move your toes?'

Chapter 10

The Walking Wounded

After much swearing and grinding of teeth, John Cochran had finally succeeded in getting his trousers, socks, and shoes on with minimal bending of his back. X-rays had cleared him of any serious spinal injury. After an overnight admission for observation and a final medical examination, he had been granted his discharge.

It was nine thirty Friday morning, and Cathy Johnson had arrived early, both to check on the inspector's condition and pass on an update on the investigation. John Cochran met her in the hallway as he left the ward. His gait was slow, deliberate, and bolt upright.

'Good morning, sir. It's good to see you up and about.' Cathy did her best to sound upbeat.

'I'm only up, Johnson, I'm not about. And it's a lousy morning, so don't try to tell me otherwise. I'm in pain and I feel miserable; please let me enjoy the moment.' Cochran's forlorn expression echoed his words.

'Sir, we searched Devlin's flat. No weapon was found. But we did find a micro-cassette recorder on the table, which wasn't there on our first visit. No cassette though. We also found a handwritten note, stuck on the fridge. It was addressed to Adrian Devlin.'

'Well, what did it say?'

'I've got a copy here.' Cathy handed over a folded piece of paper.

Adrian,

There's no time left for me. A man can only take so much. We've had many good times together, my friend. Beer, more beer, women, and song. Do us a favour, get all the regular guys together — Howard, Keith, Ralph, Bobby, Donger, and Wart. Have a card night and a few drinks, leave an empty seat for yours truly. Do one more thing, get that piece of furniture fixed up once and for all, it was once mine, remember!!!!!

Good-bye and good luck — S.S.

Cochran put one hand to his chin and groaned uncomfortably as he thought it through.

'What do you make of this, Johnson?' asked Cochran, adopting the role of mentor.

'I think it's more than just a farewell or suicide letter, sir. We need to see if all those names are real people and, if they are, have a chat with them. We know of Howard Morgan, so perhaps he can shed some light on the other names. And we turned the place inside out, thinking the micro-cassette might be hidden somewhere. But we found nothing.'

'Very good, Johnson, very good! Was that your idea?'

'Hogan's, sir.'

'Never mind, Johnson, there's still plenty of good ideas left in this case. I expect some of them will be yours. I don't suppose Stacey's dead, is he?'

'He's awaiting psychiatric assessment and should be transferred to the psychiatric ward sometime today. He took an overdose of diazepam. We found four empty blister packs on the kitchen floor. That's forty tablets, or two hundred milligrams. The doctor I spoke to felt it was unlikely he had taken that much. He regained consciousness too quickly. Dempsey and Hogan have been keeping an eye on him.'

'Okay then. First thing, you drive me home nice and slowly, avoiding the bumps.' Cochran walked gingerly down the hospital corridor, with one hand resting on Cathy's shoulder.

Chapter 11

Security

It seemed to be the warmer morning that had boosted the early attendance at the Bodytone Club. The previous few days had been cool, and despite the heated pool, the cooler weather usually contributed to a slower start to the day. Wendy, the receptionist, who had been busy organising numerous membership renewals, was now occupied making minor alterations to the day's program on the whiteboard. Wayne, the gym instructor, had called in sick, and a slight reshuffling of staff had been necessary. With the whiteboard updated, Wendy moved on to a quick tidy of the reception area.

The plush foyer was an impressive greeting to any potential new member. The thick, rich brown carpet, assortment of cane furniture and evergreen plants blended perfectly with the multi-toned red brick interior. Certificates and awards decorated one wall, while on the opposite side of the room hung several attractively framed colour photographs of super-fit male and female bodies. The custom-built reception desk, made from Tasmanian Blackwood, was the piece de resistance, and a touch of brilliance from the brain of Charlie Madden and the wallet of Simon Stacey.

A tall man entered and walked directly up to the reception desk.

'Good morning, sir. I haven't seen you here before. Your first day at Bodytone is always complimentary. We have a brochure that explains how the club works and gives you a rundown on all the facilities,' explained Wendy. She passed the glossy publication across the counter. The tall, blonde-haired man stood with his hands in his pockets, making no gesture to accept the handout.

'Schliemann!' he said in a husky European voice. Wendy slowly placed the brochure back on top of the others. His statement did little to make her feel at ease. She broke eye contact and straightened up the small pile of brochures.

'Oscar Schliemann!' repeated the blue-eyed stranger.

'Oh, I see, your name… is… Oscar Schliemann! My apologies,' she stuttered somewhat nervously. 'Pleased to meet you, I'm Wendy. I work here; well of course I do. Obviously. I am the receptionist. I am a bit of everything, really.'

'Yes, I see. Thank you. Would Charlie Madden be here?'

'You wish…to see…Charlie, our manager?' said Wendy in slow, staggered speech. 'You wait there,' she said, gesturing with an open hand like a policeman halting the traffic. 'I'll see…if Mr Madden…is in…okay?'

Charlie Madden's office door was partly open. Wendy knocked and entered.

'Excuse me, Charlie, there's an Oscar Schliemann wishing to see you.'

'Fine, Wendy,' said Charlie, leaning back in his chair, his face obscured by the morning newspaper. He heard her voice, but not her words. The Stacey story had his full attention. Had it not been for the items 'Police Corruption Enquiry Looms,' and 'Babysitter Kidnaps Child,' the story would have made the front page. Charlie slowly read it through again.

HOUSE FIRE WAS MURDER — THREE DEAD

A police spokesman has revealed the fire that claimed the lives of Mrs Alison Stacey and her child in the early hours of Wednesday morning was deliberately lit. A third body, found later at the scene by police, has yet to be identified. The man, aged 35-40, 1.8 meters tall and weighing about 80 kgs, was believed to have been naked at the time of his death. Well-known identity and husband of the dead woman, Mr Simon Stacey, is assisting police with their enquiries. Police are appealing to anyone who witnessed the blaze or who can aid in the identification of the dead man to come forward immediately.

'Dear oh dear,' said Charlie quietly, shaking his head both in sympathy and disbelief. As he lowered the newspaper he jumped with fright as the huge man standing quietly in front of the desk came into view.

'Excuse me, sir, but the reception area is just outside,' said Madden, his voice a little higher pitched than usual.

'Ah yes, Wendy. We met. Funny lady,' smiled Schliemann.

'How can I help you?' He moved uneasily in his chair.

'Oscar Schliemann.' The man's hand reached forward. Madden stood and took a deep breath.

'Thank God!' exclaimed Charlie. The penny had finally dropped. 'I'm sure glad you're on our side. I'm Charlie Madden.' The two hands met across the desk. Schliemann's grip was like a vice. Charlie's fingers doubled over onto one another. 'Can I show you around the club?'

'No need,' said Oscar, still smiling.

'It's quite all right, I have plenty of time, and I'm sure you'd like to know all the ins and outs.'

'I do.'

'What? I mean, I beg your pardon,' exclaimed Charlie. 'You know already? But, it was my understanding that you hadn't been here before.'

'Last night.' Schliemann displayed the key he removed from the fob pocket of his shorts.

'And the alarm system? A key also?' asked Charlie. The big European nodded his reply. 'Can I tell you about the staff, or do you already know that, too?'

'I know about most of them, but I am not familiar with all their faces yet. I should be after today. It might be easier if you introduce me as a new gym instructor or club supervisor,' said Oscar.

'I'm sorry to say, most of the staff already know that a security guard will be working here. We had a meeting yesterday,' said Charlie regretfully.

'That's unfortunate,' noted the security officer. 'But these things never stay quiet for long anyway. In future, you can discuss such matters with me first. Let us meet some of those faces then.'

'Of course, I'm only the manager, who am I to argue?' said Charlie, catching himself by surprise. 'Have you seen this?' Charlie tapped his finger on the newspaper.

'Yes.'

'Silly of me to ask I suppose,' said Charlie, feeling a touch superfluous. He looked around his office and nodded, then posed one more question.

'I wonder, Mr Schliemann, can you tell me what is in my desk drawer?'

'Which one?'

'The top one. The locked one,' said Charlie smugly.

'Cheque book, bank statements, cigarettes, calculator, twenty dollars seven cents and your personal diary,' recited Oscar. Charlie stared at Schliemann for a moment, shrugged his shoulders and laughed. Oscar joined in with a hearty chuckle.

'How very nice. Come on then, let's go see those faces, Oscar,' said Madden as warmly as he could.

'Yes, let us do that. And you must introduce me to Deborah. Monday sounds like a promising night for you, Charlie,' said a smiling Schliemann. Both men left the office.

*   *   *

Noel Briggs sat in his vehicle in a shaded area of the Bodytone Club car park reading his novel *The Bourne Supremacy*. He lifted his head as a group of three fit young women in leotards strolled by. He nodded his approval and tipped his head at the ladies, who were too involved in their own chatter to notice.

He groaned, stretched, and closed his book. 'Hmm. Oh well, I suppose I should make an appearance and chat to some of these pricks.'

At the reception desk, he was greeted by Wendy, who gave him the same spiel she had given Schliemann twenty minutes earlier.

'Young lady. As much as I would love a complimentary day here, I am not here to join. I am a detective with CIB. Detective Noel Briggs.' He displayed his ID. 'I would like to see the manager please.

It is in relation to some recent unpleasant matters concerning the Stacey family.'

'Oh dear. Yes, how dreadful,' replied Wendy, as she placed both hands against her cheeks. 'Poor Simon. How is he managing?'

'Unfortunately, I am not privy to that information. Have you known Simon for very long?'

'He hired me three years ago. We are not close or anything like that, but he is a great guy and always very friendly to all the staff. This is so tragic.'

'Are you aware of any conflicts he has had with anyone here or elsewhere?'

'Oh no. Not at all.' Wendy shook her head. 'If you ever met him you would know the sort of man he is. Outgoing, charming, and very clever.'

'Simon Stacey and I do know each other. We met some years back,' said Briggs with a half-smile. 'You might say we helped each other out a few times.'

'Yes, that's the sort of man he is. Always helping others,' agreed Wendy.

'So, the manager then?'

'Oh, yes. Sorry. He is not available right now. But I could schedule you an appointment sometime...' her words trailed away as the detective looked away.

Noel Briggs was once again distracted by a group of sweaty women walking through the foyer. 'Good morning, ladies!' he said brightly. This time he got a hi, two hellos and a nice smile with good eye contact. He had turned his back on Wendy and moved towards the smiling brunette.

'I'll be back Monday morning to see Charlie Madden then. Thank you for your time!' he called over his shoulder as he drew alongside the smiling lady and escorted her out the front door.

Briggs had two major failings; a propensity to become lured off track by beautiful women; and a desire to expedite investigations, often prematurely. Only two months ago, Inspector Cochran had located the final piece of evidence to convict the young woman of murdering her husband. The homicide team stormed her house, only to find Briggs in bed with the attractive killer, probing for more information.

Chapter 12

Under Lock and Key

The heavy door had a narrow glass window, through which a small room, about the size of a large elevator, could be seen. To one side of the entrance there was a small black panel with a central red button and a message in bold white print: 'To enter. Press once and wait.' Simon's companion ignored the sign and produced a key from his pocket and unlocked the entrance to the secure psychiatric unit — Ward 21. Once inside the anteroom, the door was locked behind them. The ever-vigilant escort looked through the second window and surveyed the corridor ahead through the convex mirror mounted on the ceiling of the hallway.

Simon stared at the distorted image of himself clad in his faded blue hospital pyjamas. A nebulous, almost lifeless-looking figure. Devoid of character. A factory product. One of thousands who have and would continue to file through these doors. As if to check the image was real, he lifted the large brown paper bag he was carrying to his chest. He nodded in silent submission as his reflection did likewise. He clutched the bag a little tighter. There was not much in it, but it was all he had to remind himself of who he really was. His escort had thoroughly checked his belongings, removing the pair of brown leather shoes, belt, wallet, and watch. All these dangerous items were to be kept under lock and key, only to be returned on discharge.

The strategically placed mirror revealed there was no one either in the hallway or lurking at the base of the second door. The two men entered, and after the last opening was secured, proceeded down the corridor.

The cries of a woman in distress grew louder with every step. Stacey looked back at the doors. He wondered about his wisdom in telling the psychiatrist that he wished he were dead. He wondered how long it would take to get out of this place, and if he would find what he was looking for. It was difficult to think clearly right now.

The diazepam was still clouding his thoughts and tiring his muscles. There was a plan, and it was clear in his mind yesterday. Tomorrow he hoped the finer details would return.

A final set of unlocked swinging doors opened into what looked like the nerve centre of Ward 21. The woman's cries were now screams. Simon could see her face pushed up against the window in one of the side rooms. Tufts of her knotted, long, black hair were jutting in all directions. Despite her facial features being partly obscured by smears of tears and saliva, her wide eyes and open, panting mouth clearly depicted an absolute fit of terror. She clenched her fists and began striking the window. A young man pacing up and down in front of the woman's room seemed to be disturbed by the scene. He quickened his pace and began slapping himself on the head with his hands. Simon was asked to sit down and wait, which he did without question. There was some activity in the staff camp. Four men seemed to appear from nowhere. Simon presumed they were staff, it was difficult to tell without the traditional white uniforms. They were quickly joined by two women, one who was holding a green plastic tray. The woman had backed away from the window and was standing on the low-set bed. Her screaming was now interspersed with swearing.

'Bastards! You bastards!' shouted the woman, as if she was aware of what was about to happen. 'Don't kill me! Please, don't kill me!'

As one of the men started to close the thin venetian blinds nested between the double glass, she jumped at the window, feet first, but the glass only bent slightly and catapulted her backwards across her bed. The door was quickly unlocked. The male staff were first in the room. The screams were now high-pitched. The door closed, and the activities of the six staff were hidden from view. A conglomerate of disturbing sounds continued for three minutes, then the shouts became softer and less frequent, until they ceased altogether. The distressed young man now sat with head down on the edge of an armchair. His fists trembled as they held a firm grip on his oily hair. Tears were streaming down his face. A few metres away sat an overweight teenager, completely oblivious to the commotion. The jigsaw laid out on the table had her complete attention. A smile stretched across her face as a piece settled into place. She giggled and clapped her hands together in a clumsy manner before settling down to further serious concentration.

Five of the medication marines emerged, task completed. The round key slid into the hole in the window frame. It turned, and the blinds opened. The sixth member was sitting on the side of the bed, feeling the pulse of the now sleeping woman. For Simon, this was a completely new experience, and one that he found extremely disturbing. He felt a deep sense of sympathy and concern for the sedated lady, and for the sobbing sentinel near her bedroom door.

'Hello, Simon, I'm Eddy, one of the nursing staff. You and I will be seeing a lot of each other. I'm your nurse therapist.' Eddy extended his hand to greet the new arrival. Simon turned his head on hearing the voice. He looked the thickset man up and down.

'Have we met before? Your name and voice sound familiar,' he asked.

'No. This is your first admission. We have never met.' Eddy withdrew the offered hand. His shoulder-length blonde streaked hair seemed odd for a man of around fifty years of age, a bit like a pretence to be something that he clearly was not. That fixed, dominating stare and stern, tight mouth were rather disconcerting. His loose-fitting short-sleeve shirt showed large forearms and biceps, but was not quite loose enough to disguise the slight outline of a rounded belly. *Piss pot,* thought Stacey immediately. A silver chain was secured to his belt and disappeared into the pocket of his jeans. He reminded Simon of a fat, smelly bouncer who once accused him of cheating and evicted him from a card game. Yes, thought Stacey, this tin god meant trouble.

'I said, my name is Eddy, and I am your therapist,' repeated the man sternly.

'Yes, I know what you said, but I have no need for a nurse therapist, or any other sort of therapist, for that matter. Thanks all the same,' replied Simon, looking up at the burly figure hovering over him.

'You'll get one anyway. Everyone gets one. *Them's* the rules, champ,' said Eddy, as he sat down next to Stacey. 'It's unfortunate you arrived during that little outburst.'

'I'm starting to think it's unfortunate I arrived at all. Is that little outburst a regular thing round here?'

'Let's get a few things clear from the outset.' The *therapist* leaned across close to Simon's ear. 'You play by the rules, keep your nose clean, and we won't need to bounce you, will we?'

'Bounce me? You are the therapist? Right?' said Simon through his teeth. He knew his first assessment of this creep was now completely justified.

'Rule one. Be polite to the staff, arsehole. Remember, I have the name tag, I have a door key, and I'm the fucking boss.' Eddy stood, walked a few paces and turned his head. 'We'll talk later then. You're in bed number eight.'

An old, bearded man sat in the vacated chair. He smiled, revealing a mouth of blackened teeth.

'Watch that one, especially when he bathes you. He's rough, and he never dries between your toes or behind your balls,' croaked the old man.

'There are some people in this world I just don't understand. How can a *so-called* professional behave that way? He's no therapist. He's just a thug with the right set of keys,' said Simon, not really expecting an answer.

'I understand perfectly,' said the old gentleman. 'I believe he's an emotionally detached and socially challenged man. I suspect he suffered maternal deprivation and paternal abuse from a drunken, intolerant father. He now strives for control and recognition in whatever form he can receive it.'

'Well, of course,' laughed Simon weakly. 'That explains everything. But whatever the cause, it makes him no less of a prick. But thank you for enlightening me. I'm Simon Stacey. What's your name?'

'Rasputin, the mad monk, but as we're friends you can call me Ras.'

'Ras, eh! That's fine. Ras it is then.' The two shook hands firmly.

'Some people here call me George, but you and I know better, don't we?' said the delightful old man, with a nod and a wink. 'You have missed afternoon tea.'

'I think I'm pretty well hydrated. They had a drip in me all night and morning.' Simon displayed the small dressing on his forearm.

'Ah, death eludes you for now. Overdoses are not a precise science.'

'I wasn't planning to die.'

'Obviously.'

The unusual conversation continued for some time. Simon was most taken with his new acquaintance, whom he found to be amusing, observant, and intelligent. Ras confessed to being in Ward 21 for the seventeenth time.

'Seventeen times! What's the attraction?'

'It seems the public are not too keen on me attempting to cast spells in the shopping mall,' said Ras. 'Besides, there are times when I feel safer in here than out there.'

'I can sort of understand that. But I reckon...' Simon let out a long yawn. '...this place has its own risks.'

'I make sure I am in here well before every Friday the 13th. There's one coming up in exactly one week. And it sounds like you should go to bed, my friend.'

Simon nodded. After the two had arranged a date for a chess game the next morning, he excused himself and trudged off to find his room. The walk from the intensive care ward to Ward 21 seemed to have drained what little energy he had remaining, and he now regretted declining the offer of a wheelchair.

There was little to recommend room eight as a place to stay for an extended period. The low-set bed was a permanent fixture to the middle of the floor. There were no railings, towel racks, interior door handles, wardrobes, or cupboards, just three soft plastic stackable trays. The bare walls were a tan colour and looked like Gyprock, but felt like solid timber. Two bedroom lights, covered by unbreakable glass, were set at either side of a small, round air conditioning vent in the ceiling. All light switches were outside the room on a panel to the side of the door. A towel, face washer, and pyjamas were neatly folded in a pile on the bed. A solitary piece of motel-size soap lay on the pillow.

Simon picked up the few items from the bed, placed them with his paper bag on the top plastic tray, and lay down. From his reclined position, he could clearly see the elevated central office through the double glass windows of his room. It was obvious that very little would go unnoticed. He fell asleep within a moment.

*   *   *

Disturbed by the chiming of a bell, Simon woke in what seemed like only minutes. It was evening — eight thirty. Medication time. He sat up on his bed and saw a procession of mournful-looking people lining up. A nurse was passing out plastic medicine cups to each in turn, while two other staff supervised the swallowing. Some patients were examined closely, being asked to open their mouths and lift their tongues. Others were not.

'Come on, Stacey, get in line.' It was Eddy, the nurse therapist, sticking his unwelcome face through the door.

'Thanks, but no thanks,' said Simon, as he lay back down on the bed.

'It's eighty thirty, you'll get in line,' demanded Eddy. 'If you're not on any medication for your mental disorder, you may then return to your bed.' His words were clear enough, and he obviously wasn't ready to debate the issue. Simon thought it best to comply, so he reluctantly joined the queue. His therapist gave him a gentle push along, just to remind him of how their relationship stood. Simon's turn soon arrived and he stood patiently in front of the window that resembled that of some banks, with a small gap at the bottom where items could be exchanged. He crossed his fingers, hoping he wouldn't be compelled to make a withdrawal.

'Hello, Simon, I'm Kym. I'll just check your sheet.' She sounded pleasant enough, thought Simon, but then so did meathead for his first sentence. The Asian nurse flicked through the clip folder under 'S', then turned and checked one of the many small wooden pigeonholes behind her. Each one was marked with a name and bed number, and most contained several bottles or packets of pills. She ran her hand along the top shelf and stopped at number eight. It was empty.

'No, nothing tonight. Doctor will review you tomorrow. He may then decide on some medication. Good night, Simon.'

'A good night to you, Kym,' said Stacey with much relief. He walked directly back to his room, completely ignoring Eddy's scowl. Lying back down on top of his bed, he folded his arms underneath his head and stared at the ceiling. He thought deeply about recent events. At the moment, it was a constant internal struggle between collapsing into a quivering, blubbering mess, and trying to maintain some degree of control and unravel the sinister puzzle. One thing seemed clear; somehow, Teddy Duncan was involved. It was obvious to Simon that Teddy had tried to prevent him leaving on the night of the fire. He'd just wanted to keep on gambling, and this was clearly out of character. Maybe he was killed because he failed his task, or maybe he just knew too much.

Simon also recalled the distressing and perverse conversation he'd had with Romoli on Tuesday night. That man was evil. A psychopath. And Simon had not the slightest feeling of remorse for putting a bullet in his brain. How could he have possibly told anyone, especially Cochran? Anyway, Adrian had all the details on the tape, and he felt confident that his good friend would help him out. As he thought back to the phone numbers on the newspaper clipping, he realised why Eddy's name and voice were familiar. It was Eddy that answered a call and identified Ward 21 as one of the listed numbers. While his stay in the locked psychiatric ward was going to be a difficult and possibly dangerous one, his determination to uncover some hidden truths was unshakeable. He just needed his judgment and level-headedness to return to within some degree of what used to be normal. Enough mistakes had been made already. In any case, thought Simon, his admission was voluntary, so when he was ready he could simply sign himself out.

*   *   *

It was ten o'clock, and the evening nursing staff had settled down to write their reports. Eddy sat at the office desk with several files. He had intentionally left Simon Stacey's file to last, so he could take time to deliberate over his entry. As he read the doctor's notes he smiled.

'Oh great, this is really radical! This joker's going to be here longer than he thinks,' laughed Eddy. Kym stopped her writing and looked up.

'What is it that's so *radical*?' she asked.

'The doctor's report, and I quote. *In view of this man's significant personal loss, his death wish, his suicide note and attempt, it is my opinion that he represents a serious ongoing risk of self-harm and/or suicide. He should be maintained in the closed ward as a voluntary patient for now; if he attempts to leave he should be regulated and detained under the Mental Health Act,* and I quite agree, he's likely to be a difficult customer,' said Eddy.

'Gee, that's one thing that really annoys me about this place.' Kym threw her pen down on the desk. 'If they're going to keep someone here like that, why don't they have the guts to tell them? It's not fair for patients to think they are here voluntarily when they clearly are not. It's false imprisonment, that's what it is!'

'Here she goes again, on her hobbyhorse. I'm sorry I spoke.'

'And there's one other thing that pisses me off. Your attitude!' Kym looked around for her pen, which seemed to have disappeared.

She flung open the drawer and snatched up a new black biro and continued her work.

Eddy ignored her remark and completed his evening report on Simon Stacey.

9th June '86 - 2215 hrs.

Admission routine and unit policies explained shortly after arrival in ward. Attempt to explain role of Nurse Therapist met with verbal abuse. Very resistive to counselling and staff assistance. Noticed to be laughing inappropriately when in company of patient who talks very little. I find this man has the potential to be physically aggressive and needs to be closely observed. We also need to exclude the presence of any psychotic symptoms.

Chapter 13

Race Day

'Hey there, Sarge,' panted Cochran. 'I never realised that four steps could be so bloody difficult to climb.' It was ten in the morning as John Cochran dragged himself into the Alderley Police Station. 'Well, where is everyone?' he continued. 'Hard at it I trust?'

'J. C., you look like shit!' declared Sergeant Carter. The fat man's eyes were out of sight, buried somewhere beneath that excess of flesh and the now swollen eyelids. 'You look like you need to go back to bed.'

'Quite possibly. I haven't slept so badly since my haemorrhoids were removed eight years ago.'

'Not sure I needed to know that piece of information,' quipped Carter.

'And you can save the J. C. for out of work hours, if you don't mind.'

'Hey, it's just the two of us here. We're mates, in case you've forgotten. What's the big deal? Are you sure you should even be here at all?'

'Of course I should be here,' said Cochran emphatically. 'I've got work to do. Just because I have a fucked-up back doesn't mean I can't use my brain. And, mates or not, this place still stinks, Carter. Haven't you tossed those shoes out yet? Clean the damned place up, will you? This is a police station, not a bloody footy change room.' Despite his use of the front counter for support, the large man had a definite tilt to the left.

'Ease up. Yes, the shoes are gone,' grunted Carter. 'And I'm telling you as your friend, that if I looked like you I'd be a long way from this office. I'd be taking it easy and recovering.'

Cochran shook his head and began tapping his fingers on the counter.

'Okay, well, I've said what I think, and I'll leave it at that,' added Carter.

'You'd best shut up now then. You are not helping. I'm this close to the point of maximum irritation.' Cochran held a hand up and displayed the smallest gap between two fingers. 'I think you know what I mean by that.'

Carter nodded and said nothing. He knew exactly what the inspector was referring to. There was a young prostitute who was suicidal, psychotic, and mumbling bizarre stories of demonic possession, torture, and sacrifice. She'd finally jumped to her death from Brisbane's Story Bridge after Cochran had almost talked her into living. The speeding police car with siren blaring tipped the scales. It was Carter who misunderstood the call for assistance and issued the instructions to the two speeding constables. This was the day of maximum irritation that Cochran was referring to, and a day that neither man wished to revisit.

'So, back to business matters,' said Cochran. 'What the hell is happening here? You are supposed to know everyone's whereabouts.'

'Marshall has gone to talk with the late Alison Stacey's parents. Dempsey and Hogan are trying to locate Adrian Devlin, as well as keep an eye on his flat. Johnson says she's gone shopping. Briggs has gone back to Bodytune, and I —'

'It's Bodytone not Bodytune,' interrupted Cochran.

'That's what I said, Bodytone,' said Carter, unaware of his error.

'No, you said *tune*, not *tone*,' insisted Cochran.

'As you wish, J. C. You know, I should be at home watching the wrestling over a couple of cold tinnies.' The sergeant forced a chuckle. Cochran was stone faced.

'Did they leave me any messages?'

'Yes, they certainly did.' Carter passed over a few sheets of paper. 'Go and digest that. They seem to be doing okay.'

'We'll see. And by the way, I'm doing you a favour. That wrestling is a load of horse shit. Absolute crap. You tell Johnson when she has finished her shopping I'd like to see her.' John Cochran proceeded slowly down the hallway using the wall for support and mumbling as he went. 'Shopping? Bitch. You bloody bitch.'

Alistair Carter lifted a small television from under the desk, switched on the sports program, and made himself comfortable. Despite being a great armchair athlete, he was in reasonable shape for a forty-nine-year-old. He was a keen jogger and would hit the streets at least five times a week, in addition to his frequent runs to and from work. His weight seldom varied from a comfortable seventy-three kilograms, regardless of his regular diet of beer and chocolate. Cochran and he had often joked about swapping roles, but Carter's dislike for fast cars and firearms guaranteed it would always remain just that.

It was thirty minutes later when the slender redhead arrived at the police station, plastic shopping bag in hand, and a light-blue imitation leather handbag over her shoulder. Carter was reclined in his office chair with his feet stretched out on a stool, watching the fight. The hooded, 'Stalking Shadow – AKA the Finisher' was in action against his arch-rival 'Kong of the Congo'.

'The boss wants to see you, Johnson. He's in his office.' Carter spoke without taking his eyes off the square box.

'I don't know how you can watch that, Sarge. It's really a load of crap.' Cathy shook her head in disgust.

'That seems to be a popular opinion this morning. Remember, one man's crap is another man's candy, and I wouldn't expect you to understand the finer aspects of a serious, action-packed, sports comedy, Johnson. Now be on your way.' He waved his hand for her to move along. Cathy proceeded to the inspector's door, knocked, and entered.

'Johnson, nice of you to come to work. Any good specials at the supermarket?'

'A couple, sir.' Cathy pulled out some low-fat fruit yoghurt. 'This is for you.'

'I'm not a bloody invalid, Johnson.' Cochran took hold of the container and read the label. 'Low-fat yoghurt! I have the impression there is a message here somewhere. Shit, I'm not in the mood for this. If you wanted to do me a favour, or if you just wanted to crawl up my arse, you could have got me a nice hot pie and peas.'

'Sir, pardon me for saying so, but if obesity was a crime you'd be up for capital punishment. With an injured back it wouldn't hurt you to lose a few pounds. One more thing —'

'Please go on, Johnson,' insisted Cochran. 'It seems you think insulting me is good for your career. The desk job is still open.'

'Yes, sir. One more thing, which was on special, was…' Cathy reached into her shopping bag. 'High wattage light bulbs! Each one of these is three hundred watts. Ideal for incendiary use.'

'What?' His manner quickly changed. He was interested. Some good news in the case was well overdue. Johnson knew she had hooked him. The typing pool had been avoided for the time being. She held the item up and smiled broadly.

'The man at the hardware store, just down the road from Devlin's flat, remembers selling a bunch of these last Saturday morning. He clearly recalled the sale, as they are not a popular item and he was considering removing them from his inventory. They were purchased by a well-dressed man who was driving a red Mercedes. Sounded like Stacey to me.'

'Nice work, Johnson,' said Cochran with enthusiasm and just a hint of pleasure. He jumped to his feet, momentarily forgetting about his back problem. He very nearly reached an upright position, but then crumbled back to his seat as the stabbing pain shot down the back of both his legs. 'Ah! Shit! Damn! Curse you, Stacey!' he bellowed to the ceiling. Both his hands slammed down on the desk. Cathy Johnson jumped. The fruit yoghurt bounced into the air and landed on the floor, splitting open the plastic packaging and allowing the contents to ooze out. Cathy moved quickly around the desk to offer what assistance she could. As she stepped forward to place her hand on Cochran's shoulder, her heel slid on the spilled yoghurt. Her right foot shot forward and she was unable to prevent herself toppling backwards.

'Johnson, are you…' Cochran couldn't continue and erupted into raucous laughter, interspersed with moans and groans of pain. The humour of the situation was contagious and Cathy, stretched out on the floor, couldn't help but join in. A moment later the door opened. It was Carter.

'What in the hell is going on here? You two are disturbing the peace. What's more important, you're interrupting the wrestling. Johnson, are you all right?'

'I'm fine, thanks, Sarge,' laughed Cathy.

'Despite what it looks like, everything… oh shit, my back! Christ!' Cochran pushed his arms behind his back for support. 'All's well here. More or less, I guess. You can be on your way. Thanks, Carter. You may return to… no, no bloody TV, I've got a job for you,' said John Cochran, now collecting his thoughts. 'You can get me a list of all red Mercedes owners in and around the city. Recent models, say, the last five years. ASAP!'

'I knew it was a mistake to come in here. A fellow comes to offer a helping hand and gets lumbered with paperwork, and on a Saturday, too!' stated Carter woefully as he left the room.

'You may get up now, Johnson, if you're able. Sorry about the yoghurt. Now you see what so-called healthy food does for you,' smiled the inspector through a grimace. 'If it was a pie and peas it wouldn't have fallen off the desk like that.'

'I think even a watermelon would have cleared the edge of the desk, sir,' said Cathy, now taking a seat. She armed herself with a small handkerchief and tried to remove some of the white fruity sludge from her navy blue pleated skirt.

'You've done well, Johnson. Now, let me put you in the picture.' Cochran picked up the few loose pieces of paper lying on the desk. 'Marshall has gathered a little history on Stacey. It seems our number one suspect was an exceptional actor during his high school days. Some of his teachers expected him to go on to great things. Hmmm…. What else have we here?' He checked his paperwork. 'Always in the top five percent of students; numerous gambling misdemeanours. Since school he's had several jobs as a stable hand, and he has worked with a few local bookmakers. He upset a few as well by collecting on several very large bets. But there's been no regular employment for the past seven years. He met his wife at the racetrack three and a half years ago, she also worked in the betting ring.'

'Sounds like a very clever, plausible man. A con man even,' remarked Cathy.

'Oh yes. He's definitely that. Fortunately for us, he's not going anywhere in a hurry, and should be in the locked psych ward for some time yet after that supposed suicide attempt.' Cochran ran his finger down the sheet of foolscap. 'Dempsey and Hogan have been trying to trace Adrian Devlin, but without any luck yet,' he continued. 'No one has seen him since Tuesday's card night at Duncan's. According to his employer, Devlin is on two weeks' sick leave. Rang them himself, apparently.' Cochran traced over a red line with his finger, starting at the name Devlin and finishing at Morgan. 'Ah yes! An unusual break and enter reported from Morgan's dental surgery yesterday. Only one thing missing: Adrian Devlin's dental file. Now why would someone do that, Johnson? I ask you?'

'Maybe Devlin was unhappy with Morgan's dental work and wanted a second opinion?'

'Johnson, I'd like to think you're trying to be funny, but I've got a feeling that you're serious. Please tell me I'm wrong.'

'Just thinking aloud, sir. How about impersonation? Someone plans a murder and wants to make the deceased look like Devlin.' Cathy tilted her head thoughtfully to one side and looked at the inspector.

'Well, maybe you're onto something, but don't hold your breath. You have missed the most obvious reason. Devlin's body may be very difficult to identify without his dental records, particularly if it's mutilated or burnt.'

'You think there may be a plan to kill Devlin as well? That does seem to make more sense, sir.'

'Well, thanks for the vote of confidence. For all we know he may already be dead. Now, continuing on.' Cochran referred to his notes. 'No leads on the male corpse found at Stacey's place, and that I can tell you is a real pain in the arse.'

'Any chance that —'

'Of course it's not Devlin,' interrupted Cochran, anticipating her remark. 'Unless you believe he somehow gained an extra seven kilos and lengthened his body by four and a half centimetres.'

'I guess that's unlikely.'

'I guess it is. As I was saying, the final autopsy report has cause of death as drowning. The head wound was enough to kill him, but the water did the job first. There was pool water in the lungs, and his blood was found in the pool.'

'That makes his being naked a little easier to understand then. But how did he get from the pool to the shed?'

'Don't you think that the more correct question is who, not how? Who moved him from the pool to the shed?'

'Well, that's more or less what I meant. I knew he didn't walk there or anything,' added Cathy. Cochran just stared at her for a moment.

'*More* or *less* are not good detective words, Johnson.'

'No, sir I realise that, sir. Sorry.'

'Now, our friend Briggs,' continued the inspector after a big sigh. 'He has spoken with dear old Miss Ashbridge, the neighbour of Edward Duncan. She confirms Stacey's story of the argument with Duncan, but can't be sure of the time. She also says that there was another argument at around two on Wednesday morning. She remembers being woken by the noise. She looked out her window and saw what she believed to be a Mercedes, possibly red, driving away in a hurry.'

'Surely that must have been Stacey,' reasoned Cathy. 'Haven't we got enough to charge that mongrel?'

'It doesn't add up,' pondered Cochran, running his fingers through his short, greying hair. 'You said yourself, Stacey's a con man. This doesn't sound like the work of a devious character like Stacey. I reckon on three possibilities. One, Stacey simply stuffed up and we've got him cold. An unlikely option I think.' Cochran spoke with his hands, unfolding another finger each time he spoke. 'Two, someone's going to great lengths to point the finger at him. To make us think he's guilty of this whole damned mess. And three, Stacey wants us to think he's being set up. With the help of others, he is creating some very unusual and perhaps misleading details, like the dental file, the moving of the body from the pool, the suicide note, and the murder of Edward Duncan poorly disguised as a suicide.'

'Maybe he just got careless under pressure?'

'Maybe. If only it was that simple. Stacey had that other Mercedes six months back. It was reported stolen and never located. It was white, but perhaps it's had a paint job. Johnson,' said Cochran, looking at Cathy as if trying to impart his thoughts. 'Well, Johnson. C'mon, let's hear it!'

'Someone could be using the car to set up Stacey, or Stacey could be using his first Mercedes to make it look that way.'

'Very good! Hallelujah! And God said, let there be light, and there was light.' Cochran raised his hands to the ceiling with joy. 'Okay then, let's move.'

'Where are we going, sir?'

'We're going to Eagle Farm Racecourse. I haven't been since last Melbourne Cup day. I'm hoping it will be a pleasant afternoon. We need to talk to some of those bookies that had dealings with Stacey.'

Carter was still engrossed in the television wrestling show when the two emerged. As he caught sight of Cochran, he jumped to his feet and quickly turned the volume down to zero.

'Made a start on those lists, J. C... I mean sir. More to come yet.' Carter placed two sheets of paper on the counter.

'Thanks, Sarge. You hang onto them for the time being. Get in touch with Dempsey or Hogan. I want another search of that flat. We have an empty recorder and I want the cassette tape found, if it exists. And get me another list of all missing persons and known bad guys that resemble that naked corpse, and this time cover all states and territories. Marshall can help when he gets back. We'll be at the racetrack.'

'What if I go to the races and you two do the paperwork, then we'll all be happy?' quipped Carter. John Cochran raised his middle finger in response and walked out the front door. Johnson followed.

'No harm in trying,' said Carter to himself.

'Sarge.' It was Cathy, poking her head back around the corner of the door. She caught Carter's attention, repeated the inspector's gesture, and disappeared.

'You'll keep, Johnson!' he shouted. 'You'll keep!'

*   *   *

The drive to the track, although slow while trying to avoid too many bumps, was uneventful. Cathy Johnson, in sympathy for her injured leader, dropped him off near the main gates while she found a suitable car park. The section reserved for police vehicles was packed with everything but, so she had a lengthy walk back to the entrance. The unlikely couple made their way to the grassed area in front of the main grandstand. Cochran stretched out flat on the lush turf and sighed with relief. The prolonged sit in the car had amplified his back pain.

With fifteen minutes until the first race, the immediate area was free from many patrons. Several children were running up and down near the racetrack fence, chasing each other. A few family groups were scattered about on the lawn, and the grandstand was only filled to about one-quarter of its capacity. With the gardens in bloom, the light breeze and the clear blue sky, it was a perfect day. Cathy sat down cross-legged next to Cochran, who had now closed his eyes. She knew they were here to talk specifically with two bookmakers: Harry Waterman and Martin McPhee. While it was very pleasant sitting on the cool grass, Johnson was keen to get on with their intended business. She kept glancing at Cochran, wondering when he would be ready to find his feet.

'Be patient, Johnson. You wait until you hear the starting signal, then you can go and talk with McPhee,' said Cochran, sensing his pupil's restlessness. 'He'll be much too busy to talk to either of us now.'

She smiled and nodded to herself. While still of the opinion that Cochran was primarily a rude belligerent slob, she was aware her respect for his judgement had grown since the start of the present investigation. Perhaps his sense of humour isn't too bad either, she thought.

'So, you and Carter are good friends then?' asked Cathy.

'What gave you that idea?'

'The way you talk to him. Which is often harsh, but not particularly convincing. And he called you J. C.'

'A detective lurks within you, Johnson. Yes, we've know each other for years. And J. C. is an off-work title only. So, don't get any ideas.'

'Certainly not, sir,' smiled Cathy. 'I might go for a stroll around. Be back shortly.'

'When you return, do us a favour and bring back a cold drink. My back's telling me it's time for some more painkillers.'

'How about a hot pie and peas as well, sir?'

'The woman's getting educated at last. Thank you, Johnson. That would be much appreciated.'

'See you soon.'

'I'll still be here.'

Cathy Johnson took a leisurely walk to the rear of the grandstand. The lost crowd had been discovered. Every consumer outlet was jammed with people. The bars, food counters, tote windows, and betting ring were all operating at a hectic pace. Generally, it appeared to be an orderly confusion, apart from the bookmaker's area, where pushing and shoving seemed to be the order of the day. Bodies five and six deep, waving money in the air, surrounded the stands, desperately attempting to gain the best price for their fancied runner. With a turn of the dial on the odds board, the bookmaker could disappoint up to a dozen potential customers at once. The unsatisfied gamblers were quick to withdraw the offered cash and weave their way through the masses in frantic pursuit of a more suitable price. Cathy had been listening to the shouting from the ring; one name had stuck in her mind. As she stood watching the commotion, she heard the call of another bookmaker.

'Our John's Back. Two hundred to twenty each way.' Cathy opened her handbag and joined the tote queue. She reached the window as the starting signal sounded for the runners to move into the starting gates.

'Two dollars each way on Our John's Back, please.'

'Horse number?' asked the lady ticket seller.

'I don't know the horse's number, sorry,' said Cathy. The lady sighed in annoyance and checked the list taped on the counter.

'Twelve.' she announced gruffly as she punched in the numbers.

'Thank you. Have a nice day,' said Cathy, as she collected her ticket. The public-address system was in operation, announcing the horses' names as they quickly assembled at the start. The mass exodus from the betting ring was like a stampede, all rushing to gain a vantage point from which to cheer their money to the winning post.

There were still a few punters running around in the clearing betting ring, some looking a little frantic and desperate. Within a couple of minutes of the starting signal the bell sounded, and the race was underway. The last few punters, eager to place their bets, were turned away, disappointed. Cathy approached the stand she had spotted a moment earlier; it was just one of at least forty. At the top of each stand was a name that identified the bookmaker concerned. There was a short, dumpy gentleman with greying hair perusing the writings on the oversized book at the back of the stand marked 'M. McPhee'.

'Excuse me, but is Mr McPhee here?'

'Who wants to know, lady?' replied the gentleman abruptly.

'Constable Johnson, CI Branch,' replied Cathy in her best official voice and displaying her ID.

'CIB!' said the man with surprise. 'I'm McPhee, and I didn't do it.'

'I'm pleased to hear that, Mr McPhee. I would appreciate just a couple of minutes of your time.'

'Always got time to talk to a pretty lady, love.'

'I want to ask you about Alison Stacey. I believe she used to work for you?'

'Oh yes. A terrible thing, that fire,' he said, shaking his head. 'Alison was a nice girl. Pity she got mixed up with that Simon Stacey. I told her he was trouble, but she wouldn't listen to me.'

'I'm listening. Please go on.'

'Call me Marty, nearly everyone does, and those that don't certainly wouldn't call me mister.' The initial rough exterior of the chunky man had been put aside. 'Stacey was well-known round here a couple of years back. He'd hit the ring with thousands of dollars at a time. He'd bet on only one local horse every other Saturday. The bastard cleaned us out, time and time again.'

'Are you suggesting there was something improper going on?'

'Yes, I am, but I could never prove anything, mind you, and I wouldn't want to say anything that might be found to be liable.'

'Strictly off the record, Marty,' said Cathy reassuringly.

'Well,' said McPhee, moving a little closer to the constable. 'I suspect that he was doping horses to make them lose. He'd nobble two or three of the fancied runners, and then bet on the best horse remaining.'

'What about swabs and urine tests?'

'They never showed anything, but I don't believe they routinely screen for marijuana.'

'Marijuana!'

'Shush, shush! Yes, biscuits, marijuana biscuits. The night before the race,' said Marty softly but emphatically. 'The officials tell me they can pick up anything in the testing, but I'm not convinced.' McPhee looked at Johnson; she was smiling. 'Yeah, sounds funny, I agree,' continued the bookmaker. 'Those horses still performed fairly well, but just not up to their best. Quite simply, they were still stoned, and couldn't give a shit about racing.'

'Right, thanks for that,' said Cathy unsurely. 'Can you tell me, why did Alison Stacey stop working with you?'

'I'm telling you the truth, the whole truth, and nothing but the truth, at least as I see it, lady,' said Marty, lifting his hands in the air as a gesture to show he had nothing to hide. 'Alison left after I refused to accept any more large bets from Stacey. I took a bet of forty grand, at five to one. I was only able to lay off eighty, so he took me down to the tune of one hundred and twenty thousand dollars. To bet like that you've got to buy more than the form guide. Alison and Simon worked like a bit of a tag team here in the betting ring.'

'Do you know anyone who would have liked to see Stacey or his wife out of the way?'

'If you'd asked me that two years ago, you could have had the names of every bookie here, and no one lost more to the bastard than I did. We were just glad to see the back of him,' said Marty, still using hand signals to assist his answers. 'Generally though, we've found it not a good idea to murder our winning customers. It tends to discourage the other punters.'

'I'm sure you're right,' said Cathy, not particularly amused, as she remembered the gruesome photographs of the victims. 'You must have known Alison fairly well; was there anything unusual, apart from marijuana biscuits, of course, that either she or Stacey were involved in?'

'Stacey was a keen card player. With his style, you could be sure he'd upset a few people. Apart from that...' McPhee paused, looked to the ground, and held his nose between his thumb and forefinger as he thought. 'Alison was in some sort of club years ago. I don't know much about it, only that Stacey got her out. Waterman's the one to talk to. Stacey used to work for him before he became a pain in the arse. He used to talk to Waterman, the two were friends for some obscure reason. Maybe he can tell you a little more.'

'Thanks, Marty. If you think of anything at all that may help, please let us know.' Cathy handed over her calling card. 'Just one more thing before I go; how did Our John's Back go in the last race?'

'Hey, Bob!' called Marty to his offsider. 'Where'd Our John finish in the last?'

'He fell just after the start. Didn't finish at all,' came the reply.

'That'd be right. Thanks again, Marty,' said Cathy. She screwed the ticket up and let it fall to the ground.

*   *   *

It was fifteen minutes before Cathy Johnson was served. The fruit salad looked tasty, and rather than join another queue for a pie and peas, she took a risk and purchased an extra one, together with two natural orange juices to complement the healthy snack. After a careful balancing act, Cathy reached her grassy resting place. The horizontal Cochran landmark was unmistakable.

'Our John's Back, eh,' she mused quietly, looking at the food in her arms. 'Definitely requires more training.' She took another two steps forward.

'Lunch is served, sir,' she said, raising her voice and hovering above the inspector with her hands full. He opened one eye.

'Now, sit down very carefully, Johnson,' he said, slowly. 'Concentrate, and don't rush.' Cathy smiled, and executed the task without disaster. 'I know it's a long time since I've been to the races, but I didn't think a hot pie with peas would have changed that much. And this,' said Cochran, holding up the orange juice, 'must be a chocolate thick shake!'

'I'm sure a man with your astute reasoning ability and obvious strength of character will have both the understanding and sense of determination to accept this meal for what it really is,' said Cathy firmly. 'Just in case you have any doubts, this is the beginning of your journey to a longer and healthier existence. In layman's terms it's called a weight reduction program.'

'Shit, Johnson, do you have to kick a man when he's down? And besides, you're not my bloody mother, you know!' cursed

Cochran loudly. 'Aren't you aware that injured people require nourishment to assist recovery?'

'You have sufficient reserves to replace every organ in your body twice, if necessary,' replied Cathy bravely. Despite the objections, she could sense there was a distinct lack of conviction in Cochran's voice. It was an opportunity not only to get some of her own back, but maybe to do the fat man some good at the same time.

'Now, while McPhee wasn't a fountain of information, he did have a couple of interesting things to say.' Cathy proceeded to reiterate the conversation.

*   *   *

Dan Marshall sat at the desk in the front office of the police station, perusing the shortened list of names. Sergeant Carter stood behind the service counter talking on the phone. The two men had been busy with the computer, telephone, and fax machine, and had condensed the original two hundred and fifty-two down to a short list of twenty-eight possible persons who resembled the unknown murder victim and may have been in the local area.

'I see. You saw the man yesterday, Constable. That's fine. Thank you for your help. Good-bye.' Carter hung up the receiver. 'You can cross Orson Ruscliffe off the list. He was sighted at South Adelaide yesterday reporting a stolen wallet.'

'I've heard that name before. What's he been up for?' asked Marshall lifting his eyes from the list of names.

'Suspected of dealing in child porn. Never charged though.'

'Ah yes. I remember reading about the scumbag a few years back.' Marshall nodded his head slowly and screwed up his face, grossly emphasising his crow's feet. 'Friends in high places as I recall. It's not what you know it's who, after all.'

'He wasn't found guilty, was he?' announced Carter, stressing the point. 'Just cross him off the bloody list, will you?'

'Yeah, right-o. Keep your shirt on,' said Marshall, as he drew a line through number seventeen. 'You know there's every chance that this joker isn't on our files, and it may be too early for him to have been reported as missing. Nevertheless, we need to contact all transport services to see if any of these characters have travelled recently. We should also check them against the firearms registers; maybe we'll get lucky and find a match with that .38 slug I extracted from Stacey's pergola.'

'I'd like to bet that when we find the weapon, it'll have Stacey's prints all over it,' said Carter.

'It's not when we find it, it's if we find it. We've had thirty cops combing the area on and around Stacey's land. And we've searched his car and Devlin's flat,' said Marshall sharply. 'If by chance we find the gun, and if Stacey has used it, you can be sure it will be clean. Why don't you use your brains for what you do best, Sarge; that's sitting on your backside shuffling papers. But if you wish to waste a few dollars, I will be more than happy to accommodate your gambling wishes.'

Marshall and Carter, two experienced and popular members of the force, harboured a mutual dislike for one another. More than anything else it was a clash of personalities. Both men were assertive, but differed significantly in the focus of their work. For Carter, the administration and clerical areas were paramount. He was a stickler for organisation, both in the workplace and at home. Marshall, on the other hand, viewed the paperwork as a necessary evil, and consequently was rather a slob as far as the office was concerned. He much preferred being out and about policing, not clerking.

'I only bet with reputable persons. Thanks for the offer.' Carter picked up the telephone and began dialling yet another number. A flashing light appeared on the small switchboard. 'Hey, there's an incoming call on Cochran's extension. Can you take it in his room?'

'I suppose so.' Marshall was quickly into the inspector's office.

'Hello, Marshall speaking.'

'Listen carefully, shithead. While you may be the senior detective on this investigation, when you're on my turf, I'm the boss, so don't try and fuck me around with your smart-arse comments!'

'Carter! You prick!' shouted Marshall as he slammed down the phone. The sergeant had worked many years in the front office, it was his domain, and he was never backward in making anyone else aware of the fact, especially Marshall. As Dan turned to leave the room the telephone began purring quietly once more. He grabbed at it angrily.

'Piss off, you bastard!' bellowed the detective.

'What? Who the hell do you think you're talking to, Marshall? A bit of telephone etiquette would be appreciated.' The voice was unmistakable. It was John Cochran.

'Shhh, err, sorry, sir. I, err, thought it was someone else.' He thumped his fist into his thigh.

'And who would have the pleasure of such a friendly greeting?'

'Carter, sir,' replied Marshall, opting for the truth, as no other name sprang to mind quickly enough. His grip on the phone tightened.

'Carter?' shouted Cochran. 'He's supposed to be there helping you.'

'He is, sir.'

'Is he? Well I'd be pleased if you two would stop playing childish fucking games and get on with the job. I expect to see some useful information when I return.'

'Yes, sir.'

'Have you heard anything from Dempsey or Hogan?'

'They completed another unsuccessful search of the flat, sir.'

'Tell Carter to get one of the local boys to watch the flat. I want those two back at the station,' said Cochran firmly. 'Johnson and I have had a talk to McPhee and Waterman. It appears that Stacey's wife, Alison, was in some sort of sex club when the two first met. This so-called club was founded by a bloke called George Hartley, who Waterman describes as an absolute nutter. Hartley used to stay at the People's Palace in the city. We will be calling in there on our way back. Meanwhile, you see what you can find out about this Hartley fellow. He's between sixty-five and seventy years old.'

'Yes, sir. Anything else, sir?' said Marshall sheepishly.

'Yes. See if you can behave like a role model, Senior Detective.'

Chapter 14

Playing Chess

'Shake a leg,' called the nurse. 'Wake up! Come on. Wake up!'

Simon Stacey groaned, and rolled from his back onto his side. His brow was furrowed and his eyes formed into thin slits as the nurse switched on the bright ceiling light.

'What time is it?' he moaned.

'Six thirty. You can have a shower and get ready for breakfast,' said the lively young lady.

'Six thirty? But it is Sunday morning, isn't it?'

'And a lovely morning it is, too. Now up you get.'

'I haven't been up at six thirty on a Sunday morning since I was being breast fed,' replied Stacey, opening his eyes a little wider. 'Besides, I don't want breakfast, even if it is breast milk.'

'That's not on today's menu. Are you awake? I've got other patients to attend to.'

'Yes, okay, leave me be. I'm awake. Am I your favourite patient, or are you this nice to everyone?'

'All patients get up now except for those in seclusion; that's left for the day staff. Now there'll be no need for me to return with a bucket of cold water, will there?' said the night nurse as she left the room, not waiting for a reply.

'I bet you would too, you cow,' muttered Simon under his breath. The hospital routine was opposite to his usual pattern of late nights with a long sleep in the following morning. He looked at the wall clock in the foyer and estimated he must have had six hours sleep; not too bad, he thought, considering he hadn't felt in the least bit tired when he was bedded down at ten. Simon wondered if the two small yellow pills he took an hour before bed might have helped. It was yesterday morning when the encounter with the red-bearded psychiatrist had resulted in the prescribing of the anti-depressant medication. Simon didn't have any success with his continued insistence that he simply needed a few days of rest without any regular medicine. Doctor Hutchinson nodded patiently and paraphrased Simon's remarks every time he repeated his request...

'I'll be fine, thanks. I just need a bit of time to sort myself out.'

'I hear you say that you'll be okay, Simon, but I feel your stay here will be shortened by taking a course of medication.'

'I don't want to take any drugs.'

'It seems to me that there is something about taking anti-depressants that worries you. Perhaps we can talk about that.'

'I'm a voluntary patient here, surely I can have some say in my treatment,' explained Simon calmly, making a deliberate effort to keep his annoyance under check.

'So, as I understand it, you'd like some involvement in your care. Can you tell me more about your ideas?'

'For one thing, no medication. Let's see how I do just being observed for a few days. What about group therapy or something?'

'I'm interested to hear your suggestions. Group therapy can be organised. I'd like to know more about your objection to medicines.'

'I simply don't think it's necessary. I just need rest.'

'You're telling me that relaxation is all you need, Simon?'

'Exactly, that's exactly right. A good helping of rest and relaxation and I'll be back to my usual self in no time.' Simon felt a glimmer of hope that his message had finally been received. His optimism, however, was short-lived.

'It's good we both agree on a couple of points, Simon. One, that a short period of recuperation is required, and two, that you're not your usual self. The medicine I wish to prescribe will address both problems.'

The conversation went on, with Simon finally relenting and agreeing to a trial of anti-depressants, starting with two tablets on the first night and building up to five after one week. He was discouraged to learn that he would need to be on the medication for at least two weeks before any noticeable effect would be gained. This was definitely not part of his short admission objective. On the positive side, there was a possibility of his transfer to the unlocked psychiatric ward by Wednesday, bed availability permitting. This, thought Simon, was fine, as by then he should have the information he was looking for.

After the obligatory morning bathroom routine, Simon strolled past the central nurses' station on his way to breakfast. The dining room was situated at the eastern end of Ward 21, to the left of the corridor through which he had entered two days earlier. Being last in, he had avoided the queue and presented himself at the counter. His meal of porridge, one scoop of scrambled egg and a slice of cold toast were presented on a tray beneath the security grill. Four staff — three men and a woman — stood at strategic locations keeping a close eye on the assortment of socially unusual individuals. With the ward only three-quarters full there were several spare seats. Stacey sat down next to his new friend and formidable chess opponent, Ras.

'Good morning, Mr Spassky. Tell me, what does a chess master eat for breakfast?'

'Well, a master would eat live monkey brains with a generous helping of chips,' said the old man with a grin. 'That's silicon chips, of course. As for the brains, I doubt that these apes on guard duty would cooperate, not that they have much to contribute anyway.'

'Good point,' said Simon with a smile. 'You really gave me a thrashing yesterday. What about a rematch? I've got a new strategy.' Ras lowered his head and began eating his scrambled egg, not responding in any way to Simon's question. 'What's wrong, my friend? Have I got you worried?'

'Hey, Stacey!' It was Mike, another one of the heavies and therapist nurses, standing right behind him. Simon wondered for a moment whether the male staff had been secretly cloned for the job. 'It's difficult enough to get the old man to eat without you distracting him. If you want a conversation, go to another table. I don't know why you persist in talking with someone who usually answers only in monosyllables or psychotic riddles.'

'I prefer to stay at this table. You'd be surprised what Ras has to say when he wants to.'

'His name is George Hartley, and I would appreciate your calling him by his correct title. It's of no benefit to him or us if you continually reinforce his delusions.'

'Thank you for your advice,' replied Simon. 'Can you leave us to our breakfast now?' The tall, well-built man walked slowly back to his position near the door. The table was in silence and remained that way until the sitting was complete. All patients were required to stay in the dining area until the count of all cutlery items was correct. Anyone too disturbed to remain was escorted to a locked single room until all items had been accounted for.

'Okay, Dougy. Hand over the fork.' Mike walked over to the short, timid man who always sat at the corner table. Doug had his head down, staring at his lap. He immediately unzipped his track suit top and removed the fork from his shirt pocket and passed it over to the waiting hand. Doug gave a series of rapid, frightened glances at Mike's feet but never raised his head.

'Count is correct. Everybody out!' announced Mike.

As the patients vacated the room, the staff unlocked the door to the kitchen and began helping themselves to the remainder of the scrambled egg.

*   *   *

The spacious courtyard, usually referred to as the 'greenhouse', was a popular area for both patients and staff alike. Located on the western side of the building, it overlooked the attractive hospital grounds with a clear view through to Mount Coot-tha in the distance. The many large expanses of unbreakable glass gave the illusion of openness, a pleasant change from the ward interior. A thick, square-shaped metal mesh, partially disguised with creeping vines, provided a secure roofing. Despite the emphasis on security, the courtyard design allowed in enough sunlight and fresh air to make the area reasonably comfortable and relaxing. The fully grassed enclosure included a volleyball or badminton court, several garden settings, complete with all-weather umbrellas, and two fern gardens.

All the regular or long stay residents — that is, those conditioned to queuing for pills, showers, and meals — habitually gathered at the greenhouse entrance half an hour before scheduled opening time. There they awaited the sound of rattling keys. Dependent upon staffing levels, the courtyard would usually be open from ten till twelve in the morning, and again from two through to four o'clock in the afternoon. Sunday was special, and the greenhouse was available for an extra hour, until five.

It was during this bonus hour that Simon Stacey lay on the grass, chin cupped in his hands, considering his next move. It was their second game, and once again Ras had by far the superior position.

'Your new strategy, I'm afraid, is worse than your old one. It's always risky to bring your queen out too early. You should save your most powerful weapon until you can use it to your best advantage.'

'Sounds like a good philosophy, not only over the chessboard,' said Simon.

'Why do you think I choose when, and to whom I speak?' explained Ras. 'As soon as I'm ready to leave, I'll say the right things, to the right people, at the right time.'

'Why stay in here at all? Surely there must be other places where you can feel safe.'

'Free food. Free shelter. And you are locked in. Which is not a bad thing as black Friday approaches. Sure, you are locked in with some heavy dudes, but not with anyone that wants to kill you. I'll be out of here in a week or so.'

'You only leave this place when they're good and ready,' said Simon, glancing at the staff. He leaned forward, close to Ras's face, and spoke softly. 'That Asian nurse, Kym, had a quiet word in my ear. Even though I'm here voluntarily, I can't leave. As soon as I make any sounds about discharge they'll slap a bloody order on me. How do you beat a system like that?'

'The secret, my friend, is to make them believe they're ready to let you go,' chuckled Ras lightly.

'Then you can go casting more spells on unsuspecting people?'

'No, no, no!' whispered the old man loudly. 'I only did that because they wouldn't listen to me. I warned them repeatedly, but I was just ignored. You know, there are some things in this world one should not become involved with, and that's witchcraft, devil worship, and necromancy.'

'Huh!' Simon sat back, somewhat stunned on hearing those words.

'It's your move.' The old man crossed his arms and focused his attention on the chessboard. Simon had lost interest in the game.

'What do you know about such things?' he asked.

'Experience. I've seen the deeds of evil people. I've seen their eyes. Their devil eyes.' Ras paused. For a moment, he seemed a long way from Ward 21. He shook his shoulders and gave a short gasp, as if feeling cold. 'Sure, I go over the top sometimes, but if you don't create a scene, who's going to listen? It's still your move.' He gestured to the chess set with a nod of his head.

'Yes, I know.' Simon glanced at the board briefly. The topic of conversation was compelling. He wanted more information.

'Queen to f5,' muttered Stacey, as he pushed the piece forward. 'Tell me, Ras, what involvement have you had with those evil things?'

'That's a terrible move. It's now mate in three. Would you like to try again?'

'No thanks, please tell me what you know, my friend.'

'I don't like to go back that far, it upsets me.'

'I'm sorry to pry, but I think it could be important for me personally.'

'To you personally! I don't understand how that could be. I suppose we all have our secrets, but witchcraft and Satanism you should leave well alone.' Ras looked at Stacey with some concern. His lips moved rapidly up and down, never parting more than a centimetre. There was a rush of faint whispering words that were far too soft for anyone to understand.

'Are you okay?' There was no immediate response. The soft, indiscernible chatter continued. Simon looked about the courtyard. Eddy was standing near the entrance, sucking on a cigarette and trying to impress one of the young student nurses. Another male nurse was kicking a basketball at a man's feet in an attempt to extract a return kick, but the statue-like patient seemed to be more interested in studying his own toes against the grass. All was well, and so far no one had noticed his companion's unusual antics.

'Ras, are you with me?' Simon placed his hand gently on the old man's shoulder. The touch was like releasing the pause button on a cassette player. George Hartley spoke immediately.

'Very briefly then. Years ago I started a club, nothing sinister, it was just an innocent sex club. There was no harm intended. I saw it as a business opportunity with the chance of getting laid on the side. Not a brothel, and never intended to be. All arrangements were private, between consenting adults. Everything was handled discreetly. It was just like a pleasant social occasion. A chance for people to meet new friends and have some fun. It was going well until a wealthy South Australian moved in. With money and a few goons behind him, he very carefully but very thoroughly changed the emphasis from a bit of good fun to something wicked and evil. He seemed such a decent bloke at first but the demon was in him, luring, deceiving, and plotting. I should have seen it earlier. I'm well out of it all now, but I still know only too well what goes on.'

'This club, did it have a name?'

'When I operated it we simply called it the S L Club — that is, the Socially Liberated Club. Some people called it Hartley's, but the demon man changed it. They now call themselves the 13th Black Candle.'

'Holy shit!'

'Nothing holy about them. Very unholy. They hold special sacrificial services they call Bodytune.'

'Bodytune?' exclaimed Simon sharply.

'Yes, Bodytune. The 13th Black Candle. Do these names mean something to you?'

'I own a gym. A health centre called Bodytone.' Stacey was suddenly deep in thought, remembering the events surrounding the naming of his fitness club shortly after he bought out the original owners. He and Alison had argued for days. She repeatedly demanded that the name be changed, but could offer little explanation for her unusually disagreeable behaviour, other than an intense dislike for the chosen title. Simon had insisted that the name, selected by a panel of staff, remain.

'Simon, what's going on here? What does this mean to you?' insisted Ras. His eyes had widened and his voice had developed a slight tremble. His lips began to pitter-patter again.

'My wife, Alison. I think that's the club she was involved with. Who was this South Australian, what's his name?' The question drew no immediate response. Ras was staring as though he was looking right through Simon. 'What's wrong now, for Christ's sake? What are you thinking? I need to know!'

'You told me your son was killed in the fire, he was nearly two years old?'

'Yes, that's right, but why —'

'When was his birthday?' interrupted Ras. Simon found his friend's manner had changed dramatically. He spoke loudly and clearly with an uncomfortable seriousness.

'Why is that important? What is going —'

'Answer me, Stacey. When was he born?'

'He was born on the sixteenth of August, 1984,' replied Simon carefully. No sooner had the words left his lips than Ras jumped to his feet with a look of horror.

'You!' he yelled. 'You're the one. You're the one. Friday, it's you. Curse you, curse you!' Ras pointed at Stacey in disbelief and kicked the chess pieces in his face. 'Damn you, Simon Stacey. Damn you to hell!' With that he turned and ran full pace towards one of the courtyard windows. The two male staff were quickly in pursuit, but just a pace too slow to prevent the old man slamming into the resilient glass with an echoing thud. The glass bowed and catapulted Ras backwards. He landed heavily, flat on his back. Blood streamed freely from both nostrils. It poured over his lips into his open mouth and down his cheeks to his ear lobes, where it dripped rapidly onto the grass. His eyes were wide open and pupils dilated. The loud respiratory grunts could be heard clearly throughout the Greenhouse.

'Clear the courtyard!' shouted Eddy. 'Get me some combine, medication, and call the doctor!' Simon arrived at the side of his injured companion.

'Is he okay?'

'No, he's not okay, now piss off, Stacey. I'll talk to you later.'

'Can I help?'

'No! Fuck off!' bellowed Eddy. Simon left the courtyard and returned to his room. He knew that Eddy held him entirely to blame, and as he lay down on his bed, he couldn't help but believe that the male nurse was right. He was responsible for the injury to the old man. Ras had not only made him laugh, but had also stimulated him to think deeply about many things. He had quickly become a friend, and they were getting on so well. He had pressured Ras too hard for information, and in so doing, had lifted the lid off some stressful events.

It was twenty minutes later when the unwelcome but expected visitor, Eddy, arrived.

'Stacey, you've really fucked up this time. I warned you about keeping your nose clean,' he growled, pointing and shaking his finger. 'The poor old bastard is a mess.'

'Will he be all right?' asked Simon lamely.

'You'll be pleased to know he should get over this upset within a few days, although his broken nose will take a bit longer to heal.'

'I'm really sorry. I guess I just didn't understand how fragile he really was.' Simon shook his head remorsefully. 'What sort of outburst was that?'

'You're quite right you don't understand, so I'd be pleased if you'd leave the counselling to those that do.' Eddy remained firm, but not nearly as hostile as Simon had expected. 'He had a panic attack. Rather radical, eh? You may be reassured to know it wasn't his first. What in the hell did you say to him?'

'We had just started to talk about black magic, witchcraft, stuff like that. He told me he found it upsetting to talk about, but I kept on with the conversation.'

'I could have guessed,' nodded Eddy. 'That would have been the worst possible subject to bring up. He has a fixed delusion about when he was attacked years ago. He believes it was the work of a group of Satanists. His attackers slit his abdomen open with a cutthroat razor. The police found him in the gutter with his guts hanging out. And in case you're wondering, it was just two young muggers; they were arrested and charged, but you can't tell old George. He's just set on the Satanists thing and that's that.'

'Yeah, okay. A pretty touchy subject. I won't bring it up again.'

'Damn right you won't. You need to understand that when he comes out of seclusion, you will avoid him like the plague until we can arrange either his, or your transfer to another ward. You're getting off lightly, Stacey. Another prank like this and you'll be making a close inspection of these walls.'

'Right-o, I get the message.'

'Don't upset anyone else. Talk about the weather, or gardening, or something else that's equally boring.'

'Okay then. Just one thing I'd like to ask you. He yelled out "Friday" to me. Do you have any idea what he might have meant by that?'

'I thought we agreed to stick to benign topics. I want you to leave it alone.'

'I will, I promise. I simply want to sort it all out in my own mind,' insisted Simon.

'I think you are full of shit and a lying bastard.'

'No bullshit, honest. Come on, you must have a few ideas.'

'Look, it's probably a delusional thing. He was attacked on a black Friday, so he is probably concerned about this coming Friday, which is the thirteenth. I might be a psych nurse but I'm not fucking psychic. Now, can we leave it at that?' Simon nodded rather reluctantly and began to replay the afternoon's events through in his mind.

*   *   *

Simon Stacey slept little that night, still perplexed by the words and behaviour of Ras, and preoccupied with thoughts and images of his wife and son. He had tried desperately to clearly recall the meeting at the fitness centre when the club's name was chosen. He knew there was an argument and they had reached an impasse. Some wanted Bodytone, others Bodytune. Finally, it was he who terminated any further team discussion and decided on Bodytone. It sounded softer, and seemed to encompass more than simply a tune-up. But who were those who had insisted on tune in the first place? Why did the mentioning of Robbie's birthday precipitate some sort of panic attack? Each time he closed his eyes he saw George Hartley's bloody, staring face. That look of horror seemed to be imprinted on his brain. Ras knew much more, but the prospect of regaining his confidence and talking with him again seemed too distant to feasibly contemplate. But there was someone else here besides Hartley who knew about the 13th Black Candle. Ward 21 was on the list of numbers he had collected from Romoli. Unfortunately, it seemed likely that this person, whoever he may be, would not be extending the hand of friendship. Simon already had his ideas on who this could be, and Mike and Eddy were on top of the list.

Chapter 15

Breach of Duty

Wendy was attending to her early morning chores, wiping down the furniture, restocking the various piles of leaflets, updating the notice board, and altering the weekly roster. She glanced at her watch: eight fifty. There was only ten minutes to tidy Charlie's office before his scheduled arrival. On entering the room, she opened the vertical blinds to keep an eye on the reception desk. The office was often a mess, and today was no exception. Charlie's late-night working back last Friday had given her more work than she expected. The desktop could barely be seen beneath the scraps of paper, open books, assorted documents, and empty Coke cans. Numerous sheets of foolscap were strewn about the floor near Charlie's chair, and several balls of screwed-up paper surrounded the small half-full rubbish bin near the corner. The club manager had an annoying habit of playing basketball with his rejected ideas; some underhand, others lobbed high in the air, and if feeling adventurous, occasionally left-handed behind his back. The two had agreed on a system to keep both parties happy. Any ball-shaped items could be incinerated. Those that looked like rubbish but had Madden's signature on the bottom corner were to be attached to the clipboard on the side of the desk. Any doubtfuls were to be placed in the emptied waste paper bin, and if still there next morning, could be disposed of. Wendy made a start on the desk, placing several items with the many others already on the clipboard. She picked up the books and placed them on the appropriate shelves. As was part of her tidying routine, she slid open the second drawer of the desk to remove the ashtray. Charlie was not a heavy smoker, just three or four a day, but he was careful not to smoke in front of club members or staff. As Wendy picked up the ashtray, the open book on which it was resting caught her attention. She lifted it up and was mesmerised by the grotesque picture on display. She walked slowly to the waste paper basket with the book in one hand and ashtray in the other. The picture had her complete attention. She emptied the dirty receptacle, not realising that three of the four cigarette butts landed on the carpet. She returned to the desk and sat down. Keeping her finger at the opened section, she turned the book to see the front cover — Sorcery and Magic by Oswald Madison. Looking back to the marked page, she read the caption under the illustration: '*The Consecration of the Feast*' depicts four witches preparing a child for a sacrificial ritual. Despite finding it extremely offensive, Wendy found herself staring at the picture with ghoulish curiosity. It seemed to be set in some sort of barn. There was an assortment of carpenter's tools, mainly saws of various sizes, hanging on the wall in the background. The four naked witches were incredibly ugly with sinister, distorted smiling faces. She wondered what sort of sick individual would paint such a picture and why on earth Charlie Madden would be reading such rubbish.

'Hello, Wendy!'

'Aaah!' she squealed with fright. Her body jolted, and the book fell to the floor. 'Oh, Oscar, it's you. You scared me half to death. You shouldn't sneak up on people like that.' Wendy picked up the book and placed it back in the drawer.

'Who's sneaking? I just walked in the door,' smiled Schliemann, pleading innocent to the charge. 'Sorry to startle you. What were you reading? It must have been interesting.'

'One of Charlie's books, I guess you'd call it a horror story.'

'*Sorcery and Magic*, I know the book. I've read some of it.'

'That's awful. You shouldn't read that sort of stuff. It's not healthy.'

'I don't. Charlie left it in the staff room. I gave it back to him on Friday night.'

'He shouldn't read it either. It's probably not his anyway,' grumbled Wendy.

'People have a habit of coming up with surprises, even for those that know them well,' said Oscar. 'I investigated a forty-year-old religious fanatic. A lovely fellow. In the evenings, he loved nothing better than to insert a variety of phallic —'

'Stop!' interrupted Wendy sharply. 'Don't tell me any more. I get the idea. There's plenty of nice romance or adventure stories available. If I read a book like that I wouldn't sleep for weeks. A friend took me to see that awful film, *The Keep*. I was so scared, I moved back in with my mother for a fortnight.' The big European grinned.

'What are you grinning at?' she asked.

'You.'

'A comedian I'm not, although I do seem to provide some people around here with a good laugh,' she said self-consciously. 'Now, can you leave me to get on with my work?'

'I didn't mean to upset you. You're a very nice person.'

'And I think your big blue eyes are very nice too, but they obviously need glasses.' Wendy felt slightly embarrassed and continued with her cleaning, avoiding looking at Oscar.

'Good morning all.'

'Good morning, Charlie,' said Wendy. Schliemann nodded his greeting.

'Everything okay, Oscar?'

'Appears to be. We were just talking about that book you're reading.' Wendy glared daggers at the blonde giant.

'Which book? I'm reading several.'

'The one I gave back to you on Friday.'

'That one? A bit boring, really. What about it?' asked Charlie, as he placed his briefcase beside the desk.

'I was wondering where you'd buy such a book.'

'Who knows? It's not mine, I found it in the gym.' Wendy looked at Oscar and forced an 'I told you so' smile. She licked her finger and drew an imaginary number one in the air.

'If you're not quite finished in here, I might go on my morning rounds now and leave you to it. Is anyone off sick today?'

'No calls as yet. Angela's still away, but Wayne is back after being off sick last Friday. I should only be a few minutes cleaning up here.'

'Oscar, would you like to come for a walk? There's a couple of things I want to talk to you about.'

'Sure,' he replied. The men left the room while Wendy quickly attended to the domestic chores. She felt her routine was a little behind schedule, and was annoyed at herself for not having Charlie's office completed prior to his arrival. The staff meeting and tea rooms still required her attention. Some movement in the foyer caught her attention. It was Detective Briggs.

'Just one moment!' called Wendy. She pulled the plastic liner out of the bin, cussing as she noticed the contents of the ashtray on the floor. She picked up the butts then attended the reception desk, closing the office door behind her.

'Detective. You've just missed our manager, Charlie Madden, by only a moment. I was wanting to give you an appointment on Friday but you left before I had a chance."

'Yes, sorry for that. When do you expect him to return to his office?'

'Possibly about thirty minutes.' She looked at the diary on the reception desk. 'I could squeeze you in then, but only for fifteen minutes.'

'Lovely. That sounds fine. Thanks.'

'Anything I can help you with in the meantime?'

'Ah, no, I don't think so. I'll just have a browse through the fitness shop and flick through a couple of magazines while I wait.'

'No worries.'

The glass door to the Bodytone sales centre was directly opposite the reception desk. The shop had a large range of aerobic and sports clothing, gym equipment, and health foods. Apart from the many well-known brand names, much of the clothing carried the Bodytone label. This was another successful innovation, thought up by Madden and financed by Stacey. Briggs entered the store, keeping a subtle watch on the activity outside. Wendy was now answering the telephone; she had the rubbish bag in her other hand.

Briggs watched as she finished her conversation, hung up the phone, then disappeared from the foyer with the garbage bag. No one else was in sight. He casually moved from the shop back to reception. After a quick glance left and right, he slipped behind the desk and then entered Madden's office and locked the door behind him. After closing the blinds, he sat at the desk and began rummaging through the drawers. The bottom two contained little to spark Brigg's interest. There were a few glossy fitness and interior decorating magazines, health equipment catalogues, an ashtray, and the book on sorcery and magic.

'Weirdo!' said Briggs softly as he replaced the book. He pulled at the top drawer. It was locked, but he smiled confidently as he removed the small black wallet from his hip pocket. Two of the small implements probed the lock for a few seconds until the click of success was heard. As Briggs perused the bank statements and cheque butts, two entries caused him to put pen to paper; a cheque in February and another in late May, both for five thousand dollars, and both payable to Charden Enterprises. Noel recorded the details and placed the piece of paper in the fob pocket on the inside of his shorts. Reaching to the back of the drawer, he pulled forward a small white envelope. Inside was a gold chain bracelet with 'Bodytone' engraved on the tag in old English-style writing. The reverse side had the words, Alison — all my love — Simon. Briggs raised his eyebrows in surprise. He replaced the jewellery, closed and locked the drawer, then had a quick flick through the diary on the desk. A couple of appointments caused him to raise his eyebrows. There was an appointment tonight with a Deborah and another for Saturday with an Alison. 'A bit of a ladies man, eh?' he mumbled. He moved on to Madden's briefcase. Squatting on the floor, Briggs opened the case. There was little to get excited about here either; a set of keys; a collection of new pencils and biros; a coffee mug; one pair of near new heavily treaded jogging shoes, and a few drawings of building projects. Noel frowned and gave a soft, disappointed growl. With the sound of a key sliding into the office door lock, he hurriedly closed

Madden's case, but had no time to do much else before the towering figure of Oscar Schliemann was standing over him. Briggs promptly started groping around on the floor.

'Can you help me? I've lost my contact lens,' he said weakly.

Oscar closed the door, grabbed the detective by the back of the neck with his right hand, and in one movement lifted him to his feet and threw him backwards against the closed door. He then placed his other hand securely around his throat and pushed upwards until the detective's feet were kicking about in the air.

'You disappoint me. I expected something better than the contact lens story,' remarked Oscar quite calmly. The live wall hanging tried in vain to pry the vice from his neck. In desperation, he attempted to kick Schliemann in the groin. This was a mistake.

'Now that is not a nice thing to do.' Oscar's right hand shot up between Briggs' legs, and his fingers wrapped firmly around an unsuspecting pair of testicles. 'It might save us both some time if you tell me the truth.' Briggs could do nothing but grunt and gasp for air. 'Could you speak a little more clearly? I am finding it most difficult to understand you. You're not one of those bloody foreigners, are you?' The detective tried hard to make some intelligible sound. His face had turned crimson. Oscar relaxed his grip on the throat, but continued to hold Briggs off the floor by pushing up on his groin. With a loud wheezing noise, Briggs sucked in air, coughed, and sucked in more.

'Would you care to give me the courtesy of a conversation now?'

'Yes, yes... give me... a... moment... to breathe,' he gasped.

'Let's start with, who are you, and what are you doing in this office? And no crap, or I promise you'll be searching the floor for more than a contact lens.' Schliemann twisted his hand sharply in Brigg's groin just to make the message clear.

'Put me down. Please.'

'You're in no position to give orders, just answers.' Oscar slightly tightened both his grips.

'Okay, okay. I'm a cop. Detective Noel Briggs. I'm working on a homicide.'

'If that is true then you are not a very good cop, and an even worse detective.'

'My back pocket. My ID.' Schliemann lowered Briggs' feet to the floor and turned him face against the door. With one hand round the back of his neck keeping him pinned, he removed a black leather wallet from the detective's pocket. Briggs' eyes strained to see what was going on. 'No, not that one. The other wallet!' Using his teeth, Oscar opened the zip.

'So, this is your detective equipment.' He threw the small tool case on the floor.

'Oscar, is everything all right in there?' shouted Madden.

'Fine, thanks, Charlie. I've got a surprise for you.' Schliemann pulled Briggs away from the door and forced him down to the floor. 'Now, you lie there like a good man, so I don't have to break your neck,' he said most politely. 'Come in, Charlie!'

'What the hell is going on?' asked Madden nervously as he made his entrance. He looked down in amazement at the man on the floor.

'This clown has been going through your office. He says he's a cop.'

'I am a bloody cop!' he snapped. 'If I can show you my ID.' His hand moved towards his trousers. Oscar reacted immediately.

'Easy!' The European's foot struck Briggs across the back of his neck. His nose and lips squashed hard onto the carpet. 'Steady, Briggs, or whoever you are. I feel much happier when you move slowly and with my permission. Now easy does it.' The detective slowly pulled his wallet from his pocket and flicked it across the carpet to Madden's feet. The ashen-faced administrator examined the badge and photograph.

'He's right, Oscar,' stated Charlie with a rather high-pitched squeak in his voice.

'Yes, a bloody cop. A very foolish cop,' grinned Schliemann, totally unmoved after glancing at the open wallet. 'There's an outline of something else in his pocket. What can that be?'

'Nothing else that concerns you,' said Briggs.

'I think I'll be the judge of that.' Schliemann slipped his hand into Briggs' back pocket and removed two small, but neatly folded, squares of clear plastic. Both contained a white powder. 'What have we here? Drugs?'

'Please, that's something I obtained from a suspect earlier today. I intend to get it tested.'

'Bullshit. I'm keeping it,' said Schliemann, as he pushed the plastic envelopes into his own pocket. 'I would recommend in future, if you want information you should either ask for it, or produce a search warrant. You may leave now, and it would be in the best interest of your ongoing health not to return.' Noel rose slowly to his feet and dusted himself down.

'You haven't heard the last of this, I can assure you,' he retorted. 'And I would like those packets back.' He snatched his wallet from Madden.

'Get out of here while you still can, Briggs,' said Schliemann calmly. Briggs pointed his finger in a stabbing motion at the security officer and made a growling sound, but said nothing further. He then turned and scurried off.

'What was he doing here, Oscar?' asked Charlie, trying to put on a brave voice.

'Looking for evidence, possibly against Simon. Either that, or information to incriminate someone else here.'

'You mean he thinks Simon murdered his own family? Or someone here is responsible?' exclaimed Charlie. 'That seems ludicrous.'

'Perhaps. It may be that Simon is their only suspect. You know what I think?' mused Oscar. 'I think Briggs will be in serious trouble when he gets back to the police station. He would have been sent here to interview staff in the regular manner, not to be breaking and entering.'

'What about those packets. Are they really some sort of drug?'

'Oh, I'm sure they are drugs. I'm guessing heroin, but I will check that later. I have an old friend who will be very interested in this information.'

Charlie looked towards the open office door where a small group of spectators had gathered. Wendy, Deborah, Wayne, and a few club members were chatting softly and staring. Oscar Schliemann walked out to the group.

'Everything is fine,' he announced. 'We just had an unwelcome intruder. He won't be back and there's no harm done. You can all carry on as usual.' The inquisitive group began to slowly disperse.

'Deborah!' called Charlie. 'Can I see you for a moment?' The sweaty brunette turned and sauntered back towards the office. Madden now had another reason to justify his rapid pulse. Oscar smiled, gave a wave, and wandered away.

'Hello, Charlie. Are you okay?' said Deb softly, taking his hand and cupping it between hers.

'I'm fine,' lied Madden. 'I wanted to confirm our arrangements for tonight.'

'All systems are go. I'm really looking forward to it.'

'Ah... me too,' he replied, feeling a little uneasy about Deborah's caresses of his hand in full view of those still around. 'My place, shall we say, seven thirty?' Deb winked in response and scratched his palm with her fingernail. Charlie replied with a gentle squeeze of her fingers.

Chapter 16

The Red Scarf

'J. C., do we still need to keep a twenty-four-hour watch on Devlin's flat?' asked Carter. 'I had a call from the traffic branch half an hour ago. They're short-staffed. I said I'd talk to you and get back to them.'

'I guess not,' replied Cochran, as he looked through the names of the missing persons. Of the short list of twenty-eight, only two possibilities remained, both of whom had been reported missing well before the time of the fire. 'Another futile exercise,' he mumbled to himself. 'Yes, that'll be okay, Sarge. We can keep an eye on things ourselves. I want you to call Devlin's place every couple of hours. If there's any answer, let me know. One of us will drive out there again this evening and have another talk to the neighbours.'

'Great. And Briggs is in your office. He doesn't look too happy. He doesn't look too well, either.'

'What's he done this time?'

'Best you ask him. Nothing to do with me, that's for sure.'

'I don't like the sound of this already.' Cochran made his way to his room. He had a slight limp and left-sided tilt, but was steadily improving. Cathy Johnson had managed to obtain an ultrasonic vibrating massager from a physiotherapist girlfriend, but she drew the line at providing the service herself. After a few simple instructions, Cochran's wife, Emily, had proved more than capable of attending to the needs of her injured husband.

The inspector sat at his desk, temporarily ignoring Briggs, who sat anxiously opposite. Cochran was aware that something had gone wrong, and was taking his time to get comfortable and relaxed.

'It's a lovely day, Briggs.' He leaned across the desk. 'Now just watch some bastard come along and fuck it up.'

'Sorry, sir, but I'm afraid that's going to be me,' muttered Noel.

'Of course it's going to be you, Briggs, you've had practice. And you should be afraid! But, let's keep calm,' said Cochran, consciously changing his tone, placing both his hands softly on the desk and reclining gently back to his chair. 'You tell me where you bought that new red scarf of yours.'

'What scarf?' he replied, looking around the room.

'Are you thick, or just stupid? Your neck! Dickhead! Obviously, someone has tried to throttle you before I had the chance.'

'Oh, that,' said Noel, feeling his neck with his hand. 'This Oscar guy assaulted me. Threatened to rip my balls off. Nearly choked me to death for Christ's sake.'

Briggs described the events at Bodytone, making sure he placed as much emphasis as he could on any personal harm or threat. He told the inspector the office door was open and he was looking for Madden. He conveniently omitted his tampering with the lock of the desk drawer. Cochran was seething. His teeth were clenched, and the angry red colouring had filled his cheeks. He continued to listen to Briggs, becoming even angrier as he recognised the signs of his own irritability.

'I've heard enough!' he shouted. 'You knew that your performance on this case was vital to your remaining a detective, and you've gone and blown it. You're stupid, Briggs. In fact, you seem to be working hard to make a success of being a failure!' The inspector stood and paced around the office, waving his hands in all directions, while Noel remained seated. 'I suppose you're hoping they won't lay charges,' the Cochran barrage continued. 'Well I hope they do. How do you think your record will stand up in court? Who the hell do you think you are? You're not the invisible fucking man! You're no super bloody hero! Your shit stinks just like the rest of us, except yours is worse. It makes me want to throw up. You had specific instructions. *By the bloody book,* I said! You're unbelievable. On the last case, you were screwing the suspect, and now you're screwing with me — and guess what?' Cochran put his mouth next to Noel's ear. 'I don't fucking like it!' he shouted. The inspector returned to his seat and took a few deep breaths.

The noise could be heard across the corridor in the debriefing room. Cathy Johnson and Dan Marshall had been reviewing the case and hoping for some divine intervention to ease their frustration. Their conversation had stopped while both listened to the Briggs battering. Cathy turned to Marshall, shaking her head.

'That man is going to burst a blood vessel one of these days. Maybe he needs some hypnosis to help him relax.'

'Are you going to tell him?' Dan asked.

'Sure, I'll tell him. But not right now if you don't mind.'

'Briggs brings these things on himself. Always looking for a short cut or some angle to benefit himself or get laid. I don't know why the boss gave him another chance. We all know what he's like.'

'Maybe he did it deliberately, to have a good reason to get rid of him?'

'If that's true, he's only got himself to blame for the stuff up. Anyway, enough of that; what have we got on Stacey?' Marshall opened the manila folder. 'An alcoholic storekeeper who is fairly sure that he sold him high wattage light bulbs, yet he can't pull Stacey's photo out of a group of only three. An old woman who thinks she saw a Mercedes at Edward Duncan's house at the time he was murdered. Stacey unwilling to give an account of his whereabouts between twelve and four Wednesday morning, and then faking a suicide attempt to possibly escape further investigation. A recent increase in his wife's insurance policy.' Marshall shook his head. 'It's not what you'd call a rock-solid case, but it does all point to Stacey.'

'Stacey's concealing something,' said Cathy. 'And what about the missing dental files? What about the naked body and the .38 slug? What about this sex club his wife was in and that suicide note? Oh, Dan, I'm so confused.'

The discussion between the two investigators continued, with the occasional interruption as they paused to listen to the shouts from John Cochran.

Dempsey and Hogan were out, once again, talking with friends, acquaintances, and family of Simon and Alison Stacey. So far, the only people willing to talk freely were the dentist, Howard Morgan, and some of the relatives. From Stacey's suicide note there were still three left to talk with: Donald Granger, alias 'Donger', Warren 'Wart' Tarrasch, and finally Ralph, who remained the only name not yet identified as even being a real person.

The Cochran task force believed those few lines written by Stacey were much more than a farewell message to his friend, Adrian. The group had spent two hours on Sunday attempting to break down the coded message. After an interesting but largely unsuccessful brainstorming exercise, Cochran asked each of the group to use their imagination and write down at least two interpretations of the note, however bizarre their ideas might have appeared to be. Cathy Johnson, with her passion for crosswords and anagrams, had surprised and entertained everyone with her rearranging of the letters in parts of the note. She discovered that the letters from the names listed in the note formed the words, THINK LOBBY WARDROBE, WHO'D RAPE GARTH. Cochran, amazed with Johnson's hidden talent, had supported her efforts to unravel the message. While no one knew of any *lobby wardrobe* or anyone called Garth, he had praised her for her creative thinking and application to the task. With their collective thoughts, the investigators had returned to Devlin's flat and explored each possibility. References in the note to time, beer, furniture, cards, and music had everyone checking clocks, the fridge and contents, chairs, and stereo, all to no avail.

*   *   *

It was 3.00 p.m. Monday afternoon when Dempsey and Hogan returned to the station. Cochran immediately summoned the team, including Carter, to a meeting for an update on developments and consideration of new strategies.

'Before we hear from the dynamic duo, I want you all to know that Briggs and I have had a long talk,' said Cochran calmly. He paused momentarily and, as was his habit, leaned forward across the desk. 'It has been decided that he will be helping Sergeant Carter for the rest of this investigation, unless for some good reason I determine otherwise. Now, if some of you inquisitive persons wish to know why I have made this decision, it involves searching without a warrant. You can ask Detective Briggs for the finer details. Is that in order, Briggs?'

'Yes, sir,' nodded Noel sheepishly.

'Despite this morning's problem, there are a couple of possible leads that need some careful follow-up. When I say careful, I mean careful. Any information or evidence gained through an illegal search cannot be relied upon to use in court. At the same time, I'm not prepared to ignore anything that may help us in this investigation. It's your contribution, Briggs, you can share it with everyone,' said Cochran with some regret. The detective went on to describe what he had seen in Madden's office, with special emphasis on the gold bracelet, the two cheque butts, and the appointment with Alison. As he spoke he became more enthusiastic about his discoveries, and seemed to be showing little regard for his unorthodox method of information gathering.

'I have made some enquires,' he went on, 'Charden Enterprises is a registered business under the names Charles Madden and Alison Stacey, supposedly providing management services. I wonder what sort of relationship these two really had. I think we should talk with Madden.'

'You won't be talking to anyone, Briggs. Let's get that perfectly clear,' said Cochran firmly. 'I can't help but get the impression that you seem to have already forgotten the quiet chat we had earlier.'

'No, sir, I haven't forgotten,' replied the detective, brought back to reality by the inspector's voice. 'There's just one more point to make,' continued Briggs. 'There's a girl called Angela who works as a part-time personal trainer. I haven't been able to establish if she is the same Angela who was seeing the elusive Adrian Devlin.'

'Okay, there's a job for you two, Dempsey and Hogan. See Madden, eat a bit of humble pie, apologise, and find out what you can. Now, listen up, all of you!' barked Cochran. 'We have located that old fella, George Hartley. He's the bloke who started the sex club that Alison Stacey was involved with. And surprise, surprise, he's in the psychiatric ward. In Ward 21, with Stacey. It would seem Stacey is remaining one step ahead of us. Hartley is off the planet, under sedation and in isolation, but we're in regular contact with the hospital, and I have been informed that as soon as he comes round, we will be able to have a brief interview. In the meantime, we need to make more of an effort to find out what we can about this club. It may turn out to be another dead end, but I want more information, and I want it quick. Dempsey, what have you got for us?'

Detective Richard Dempsey flicked through his notebook. He was fanatical about recording every snippet of information.

'Come on, Dempsey!' ordered Cochran.

'Yes, sir, I've got it here,' said Dempsey. 'We talked to everyone we can think of, but no one seems to know this person called Ralph mentioned in the suicide note; it's as if he doesn't exist. No joy either in finding out where Adrian Devlin is. As for enemies of the Stacey family, another blank really, apart from a passing comment by Donald Granger that one or two bookmakers didn't like him, but that was a couple of years back.'

'Okay Dempsey, you've told us what you didn't find out. Now please tell us something you did.'

'Stacey's not normally a big beer drinker,' continued Dempsey. 'He has a reputation for throwing up after a few stubbies. He usually prefers scotch or red wine. It could have been his bottle that was forced down Duncan's throat.'

'Maybe. Anything else?'

'A little more concerning that suicide note. Apparently, none of the furniture in the flat was ever Stacey's, and while some is old and a little out of shape, none of it is broken; at least it wasn't before we got stuck into it,' quipped the detective, only managing to amuse himself. 'The only things in the flat that belonged to Stacey were a couple of framed pictures.' Cochran was still leaning over the desk, but was now staring at the ceiling. The room was in silence.

After a moment, Cochran slapped his hands together. 'Bingo! Framed pictures, of course! Does anyone recall the picture on the inside of the bathroom wall? It depicted a chimpanzee with its head stuck in a toilet bowl, the caption below read, *"Good-bye Cruel World"*. Hogan, did you check out Devlin's toilet?'

'Yes, sir, I looked in the cistern.'

'Well next time, Hogan, perhaps you'll be a little more thorough. Who knows? It might be just the incentive you need to stop biting your fingernails. Ralph, that name from the suicide note exists, all right. Ralph is in fact the toilet bowl, and I'd like to bet that there's something else in there, too, maybe that tape.' Cathy Johnson looked perplexed and turned to Marshall.

'I don't get it, Dan,' she whispered.

'Ralph, vomit, throw up. It's slang. You know, the sound you make with a good chuck — rrr...alff! It's a reference to the toilet bowl, as is the picture of the chimp with its head in the dunny. And Good-bye Cruel World is also a suicide reference. It all fits. We should have seen it sooner.'

'You mean my *Think Lobby Wardrobe, Who'd Rape Garth* wasn't right?' said Johnson, dropping her bottom lip in a half-hearted search for sympathy.

'Sorry, Cath,' laughed Marshall, as he patted her on the head.

'Okay, let's move!' grunted Cochran sharply. 'Johnson and Marshall, you come with me. Dempsey and Hogan, chase up Madden and talk to that Angela girl. I'm sure Madden will have her details. Carter, get on that telephone and call some of the local escort girls, see if they know anything about this sex club. I'm sure Briggs will be able to supply you with the phone numbers. And Briggs, remember I said telephone *only*; if there's any visiting to be done, Hogan can do it when he gets back. C'mon, let's go then, there's no time to lose. I've called off the bloody watch on Devlin's flat!'

*   *   *

Adrian Devlin's bathroom was a typical one for most of the lower-priced flats in the area. The only architectural dilemma being how to squeeze all the basic facilities into the six-square-metre floor space. The shower was mounted over a square bath, the size of which would guarantee a close inspection of the bather's knees. Cochran squatted down in front of the toilet bowl, placed one hand on the white plastic seat and lifted it up. The seat and lid fell to one side. Both holding brackets were broken.

'*Fixed up once and for all* — that's what Stacey said in his note, and this is what he meant,' explained Cochran, holding up the toilet seat as if it was a prized personal possession. 'Marshall, check that cistern again, will you? Dear Detective Johnson, can you answer a simple question for me?'

'Well, I'll try to, sir,' replied Cathy hesitantly.

'How many men do you think it would take to effectively search this flat?'

'I'm not sure what you're getting at, sir. Three or four I guess.'

'And how many men to give this bathroom a good going over?'

'Time permitting, just one should do.'

'Wrong, Johnson!' barked Cochran gleefully. 'The answer is none, because it's not a man's job, is it? Now stick your hand down this toilet bowl, and don't forget to check under the rim.'

'Sir!' squawked Cathy in horror. 'That's not at all fair! After all I'm just new to this sort of thing. I think you should show me how it's done. I personally prefer the rule, *finders keepers*.' John Cochran closed his eyes and sighed.

'Marshall, anything in that cistern?' Detective Marshall lifted the ceramic lid, placed it on the shower floor, then peered inside.

'Yes, but nothing that shouldn't be here.'

'Well, check in here then.'

'Sorry, sir, I think Johnson was right. Besides, my hands are too big for the gloves provided,' replied Marshall, trying hard to hold back a grin.

'Okay, you two.' The inspector pulled a latex glove from his pocket.

'Now pay attention. There's a lesson to be learned here. In the pursuit of evidence, no stone must be left unturned, and a detective inspector's job is to occasionally lead by example. So be aware, that if my demonstration reveals nothing, it's into the sewerage pipes for both of you.' With that, Cochran plunged his gloved hand into the toilet water. His fingers reached up around the 'S' bend. He cringed as he felt the slimy surface. He probed his thick forearm further forwards.

'There's something in here. It's firm and round,' grunted the big man as he tried to grip the item. Dan, who had been trying hard to contain himself, erupted into laughter. 'Shut up, Marshall, it's not what you're thinking. Ah, got it!' Cochran pulled the object free, after a little difficulty negotiating it past the bend. He threw it down on the bathroom floor, sending droplets of water over Dan's shoes. At first glance it looked like a rolled-up magazine wrapped in plastic. Marshall knelt, took a penknife from his pocket, and cut the single piece of string from the middle of the cylinder. The mystery item unrolled slightly, revealing a tied plastic bag. He sliced open the rough packaging and spilled the contents onto the floor. A name protruded from the top left-hand corner of the bent cardboard file: Devlin, A. R.

'Devlin's dental records!' exclaimed Marshall. 'I don't believe it. What the hell are they doing here? It doesn't make sense.'

'Give me that penknife,' demanded Cochran abruptly. Dan passed it over, and the inspector's arm once again disappeared into the bowl. He felt the strain in his lower back as he twisted himself awkwardly to get his hand at the best angle to use the penknife.

This time he found something smaller. He stood, holding something barely discernible between his fingers. 'Now I ask you, who would put silicone gel on the inside of a perfectly good toilet bowl?' Cochran's two colleagues offered no immediate answer. 'My guess is someone like Simon Stacey, to secure and hide something small. Perhaps something like a micro-cassette tape?'

'Is there anything else in there?' asked Johnson.

'Yes, but as Marshall would say, nothing that shouldn't be there. There's no tape. Some bastard's been here before us! Two questions; how did they know to look here? And who the hell was it?'

'I don't think it would be Devlin. He hasn't shown up anywhere,' said Johnson. 'What about Madden? Stacey told us what a resourceful guy he is and how he knows all of his friends' details. He had the bracelet in his drawer and an appointment with Alison in his diary.'

'Johnson, I like your thinking. Hopefully Dempsey and Hogan are catching up with him. I wouldn't mind a chat with him myself.'

Chapter 17

Dinner is Served

It had been a frantic afternoon, but Charlie was sure the fruits of his labour would be well worth the trial of the shopping trolley derby. He'd left Bodytone early and scampered through numerous food stores, carefully selecting all the ingredients for the special evening meal. One by one Madden crossed them off the list he had thoughtfully prepared the previous night. He was like an excited adolescent nervously preparing for his first date.

It was seven thirty. Charlie had finished cleaning his teeth and gargling with breath freshener for the second time. The moment had finally arrived to light the dining room candles and select the music to suit the mood of the evening. He flicked through his extensive collection of LPs. Rejecting the large variety of contemporary music, he ultimately settled on a classical choice — Mendelssohn, beginning with the 'Spring Song'. Madden smiled as he placed the record on the turntable and let the stylus hover in readiness above the first track. Wandering through the house, he checked each room once again, making a few final adjustments. He put down the toilet seat, fluffed up the pillows on the double bed, switched on the lava lamp, rearranged the cushions in the lounge, and polished some of the cutlery with a clean handkerchief. A last look in the kitchen and he could sit down and quietly await the beautiful brunette's arrival.

The first course, a vegetable platter with a curry mayonnaise dip, was ready to serve. Charlie had selected the recipes and ingredients carefully. The meal needed to be distinctive and palatable, but at the same time not too heavy on the calories; Deborah would like that. He had decided on foil-baked snapper with a tossed salad for the main course, followed by a small serving of strawberry and mango cobbler for dessert. The Krug, a vintage French champagne he had specially ordered last Friday, would be like liquid gold, and the perfect prelude to the remainder of the evening. Leaving the kitchen, Madden glanced nervously at his watch: 7.45. Deborah was running late. He looked at the shimmering flames on the dining room table; the wax drops were slowly forming narrow pink stalactites down the sides of both candles. Once again on his feet, Charlie moved closer to the table, repositioned the serviettes and looking at his wrist: 7.48. Time was almost at a standstill; minutes seemed like hours.

'Come on, Deb,' cursed Madden anxiously, as he ventured again to the toilet. He freed himself from his new blue denim jeans and squirted an infinitesimal amount of clear urine into the bowl.

'Listen, dribble dick, you must be as nervous as me. I expect you to do your duty tonight, stand and be counted. I'm told it's not size that counts, so let's hope that's not just an urban myth to make us both feel better.' The chiming of the doorbell interrupted Charlie's private conversation. 'It's action stations, I'll see you later!'

On his way through the lounge he released the stylus arm. A soft crackle of needle on vinyl preceded Mendelssohn. Madden cleared his throat and opened the door. His pounding heart sank to his boots as he looked at the wrinkled face of the old man from across the road.

'What do you want?' he said sharply.

'Well, that's a fine greeting for someone who came to extend the arm of friendship and hospitality,' came the surprised reply.

'Leo, mate, I'm sorry. I didn't mean to be rude, it's just that I was expecting someone else.'

'Your face is as long as a fiddle. It must be a woman.' Leo peered around Charlie into the unit. 'Candles. Nice table setting. Classical music. Shit, you are serious!'

'Serious? Yes, seriously nervous. How stupid is that?' Charlie looked apprehensively at the car lights slowly moving up the street. The vehicle pulled into his driveway. 'That's her car, she's here!'

'Well I'd better be going then. I was going to invite you over for a quiet drink, in consideration of you being on your own and all that, but maybe this is a bad time. Wow, she's stunning. If she's got a sister let me know.'

'You couldn't handle the pace. Go on, get out of here, Leo, you animal.'

'See you tomorrow then.' The old man winked, punched Madden gently on the shoulder and headed for home. His aged friend was right, Deborah looked dazzling. The black cropped bolero and rich, red velvet strapless dress highlighted her streamlined figure. Her long, dark hair was swept to one side, resting almost teasingly over her left breast. She sauntered up to her date, placed her hands on his shoulders, and pecked him softly on the cheek.

'Hi, Charlie,' whispered Deb, breathing into his ear. 'Sorry I'm a bit late. Are you ready for me?'

'Jesus, Deb!' exclaimed Madden.

'I'm not embarrassing you am I?' said Deb, now kissing him on the neck. 'I certainly don't mean to. It's just that…well, I've been so looking forward to spending some time alone with you.' Charlie quickly glanced around, checking there were no witnesses to the conversation. Leo was still gawking from the other side of the street.

'I think we should go inside.' Madden placed his arm around Deborah's waist, anxious to get her behind closed doors. 'We'll be more comfortable talking in the dining room.'

'Hmm…or panting in the bedroom,' she replied.

'Holy sh_t, you must be the sexiest woman I've ever met.' The feeling in his jeans had stirred from slightly above dormant to maximum in only seconds. The door closed and Deborah pushed herself up against Charlie, forcing him two paces back up against the wall. Her groin writhed hard into his.

'Wow!' said Deb, glancing down at Madden's groin. 'It has been a while, hasn't it?' The back of Charlie's head bumped loudly against the wall as Deb forced it back with the pressure of her mouth on his. She plunged her tongue deeply, then stopped suddenly and pulled back. She gazed eagerly into his eyes. 'I'm hungry, Charlie. I want to eat.'

'Ah, well, um…everything is ready,' he said, momentarily confused.

'Yes, it most definitely is.' She dropped to her knees.

Right at that moment there was a loud rap on the door, followed by the words, 'Mr Madden, this is the police!'

Chapter 18

Sweet Dreams

Simon joined the eight thirty queue for the Monday evening round of medication. He thought through another day in the locked psychiatric ward. Overall it had been a day of recovery and not discovery. And while he was pleased to have no further symptoms from the overdose of diazepam, it was disappointing that there was no clear indication as to who may know something about the murder of his family. He felt he was relying more on intuition than anything else.

Everything in Ward 21 was structured to timeframes from the moment of being woken early to going to bed at night. The three meal breaks, morning tea, afternoon tea, and supper all ran like clockwork. Monday to Friday there was always a nine o'clock morning meeting for 45 minutes for all patients well enough to attend, and in the afternoon from one o'clock on some form of supervised physical activity. On top of all this there were various appointments with psychiatrists, social workers, and others to slot in. Despite all this scheduling, Simon had been trying to talk to as many staff as he could with the thought of tracking down whoever may be the link to the 13th Black Candle. Some staff were forthcoming with some personal information about their off-work activities and others were not. Mike and Eddy gave him nothing at all.

Simon arrived at the front of the queue.

'Hi there, Simon.' It was Kym, the pretty Asian nurse. At least she was someone who would talk to him. He knew she liked animals, did some jogging, and enjoyed cooking. 'How did you manage on your first dose of medication yesterday?'

'Yeah, quite well thanks. No ill effects,' he replied. 'Have you cooked up anything special lately?'

'I did a tasty red snapper in coconut and tamarind sauce yesterday.'

'Sounds way better than hospital food.'

'Here's your tablets.' She passed two yellow pills in a small medicine cup through the opening below the medication room window.

'Right.' Simon looked at the two tablets as he turned away from the window. 'They look sort of more yellow than the last lot.' He felt a push on his shoulder. It was Eddy. He held out a small cup of water.

'Just take them, Stacey. Don't fuck about,' he demanded.

'Yeah, yeah. Okay.' He took the water.

'Good night, Simon. See you again soon,' said Kym. Simon took the tablets and half-turned back to Kym. He raised his water.

'Night, Kym.' He swallowed the tablets and handed the cup back to Eddy. 'Can you tell me how old George is doing?'

'Didn't we have a chat about this?' said the male nurse. 'You are not to go anywhere near him.'

'I know. I don't even want to see him,' lied Simon. 'I was just concerned for his welfare. He seemed such a nice man.'

'I don't believe a damned word you say, Stacey. But in summary, he's still as crazy as a shithouse rat. Just leave it. Goodnight.'

'Okay then.' Simon moved away to his room, turned off the light on the panel outside the door, then dropped onto the bed and stared at the ceiling.

*   *   *

Some time later, he opened his eyes and slowly looked around. It was still dark, and for some reason he was lying on the cold grass of the greenhouse. Not a soul was in sight. The courtyard was closed. He sat up and checked out his surroundings. In the dim lighting, he could discern the outline of the garden furniture and badminton net. Looking through the expanse of glass and beyond the confines of his secluded area, he could see a scattered but varied assortment of flickering lights. Each seemed to have a radiance of thin, shining spindles surrounded by a faint halo. The smallest and most distant sparklers, set back in the hills, reminded Simon of how things used to be only a few days ago. A cool night rugged up in front of the fireplace with Alison. Robbie lying asleep in his arms. A large mug of Irish coffee at his side, and in the background Phoebe Snow singing 'Don't Let Me Down'. He would carefully tuck his son into bed, kiss him on the forehead, turn on the Donald Duck night-light and return to the warmth of the fire, and Alison. He smiled at the thought.

Simon's escape into fantasy was strangely interrupted by a soft tapping sound. A swarm of moths, attracted by the glow of an interior light, flicked themselves lightly against the glass of the closed greenhouse doors. Simon slowly stood as he stared at the suicidal creatures. They must have been at least ten metres away, yet he could still hear them fluttering clearly. He scratched his head as he wondered how long he had been sleeping and why he had been left alone. There seemed no rational explanation. Surely the staff, despite their many shortcomings, must have noticed someone asleep on the grass before they locked up. After some moments assessing the situation, he decided that he had been deliberately locked out of the main ward area to teach him a lesson. He stared again at the moths. Their fluttering sound had become louder. There seemed to be more of them than before. Simon swallowed heavily, and almost in slow motion proceeded towards the locked doors.

'Eddy, you arsehole!' he muttered, fully aware of whose idea it would have been. Simon also blamed the small yellow tablets. He could recall being firmly directed to take them, and he assumed that somehow, in some sort of vague state, he had crossed swords yet again with his thump therapist.

A second noise became more audible with every step. Stacey placed his hand on his chest. Now he could even feel the sound. It was his heart pounding. An intense fear was welling up from his stomach. That petrified feeling resurrected a memory that had been buried for years. He was twelve and alone in his bedroom with an American Playboy magazine. Completely absorbed by the furry triangle of the centrefold and only seconds away from orgasm, he had not heard his father come in. Simon was never sure whether it was the fact of being caught dick in hand, or making a mess over his old man's magazine that had caused so much hostility. He had experienced fear that day, but this was worse, much worse.

The moths seemed to have doubled in size and were now flapping against the glass with frightening intensity. He looked down at his hand still on his chest. It vibrated in time with the hammering of his heart. Sweat ran freely from every pore in his body. The tip of his nose dripped like a tap, and his eyes stung as the salty liquid partly obscured his vision. He thought he had stopped moving his legs, but his body glided inevitably towards the moths, now the size of small birds. Breathing was becoming difficult. That dry, burning feeling in his throat stimulated further memories. The darkest corner of the park, his good friend Adrian, and a huge joint the size of a cigar. Walking proved an unusually difficult task. The ground was rolling side to side. If he could have urinated he'd have drunk it to quell the fire in his throat. Simon desperately wished he could make a permanent escape into one of his vivid memories but he continued to be drawn closer. Neither could he turn his gaze away nor control his unwilling forward motion. Every hair on his arms stood upright as he felt the hot air from those huge wings against his clammy skin. His respirations had deteriorated into a loud, squeaky wheezing; Mum and Dad's farmyard gate; Cochran's car suspension; Robbie's futile struggle for air in the smoke and heat. Simon opened his mouth to scream. He had barely enough air to breathe. All sounds were now drowned out by the clattering of the giant creatures whose wings now slapped against his face.

'Hang onto him! Hurry up with that medication!' bellowed Eddy. 'Stacey, settle down. No one is going to harm you!' Simon's eyes opened. The creatures were changing. Wings became fingers and hands all over his body, stopping him escaping. Trying to stop him breathing. The noises changed to voices, shouting, ordering and threatening. Simon was staring straight ahead. Amid the moths, hands and arms, a face was forming. He squeezed his eyes tightly and then looked again. The head of the biggest moth of all morphed into the face of Eddy. Stacey summoned every ounce of his waning energy, lunged forward, and released a prolonged, ear-piercing scream. His forehead struck hard at its target and then fell back on the bed.

'Fuck!' Eddy shook his head. Spots of blood sprinkled across the sheets and Stacey's face. 'Get that bloody needle in. Give him the lot, for Christ's sake!' Simon felt a sting in his left forearm, followed by an ache travelling up his arm to the shoulder. He was beyond resisting any further. A black curtain began to fall. Simon partly opened one eye. The biggest moth was squashed over the locked doors. He smiled and fell into a deep sleep.

Chapter 19

An Innocent Man?

'Good evening, Mr Madden,' said John Cochran politely. 'Thank you for coming down to the station. Detective Dempsey and Hogan did try to catch you at work this afternoon but they were advised that you had left early on business. I'm very sorry to interrupt your evening like this. I realise it's quite late, but nevertheless it is very important, as I am sure you understand.' The inspector had adopted a conciliatory approach. Gerry Hogan, occupying a seat to one side of Cochran's office desk, slowly lifted his hand and placed one finger over his lips as if to prevent some sarcastic utterance. Cochran walked around his desk and sat down and faced Madden. He stretched backwards, with his hands holding the back of his head and groaned loudly, as if gaining some pleasurable relief, then placed his arms in front of him across the desk. 'I must also apologise for the behaviour of Detective Briggs earlier today. He was totally out of line and will be severely dealt with by the department.'

'I would have been happy to talk with him. He had no need to go sneaking about looking in my drawers and briefcase. I have nothing to hide.'

'Very good. As I say, I am sorry about that. He will not trouble you any further.'

'I'd really like to get this over with. I've been waiting nearly an hour already and I haven't had dinner yet,' said Charlie in a quiet but deliberate manner.

'Actually, it's forty-five minutes, not an hour,' remarked Cochran almost pleasantly, as he glanced at his watch. He then paused for a moment and reminded himself of his plan, and continued in a most courteous and uncharacteristic style, 'Would you care for some coffee, Mr Madden?'

'No thank you, but I would very much like some questions so I can return home.' Charlie thought of Deborah. He squirmed in his chair and tugged at the crotch of his jeans. He slowly extended his leg, pushed his heel firmly into the floor, and transferred weight to his left buttock.

'Is something wrong? You look concerned,' said Cochran.

'No. Nothing,' he replied.

'Are you in some pain or discomfort?'

'I am fine.' Charlie tried to replace the painful grimace with a relaxed smile. 'Do you think you could stop the paper shuffling and get on with this?'

Detective Dempsey popped his head around the door. 'Sorry to interrupt, sir. A call for you. I think you might want to take it out here.'

'It better be important,' sighed Cochran. 'Excuse me.' The inspector stood and left the room. Charlie Madden pushed at his forehead with his fingers and looked at the floor.

Cochran walked up the corridor alongside Dempsey towards the reception area. 'Well, who is it?'

'It's some European guy called Oscar. He says he's the security officer at Stacey's fitness club. He was very insistent and quite sure you would want to talk to him,' replied Dempsey.

'Hmm… thank you, Detective. I'll take the call privately if you don't mind.'

'Yes, sir. Absolutely.'

*   *   *

It was ten minutes later when Cochran returned to his office to continue his interview with the frustrated Charlie Madden.

'So, tell me, what was the extent of your relationship with Alison Stacey?'

'There was no romantic involvement if that's what you mean. We met at the club a few times. There were a couple of occasions when we even had dinner together. We were to catch up this weekend. We were good friends. Stacey knew all about it.'

'A very nice arrangement indeed. And what sort of things would you both discuss over dinner?'

'Mainly financial and club matters. Boring stuff, I'm afraid. We have a registered business called Charden Enterprises. It is a business of convenience, nothing more. It helps me get a good bonus every now and then, gives Simon taxation benefits, and it gave Alison some pocket money.'

'Pocket money! She really needed that, didn't she?' Cochran stood and began pacing. He continued with his tolerant pretence. 'So, the club's manager and the owner's wife sold management services to their own club?'

'That's basically how it works, yes. It's all quite legitimate.'

'Oh yes, of course it is. I'm sure you'd have seen to that,' said Cochran, nodding his head sarcastically. 'Did you see her on the night of the fire?'

'I certainly did not. I never had any improper dealings with Alison, and perhaps I should add that I know nothing whatsoever about the fire. The whole matter has been very distressing for me and a great many others!' snapped Charlie gruffly. The inspector stopped his pacing and squatted quietly next to, and slightly behind, Madden's chair. His mouth was only centimetres away from Charlie's ear.

'I wish to be frank with you, Madden,' he said softly. 'I'm making a special effort here to be polite and considerate, given the present circumstances. Now that's something that doesn't come easy to me, as Detective Hogan will tell you.' Cochran moved even closer to Charlie's face. His voice was becoming progressively louder. Madden could feel the policeman's breath; he twisted uncomfortably once again.

'While you may find the questions personally offensive, I can assure you that I find four murders much more so. If by chance my polite inquisition upsets you, it's just too fucking bad!' The big man stood and began pacing again, but all the time glaring at Madden. 'Now, did she ever talk to you in confidence? Were you aware of any problems in the marriage?'

'As far as I knew their marriage was fine.' Madden opened his hands and rested them on the arms of the chair, demonstrating his sincerity. 'Alison had some concerns about whether Bodytone would be a success. She didn't like the club's name. Even the mention of it seemed to make her uncomfortable.'

'Very good. If we continue like this we'll all be able to get home, won't we? Now, did you ring anyone on Tuesday night?'

'I might have,' said Madden, pausing to think. 'Yes, yes. I rang Stacey at Duncan's house. I had a good idea about the disco.'

'And that couldn't wait a day or two?'

'He always made it clear that I could call him anytime, about pretty much anything. I made a note of the whole thing in my diary. You can check.'

'Why ring him at a party, late at night?'

'He's a hard man to catch up with. Besides, if he's had a few drinks there's more chance he'll go along with my ideas.'

'And you just happen to have Duncan's number?'

'I have all his contact details and notes from his diary. That's how we do things.'

'Really,' remarked the inspector, unconvinced. 'A guy goes to play poker with his mates, but still decides to chat to you on the phone about a non-urgent matter. I don't buy it, Madden.'

'It's his choice to take the call or not. What can I say?'

"Do you know Adrian Devlin?'

'Well, yes. I know him. He's a great mate of Simon's. I've met him a couple of times.'

'You been to his place?

'Never have.'

'But you know where he lives?'

'Of course.'

'Yes, of course. You know all Stacey's friends and contacts.'

'Most, perhaps not all.'

Cochran shook his head slowly, pushed his hand through his hair and referred to his notes. He read the report Briggs had put together. There was still the bracelet. Information obtained in such a manner needed to be handled carefully. He decided the tried and true method was his best option and continued his slow walk about the office as if deep in thought. He stopped behind Madden's chair, grabbed it firmly and dragged it away from the limited protection of the desk. Charlie tried to stand, but Cochran's hand dropped onto his shoulder and made sure he stayed seated.

'You know what I think, Madden?' shouted the inspector. 'I think you torched Stacey's house! You screwed his wife and shot some poor bastard who came to help when he saw the flames and heard the kid screaming. I think you're a psychopathic killer, Madden, and I'm going to nail you! You son of a bitch!'

'No, no, no! I did none of that, I swear!' pleaded Charlie.

'That's bullshit. You did it all right. Maybe not exactly like I said it, but you're guilty, and I'm damn sure you were fucking Alison Stacey.'

'I didn't and I wasn't!' Charlie couldn't help himself, he raised his voice. He tried again to stand, but only with the same result. 'I'm not guilty. Please! This is outrageous!'

'Why did you have her gold engraved bangle in your desk drawer then? Maybe she took it off when she dropped her knickers, eh?'

'That's not true. She didn't like the bracelet. She gave it to me to look after.'

'A woman that doesn't like gold? Hogan, have you ever heard of such a thing?'

'Should be more of it, sir,' replied the smiling detective.

'Please, it wasn't the gold,' added Madden. 'It was the engraving. She never liked the club's name - Bodytone.'

'What was it about that name?' demanded Cochran.

'Don't know. She would always say it was a woman's prerogative not to like something. Like dogs don't like cats, she used to say. There doesn't need to be a reason. I was to keep the bracelet and not tell Stacey. She didn't even want it in her house.'

John Cochran continued to needle Madden about his relationship with Alison Stacey, and past associations with Adrian

Devlin and other friends of Stacey. While the desired effect in loosening up his tongue and introducing the bracelet had been achieved, no startling revelations were forthcoming. Questions, accusations, and insults continued, and despite having no alibi for the night in question, Charlie clung steadfastly to his innocence. When eventually offered an opportunity to leave, he wasted no time in vacating the scene.

*   *   *

'Shit, what a total mess! Dirty rotten arseholes! Pricks! Bastard cops!' Charlie slammed his hands on the steering wheel. He continued driving and swearing for fifteen minutes, cursing Cochran, Hogan, Dempsey, and the entire police department. Then he started on himself. 'Why stay and put up with that, you great dickhead? Why even go in the first place you stupid, turd-faced idiot?' Turning into Acacia Drive, Charlie looked up the road to his humble dwelling. The lights were still on. 'Deb, my honey pie. Get ready. Here comes your dessert.' With a short, sharp squeak of rubber on concrete, the car stopped only centimetres from the garage door. Charlie hurried up the path, key in hand. He stopped in his tracks and looked back at his car. 'No, she can't have.' His brain was working overtime. 'Yes, she must have put her car in the garage. Of course she did.'

Charlie opened the front door. Everything was quiet. In the dining room, he could see a sheet of folded paper propped up against a champagne glass. His last hope for a successful end to a disastrous evening was fast disappearing. Charlie walked towards the table and read the note.

Dear Charlie,

I rang Dad. Mum has taken another bad turn.

Have to go. Maybe next time. So very sorry.

Love Deb.

Madden picked up a glass and hurled it against the wall. Fine splinters showered over the carpet. Next to go was the tablecloth, together with the cutlery, plates, salt and pepper shakers, and the lifeless pink candles.

Chapter 20

Poor Old George

Most of the regulars were already showered, dressed, and waiting for breakfast. Others shuffled about on the cold vinyl floor, responding rather reluctantly to the multitude of staff instructions. Therapy, such as it was in Ward 21, was underway. All manner of activities from bathing and bed making to badminton and basket weaving were included under the therapeutic umbrella. Altruism was actively encouraged, and often whether they liked it or not, residents were expected to aspire to this healthy practice and assist those less able than themselves. For the most part, the role of the staff was one of observing, supervising, prompting, and medicating. Substantial emphasis was always placed on personal hygiene and general ward tidiness.

Two custodians, Eddy and Mike, stood watching a middle-aged man frantically wiping down the bedside lockers.

'These old alco's are surely good value,' said Mike. The distraught gentleman had beads of sweat forming on his forehead. His heavily creased features and bulbous, pulpy nose, a by-product of many years of intemperance, belied his true age. 'They work like a thrashing machine, do everything you say, and never remember if you give 'em a flogging.'

'You're right, you know,' said Eddy. 'But it doesn't make sense.'

'Why is that?'

'I was thinking that they behave that way because of a deficiency in the neurone department. Right?'

'Yeah. So?'

'Well, dear Michael.' Eddy placed his arm over his friend's shoulder. 'You're the biggest piss-head I've ever known, and you wouldn't work in an iron lung!' He removed his arm and quickly took a couple of steps to one side, just out of reach. Mike gave a wry grin, nodded, and rubbed his hands together.

'Okay, dog-breath. Maybe I like to have a few beers, but look at this complexion.' Mike ran his fingers over his cheeks. 'Absolutely flawless. Now yours, I'd like to point out, is quite different. Tell me that funny story again from last night. The one about how you got that black eye and those three stitches.'

'Yeah, very funny, smartarse.' Eddy lightly touched the small dressing on the bridge of his nose. The area was still very tender, but wasn't hurt nearly as much as his pride. 'Come on, let's get old George up now. Nearly everyone else is ready to go around for breaky. Stacey, the prick, can stay and eat in his room.'

Ras was lying on his side, bed covers over his head. He had remained in the locked seclusion room since the incident with Simon Stacey on Sunday. Mike slapped his hand against the glass. 'Come on, Georgie. Rise and shine. It's your lucky day. You've got two very nice gentlemen to escort you to the bathroom.' Eddy looked at Mike with raised eyebrows and unlocked the door.

'I hope you're not going to ask him to pick up the soap?'

'It's an interesting thought,' pondered Mike. He positioned his hand over the front of his stone-washed jeans, cupped his genitals and gave a sharp shake up and down. 'I do like to make good use of my therapeutic tool.'

'You're really a depraved, evil man, you know,' said Eddy, with a grimace at the thought. He turned the handle and both entered the room. 'George, up you get. Time for a sh — ' There was a moment's stunned silence as Eddy reefed away the bedcovers. Ras was lying in the foetal position, naked from the waist down. A damp plastic bag clung like Glad Wrap to the patchy blue and grey face of the old man. His purple tongue protruded slightly from the lower corner of his open mouth. The whites of his eyes could just be seen through the partly open eyelids. The standard-issue, blue hospital pyjama pants had been secured around his neck to ensure the bag would not easily become dislodged. 'Fuck!' Eddy threw the sheets to one side, crouched, and felt for a pulse. 'Cold as a fucking maggot. He's been dead for hours.'

'Jesus, mate, this will go over like a lead balloon. How the hell did he get a plastic bag in here?'

'Stuffed if I know.' Eddy slid his hand along the sheet up to the pillow. 'I thought I saw something. There we go. Would you look at that. Looks like chlorpromazine.' He held up a large white pill between his fingers. 'It looks like it's been in his mouth. There's a couple more here too.'

'The bastard's been hoarding his medication. I always thought he swallowed his tablets.' Mike sighed and scratched his head.

'Let's get out of here,' said Eddy. 'We'll leave everything as it is, lock the door and close the blinds. We need to call the supervisor. It'll be a police matter now. This is so totally fucked.'

Chapter 21

Friends and Foes

Simon Stacey had been lying awake for ten minutes watching the clock through the blinds and wondering how he had ended up in a locked seclusion room. Events were patchy, but he recalled images of large moths, of blood, and he had some memory of his heart trying to jump out of his chest. He stood, taking a moment to find his balance, then moved to his window.

There seemed to be an unusual air of quietness and sobriety about the ward. Four staff stood in a small circle outside the office, chatting and from time to time, staring at the floor and shuffling their feet on the vinyl. There seemed to be a distinct lack of patients; only two could be seen. Dougy, the compulsive cutlery collector, sat in the corner with a fixed, fatuous grin. For some reason, he always looked untidy; a shower, shave, and shampoo seemed to grant little improvement. His beady eyes darted to and fro. He slouched even further into the corner, then secretly opened his brown corduroy jacket, removed a dinner fork, and polished it briskly on his blue pyjama trousers, then returned it to its hiding place. He wrapped his coat up snugly, folded his arms across his belly, and began to jerk his body up and down excitedly. The only other patient to be seen was the obese brain-damaged teenager who sat at the table engrossed in her jigsaw that was at last taking shape.

Simon found himself becoming more preoccupied with the unusual sensations of his own body rather than the goings on outside his room. In the reflection of the window, he looked at himself swaying to and fro. He was surprised how unconcerned he felt. His torn, unbuttoned pyjama shirt, dirty-looking hair, unshaven face and dry lips would normally demand his immediate attention. Simon broke his fixed stare by placing his open hands in front of his eyes. While his fingers trembled uncontrollably, his dulled sensorium continued to safeguard him against any emotional distress. In this intangible state, he was content to take refuge.

'The entire world is my aquarium. They're all trapped but me.' Simon pushed his face against the glass, distorting his features. 'I have the greatest freedom. I no longer worry. I no longer suffer,' he whispered. Stacey forced a smile. It helped him believe his own words. 'I don't think they see me. They look, but they see someone else. Without me they are nothing, for they can only exist while I continue breathing. My life is their life.'

Simon was so engrossed in his escapist voyage from the fish bowl to Utopia that he failed to hear the door unlock and open.

'Breakfast time, Simon!' announced Kym. Stacey was momentarily breathless as he jumped with fright back into reality. 'Are you okay? I didn't mean to startle you.'

'I was a million miles away, searching for the meaning of life,' replied Simon, catching his breath and sitting on the side of the bed. While he was somewhat displeased with the intrusion, he found it consoling to see Kym in preference to anyone else on the staff. Apart from her attractive oriental appeal, she had been polite and understanding since their first meeting. 'I don't feel normal. It's like half my brain is anaesthetised. The other half was asleep as well until you surprised me. I know I should be concerned about what's happening here, but I just feel, well, nothingness; emptiness; detachment.' Kym placed the tray on the end of the bed and sat down next to Simon. She looked to the door, nodded, and waved her hand to the male nurse standing outside. He nodded, realising that his assistance would not be required, and left.

'You were injected with some medication late yesterday evening. I imagine you're experiencing some after effects. Do you remember what happened?'

'Vaguely. I think I was hallucinating. There were giant insects. Moths.' With the help of pressure from his fingers to his forehead, he recalled some of the nightmare. 'Yes, giant moths. Sounds crazy doesn't it? Never in my life have I had such an experience, so why should I start now?'

'You've had some major life traumas.'

'Yes, but no, that's not the answer. Listen, Kym,' he said sincerely, gently placing his hand on her shoulder, 'You're one who's concerned about injustices in the world. What about forcing people to take medicines? In particular, me. Here as a voluntary patient. Falsely imprisoned, as you told me yourself the other day. This is destroying me, Kym. Very slowly, but very surely.'

'Simon, one thing you should know is that you are no longer here voluntarily. Doctor Hutchinson and Eddy completed the necessary paperwork last night.'

'Bastards! Partners in crime, I'm sure.'

'Your behaviour was really bizarre last night. You needed to be physically restrained.'

'I know this will sound like a line you've heard a thousand times, but I'm sure the medication I am being given is laced with something. It's poisoned!' Simon tried on his most honest face, and looked directly into Kym's brown eyes. If she had any doubts about his story, it was not publicised on her face. 'Now, if you're thinking I'm paranoid you're right, because there really is someone out to get me.'

'To be quite straight with you, yes, I have heard that line many times, and on every occasion it has turned out to be false. Why should this be any different?'

'Do I have any history of psychotic behaviour?'

'None that we are aware of.'

'I think I would have preferred a simple no, but never mind. Tell me, is it usual for so-called depressed patients to become paranoid?'

'Psychotic, yes, in a paranoid way? Occasionally,' replied Kym with an intended grin, which revealed a perfect set of teeth.

'I have the impression we're not doing very well here.' Simon returned the smile, both pleased he could see the lighter side of the situation, and relieved he was no longer feeling like a total zombie. 'I think you should be my therapist, not Eddy the arsehole. Just talking with you is making me feel more like a human being.'

'Being cooped up in these rooms can make you feel detached from the world. I think you're right; some company is what you need. Not mine in particular though.' Simon smiled at Kym's diplomatic reply.

'I wouldn't be so sure of that.' Stacey kept his vision locked onto the black-haired Asian nurse. She parted her lips as if to speak. Her eyes darted from side to side, quickly scanning his face. Raising her hand, she faintly stroked her index finger over his lips. For a second she sat staring, then stood and walked to the door.

'I'm going to risk being unpopular and leave your room open. Those lips are very dry. I'll fetch you some cream.' Kym turned and was soon out of sight.

Simon gave a big sigh. He smiled and nodded in a confident gesture intended to convince himself he had achieved something meaningful with Kym. *I'll be needing to get out of here before long, and Kym might just have the ticket*, he thought. Looking at his breakfast tray, Simon shook his head in disgust. All the items, the mug, dessert spoon, and two bowls, were all made of a soft yellow plastic. One bowl contained porridge, and the other bite-sized sausage pieces in tomato gravy.

'I think they forgot my high chair,' remarked Simon quite loudly. He picked up the mug of lukewarm tea, took one mouthful, cringed, and tipped the remainder into the porridge. 'Shit, I hate plastic tea!'

*   *   *

Simon pursed his lips and applied the lanolin-based cream. It gave immediate relief. He could now smile without cracking his face. He replaced the top on the tube, handed it back to Kym, then sat down on the unmade bed.

'Thanks very much. A simple thing, but it makes a big difference.'

'Starting to feel a little more like part of the human race. That's good. Would you like to talk?'

'With you, yes. About you, yes.' Stacey thought of adding something about getting out of hospital, but decided it would be premature to reveal his hand too early. Kym reached outside the door with one hand and dragged in a plastic straight-backed chair.

'I think it would be more beneficial for us to talk about you.' Kym positioned the chair on Stacey's right. She sat, crossed her ankles, gently cupped her hands, and leaned slightly forward.

'That would be a very boring story, I'm afraid. Couldn't we start on something a little more interesting?'

'Simon, I hope I'm not being too direct, but sooner or later you're going to have to talk about what's happened. About your wife and son. About the fire. I'm sure you would like to leave this place before long. Working through your grief is the start of the healing process and a step towards getting well and getting out of here. What do you think?'

'Shit, shit shit!' cursed Stacey. He looked away and studied a dried drop of blood on the floor. *Yes, I sure want to talk about that all right, but not in the same way that you do*, thought Simon. He placed his elbows on his knees, supported his chin with his thumbs, and thoughtfully rubbed the sides of his nose with his fingers. After considering his options for a couple of quiet minutes he came to a decision, then spoke firmly and clearly. 'Kym, I need someone I can trust. I don't mean to put you in a professionally awkward position, but I need a guarantee that what I am about to tell you will not go beyond these four walls.'

'I don't know whether I can make such — '

'Listen, just give me forty-eight hours,' interrupted Stacey. 'If after that time, you still feel the need to release a world exclusive, go ahead.' Simon edged closer across the bed, his eyes pleading. Their knees touched.

'Okay, you have my confidence, Simon. Let's hear it.'

He gave Kym the abridged version. He told her about how his wife, Alison, had become mixed up with some sort of cult, and that he believed it was these people that had murdered his family and torched his home. He linked this to the 13th Black Candle group that George Hartley had described, saying he believed they were one and the same. He said how he had found a note containing phone numbers, one of which belonged to Ward 21. Finally, he repeated those words Ras had screamed out: *You're the one. Friday, it's you!*

*   *   *

'You see, Kym, I'm going to need your help,' said Stacey in conclusion to his story. He had told her as much as he thought she needed to know, at least for the moment. There should only be one person who knew more, thought Simon, and that was the person with the micro-cassette tape, Adrian; but where the hell was he?

'There's no way I can get near old man Hartley,' added Simon. 'And that's the way Eddy wants it, I'm sure. You'll have to talk to Ras for me. Find out more about the Friday thing.' Stacey spoke quickly, as he looked at Kym in anticipation. She had turned away, bowed her head, and reached for a tissue from the pocket of her navy-blue culottes.

'Ask him about these Black Candle people, about where they meet and who...' Simon's words slowed as he heard the soft sobbing. Kym had her eyes covered with the damp tissue. He reached forward, placing his hand gently on her shoulder.

'What's wrong, Kym? If you don't want to do this...'

'It's not that, Simon. It's George Hartley. That lovely old man.' She sighed, lifted her head, and flicked her hair back with her hand. Her eyes were moist and red.

'Yes, yes, what's up? Is he still sick?'

'He's dead, Simon. Last night. He committed suicide. I'm so sorry.' Stacey let himself fall backwards onto the pillow and stared at the ceiling. He clenched his fists and took three deep breaths to suppress his urge to shout and scream. *You can handle it, Stacey. Get a grip on things,* he told himself. With eyes closed he began whispering instructions.

'Calm and relaxed. Quiet and relaxed. Loose, calm, and relaxed. Let go, let go and relax. Relax, relax, relax.' Apart from an unusual thick sensation forming in his tongue, his technique seemed to help a little each time he repeated the words to himself. After a moment, he sat back up. 'You know that if it wasn't for me he could still be alive. I was pressuring him to speak about the club and the Bodytune thing. I can't help but think that someone here wanted to silence him. The poor old bugger,' he said mournfully. 'It might look like suicide, Kym, but I'll bet it's not. And if you don't help me, I will be next.'

'Okay, Simon, I will keep your confidence for the time being. George's death does sound odd, and while he was often psychotic, I have never known him to be suicidal. I'll make some discreet enquires and keep you informed.' Kym blotted her eyes one final time, and picked up Simon's breakfast tray.

'Kym, you need to be careful. This is a dangerous place.'

*　　　*　　　*

The Asian nurse stood alone at the workbench in the locked medicine room. She was head down, concentrating on the task in front of her when Eddy's loud voice caught her attention.

'I'll bring him a couple of Panadol. Just wait on.'

'Damn you,' cursed Kym, as she hastily placed a bottle of pills back in its pigeonhole, not noticing as it toppled to one side. Eddy's rattling keys could be heard at the door. She pressed the plastic top down firmly on another small glass medication bottle. The medication door lock clicked, and the handle swung down with a thump to the open position. With the pressure from her thumb, the small bottle slipped against the smooth laminated surface and shot out onto the floor. The door swung open. The bottle shattered. Without looking up, Kym dropped to her knees and began collecting all the small yellow pills. A few continued rolling and came to rest between Eddy's brown, slip-on leather shoes.

'While you're down there, Kymmy?'

'In your dreams, pencil-penis,' she replied without hesitation.

'Oh dear, that's a very nasty and hurtful thing to say,' said Eddy sarcastically. 'Now, a good psych nurse would not inflict such an enormous emotional scar on a colleague.' Kym raised her middle finger, and then gathered up the last of the yellow tablets and dropped them into the pocket of her blouse. 'Do I see the nurse pilfering hospital medication?'

'No. You see the nurse picking up her own vitamins. I was just about to take my morning dose. And, if you hadn't deliberately set out to frighten me, I would not have dropped them in the first place.'

'I see, I see. This is all my fault. I'm so ashamed.' Eddy extended his hand limply forward and slapped his own wrist. Kym gritted her teeth, pushed herself roughly past the unwelcome obstruction in front of the door, and left.

The glass cabinet to the right of the individualised compartments contained most of the 'everyday' medicines such as analgesics, cough mixtures, creams, and the like. After popping two Panadol from the foil, Eddy replaced the packet on the upper shelf. The tipped bottle in pigeonhole number eight caught his attention. After turning the bottle upright, he replaced all the loose antidepressant medication — except for one. Dropping onto all fours, he groped around the floor for a couple of minutes, looking around the base of the oxygen cylinder, feeling near the wheels of the stainless-steel trolley, running his fingers down the narrow gap between the vinyl tiles and the edge of the cupboard, and finally lifting the plastic pedal waste bin. There it was, one lonely yellow pill. Eddy stood and placed it next to the antidepressant tablet retrieved from Stacey's medicine compartment.

'Exactly the same,' he whispered with intrigue. 'Vitamins my arse.'

Chapter 22

The Madhouse

'J. C., good morning. I've been expecting you. What's your interest in this fellow? Seems like an uncomplicated suicide. It's not the first in this madhouse, and it won't be the last.' Senior Constable Martin Joseph Blake and his colleague from the local station had been waiting for John Cochran. They had completed some preliminary enquiries and a partial inspection of the scene. After being advised of the inspector's concern and curiosity, they had suspended further investigation pending his arrival.

'This so-called suicide is just too convenient for my liking,' said Cochran gruffly. He crouched beside the low-set bed, lifted the pyjama jacket with two fingers, and ran his eyes up and down the blotchy body of George Hartley. 'What can you tell me, Snake?'

'He was found like this by two male nurses, at seven thirty this morning, but with the sheet and quilt over his head. He has been in solitary since going ape-shit on Sunday afternoon. The night staff record sheet has him as sleeping soundly all night. What a joke! How he got that plastic bag is a bit of a mystery; they're supposed to be banned from the ward.'

'What are these?' Cochran stood, displaying two large white pills in the palm of his hand.

'Chlorpromazine, or so they tell me. He was prescribed one every night. It has been suggested that he wasn't swallowing them. And that he may have got together a bit of a stockpile.'

'The cheeks of his arse look like a pincushion. What the hell have they been pumping into him?

'Other tranquillisers. They're all written down on his medication order form to be given as necessary,' replied Blake.

'Was that chessboard like that when you came in?'

'Certainly was. The old fella liked playing the game, but that's no position I've ever seen before.'

'What do you make of it, Johnson?'

Cathy had been standing quietly near the door, absorbing the details of the tragic scene. The chessboard sat in one corner of the room, neatly aligned with the two walls. All the black pieces formed a circle extending to the edges of the board. A row of white pawns bisected the circle. The other white chessmen lay on their sides forming two lines that crossed the line of pawns.

'It's unusual,' remarked Cathy quietly.

'Well, well! That's a bloody breakthrough. It's unusual,' announced Cochran in his usual loud offhand manner. 'I guess that's it then. Case closed!'

'There's no need to go on like that. Give me a moment,' insisted Johnson. Blake raised his eyebrows in surprise at her backchat. 'It seems to have the basic shape of a crucifix,' she continued. 'Except with an extra cross piece at the bottom and two additional angular struts at the top. I would guess it has some religious significance.'

'Thank you, Johnson. Now you're thinking. Take a photo of it, will you?'

*   *   *

The feeling in Stacey's tongue had increased. He rolled it round in his mouth with difficulty. It felt awkward and heavy, as if it was swollen and partially paralysed. A tightness was forming in the muscles of his jaw and neck, causing his head to tilt uncontrollably to the left. He wondered initially whether this was some strange neurotic reaction to the news about the demise of his old companion. Then he thought back to his breakfast and the terrible taste of that cup of tea.

'Po…pois…poishun!' he mumbled almost incoherently. His speech was failing fast. The terrifying sensations were spreading quickly. His eyes wanted to roll up and look inside his own head, while his body arched to the left, making him look like a human coat hanger. Hurrying through the door with shortened stride, he presented himself, snorting and hissing, in front of the nurses' station.

Eddy, noticing the unusual sound, casually looked up. He slowly placed his novel to one side after carefully folding one corner of the page to mark his spot.

'What have we here?' He rose from his chair and stretched out his arms as if waking from a deep sleep. 'Stacey, it's very rude to interrupt. The very least you could do is say excuse me.'

Simon was unable to focus his vision or even force his eyes to look at his nemesis. Eddy's attitude only served to reinforce his fears of being poisoned.

'If you wait there like a good fellow, I'll get a special injection for you. Would you like that?' Eddy paused momentarily, waiting for a response which he knew only too well would not be forthcoming. 'The cat got your tongue, or is there a frog in your throat?'

Stacey's heart pounded even harder as the male nurse made a move towards the medication room. *The bastard's going to finish me off for good.* He turned to move away but caught his feet around the legs of a chair and toppled headlong across a table. Jigsaw pieces went in all directions. Simon lay writhing on the floor amongst the upturned furniture and pieces of the puzzle. The podgy adolescent sat looking down at her shattered dreams. She held a single piece of jigsaw between the thumb and forefinger of each hand, the last two pieces to complete the picture. Her meaty cheeks vibrated as her trembling became intense. A loud, high-pitched shrill filled the air. She stood, took a few steps forward, and began repeatedly kicking into Simon's stomach and chest. He could do little but wave his arms as if shooing flies. There had been many times when he had contemplated death, but the thought of dying by being kicked to death by a frenzied, obese, brain-damaged, teenage girl was never one of them.

Any loud noise in Ward 21 was guaranteed to attract staff like bees to a honey pot. Eddy, despite being the only eyewitness, was not first to restrain the young girl. He allowed her to persist with the corporal punishment until two other male staff, making a hasty exit from the conference room, took hold of her arms. Only then did he assist in dragging her, screaming and kicking, into the nearest seclusion room.

With the hastily convened meeting to discuss the morning's distressing events now disrupted, plenty of persons were available to help with the more immediate problem. Kym was the first to lend assistance to the snorting and squirming Stacey.

'I know you're frightened, but you're going to be okay,' said Kym with confidence. 'This is a reaction to the injection you had last night, it happens sometimes. If we give you another needle you'll be back to normal within a few minutes. I promise. You are going to be fine.'

Kym sat on the floor next to Simon's head, held his hand, and continued to offer words of support. His only possible response was to lightly squeeze her fingers. Another nurse was quick to arrive with the syringe and swab. She stepped over the contorted body, pulled down his pyjama pants, rubbed the site, and plunged the needle in to the hilt.

The events had not gone unnoticed by John Cochran, who was peering intently through the narrow opening of Hartley's bedroom door.

'Bloody Stacey. Always up to something. I suppose I've got Buckley's chance of getting an interview now,' cursed the inspector.

'From what I could see, I don't think it was all theatrics. He's going to be pretty sore and sorry for himself later,' commented Cathy. She had been trying to get a peek at the action, but Cochran's oversized torso had obstructed her vision. Brief glimpses under his arms and over his shoulders were sufficient for her to assimilate what had happened.

'I don't like this, don't like it at all. That bastard has either gone completely troppo or he's playing us for fools. In any case, he knows enough to get himself or someone else in even more trouble. I want him out of here, and the sooner the better. He's going to the Wacol Security Patient's Hospital. I'll be making recommendations as soon as we get out of this madhouse.'

*   *   *

It was 10.30 and morning tea was being served. Apart from the dead George Hartley lying in a locked room and a plain-clothed policeman sitting at the door, the ward was pretty much back to normal. Stacey was asleep on his bed, the adolescent girl was secluded and sedated, and the other police had left. The courtyard was open, and patients were quietly helping themselves to tea and coffee from the stainless-steel trolley. Kym was mixing amongst the quiet group, passing out biscuits from a plastic bowl, while Eddy sat near the courtyard door having a cigarette. He felt the breast pocket of his short-sleeve sky-blue shirt. With his finger, he detected the small tablet he had located on the medication room floor. He looked at Kym; she was heading in his direction with the biscuits.

'Kymmy, how about a bicky for your favourite nurse?'

She stood in front of him and tipped up the bowl. A few crumbs fell onto his jeans.

'Hard luck. Looks like you dip out. What a shame.'

'What about this then?' Eddy displayed the small yellow tablet.

'Is that supposed to mean something?'

'Well it's not a bloody vitamin pill, is it?' smiled Eddy.

'Isn't it. So what?' Kym was trying hard to sound unconcerned.

'It's more like an antidepressant. You were flogging some medicine. If you're depressed, maybe I can interest you in some of Eddy's special therapy.'

Kym was quiet for a moment. She held her hands tightly and swallowed deeply.

'Okay, it's an antidepressant and I was pinching it, but everyone helps themselves to a bit of stuff here and there.'

'Sure they do,' admitted Eddy. 'But most don't lie about it when they're caught red-handed.'

'Yes, I know. I guess I've been a bit upset. They are for my aunty. She's been really sick and I'm worried about her,' replied Kym hesitantly.

'Really?'

'Yes. Can I have that pill back? I'll put it with the rest.' She sat down and extended her hand. Eddy raised his eyebrows, looked at her, and then at the tablet held gently between his fingers.

'There's plenty more in the drug room. Help yourself.'

'You have no need for that one. Just pass it over please,' insisted Kym.

'It must be made of gold. I think I'll keep it.' With that Eddy dropped it into his pocket, stood, and began to walk away.

'You prick!'

'Go to hell,' he replied promptly.

Eddy walked up to the trolley and started stacking the cups. Kym glared and clenched her teeth. A moment later, she relaxed, nodded slowly, and smiled.

'You'll go to hell, you bastard. And maybe sooner than you realise,' she whispered.

Chapter 23

Robes and Rituals

The nine thick, black candles shimmered in the breeze that found its way through the small holes and cracks of the old timber building. Several large, knotted, and almost straight tree trunks were strategically placed to support the dilapidated construction. For the moment, all seemed peaceful. The wind whistled lightly, a branch scratched against the corrugated iron roof, and occasionally the drone of a distant vehicle could be heard. The dusty room, about the size of a tennis court, had a raised wooden platform area at one end, like a low-set stage. The remainder of the flooring was simply dirt, sawdust, and wood chips.

Each of the nine candles sat firmly in its shallow earthenware holder on a long, heavy wooden bench mounted on the platform. This rustic piece of furniture, roughly assembled from heavy lumber, appeared to be the focal point for whatever business the weather-beaten haunt endorsed. Carved into the centre of the bench were two interlocking, red-stained triangles, forming a six-pointed star. Of the nine naked flames, one sat on each point, and three others on intersecting lines of the symbol.

Two other items added to the decor of the area. On the right of the bench, a solid wooden bucket bound by two rusty metal hoops, and to the left, leaning at forty-five degrees to the rear wall, a full-size timber crucifix. To the long end was attached a chain which ascended to a ceiling beam, through a pulley, and down to a hand-operated winch, the use of which would suspend the crucifix upside down. Secured to both cross pieces were numerous strands of barbed wire of a suitable length to be tied around the arms and legs of any hapless martyr.

To the front of the elevated area, lying flat on the dusty floor was a large, black diagram etched on a sheet of canvas. Two concentric circles, the area between equally divided into thirteen sections, formed a large ring extending to the edges of the tent cloth.

In each division was written a name, only just visible in the candlelight. At the top, nearest the altar, LUCIFER — and clockwise the names: BELZEBUB, ASTAROT, LUCIFUGE, SATANACHIA, AGALIAREPT, FLEURETY, SARGATANAS, NEBIROS, EURYNOME, HAKELDAMA, BELPHEGOR, and BAAL.

Inside this circle of malevolent nomenclature was a further curious formation — a central ring with six other interlocking circles of equal size, resembling a flower with six round petals. Lying crossed in the centre were two highly polished daggers with curved, dark handles fashioned artistically into the shape of a serpent.

The wind began to gust, causing a piece of roofing iron to vibrate into a monotonous tapping rhythm. A rush of air through a crack near the rear paling door whipped up a small cloud of sawdust and deposited it on the opposite side of the room. The beams from an approaching light caused the shadows to become alive. The nine flames flickered a little more vigorously, as if heralding the arrival.

The paling door rattled and opened. In single file, they entered. There were seven of them, all clad in black, hooded robes. The last two carried a canvas and pole stretcher containing an eighth person — a naked, unconscious man. The leader switched off the torch on entering the old barn, reached into his pocket, took out a cigarette lighter, and lit the candle passed to him from the second in line. The troop proceeded quietly toward the canvas sheet. The candle bearer stopped with the daggers at his feet and sat down cross-legged. His right foot protruded from under his robe revealing the underside of his shoe — the thick rubber sole, with a multitude of V-shaped protrusions, had little wear. Four of his followers positioned themselves likewise, each in the centre of a circular petal. One other wore sports shoes. The rest had bare feet.

The other two of the party proceeded to the left of the altar, lowered the stretcher to the ground, and without hesitation or a spoken word took hold of the sleeping man. One grabbed his arms, the other his legs and lifted. The man's head jerked backward and his buttocks sagged awkwardly, but the lift achieved its purpose, and the naked body descended onto the crucifix. Now closer to the candlelight, his body showed a mass of bruising, particularly on the chest and the unshaven face. His eyelids were swollen, lips dry and cracked, and both wrists carried red weeping wounds. The two anonymous performers now secured the barbed straps. Three to each arm and four around the legs. The man stirred. He shook his head several times and groaned loudly as the restraints were tightened and the twists of metal cut into his flesh. Trickles of blood ran over his limbs. Some flowed freely onto the cross and then dripped onto the already stained floor.

The two disciples re-joined the others and assumed their positions in the remaining two circles. Everybody faced inward towards the holder of the black candle. The circle of worshippers chanted in unison to their leader, who held the daggers crossed above his head.

Romoli, it is you who will lead us.
Romoli, it is you that have the power.
Romoli, it is through you we will contact the King.
Lucifer, we remain your loyal servants,
Now and forever - Amen.

'Is all in readiness for Friday's celebrations?' spoke the central figure. His speech was solemn and insistent. One cloaked head lifted and looked at the leader. The black hood slid back, revealing a head of long, black, shiny hair.

'A minor problem at my end, Romoli, but it will be resolved tomorrow.' The young woman's voice was slow and calm. 'Our plan will continue as we discussed.'

'Do you need any assistance?'

'No. I'll contact you if there's any further problem, but I don't expect there to be,' she replied firmly.

'Anyone else?' There was a short pause. The soft cries of the man secured to the cross filled the air. No other comment was made. 'Excellent! The night of our greatest offering and tribute to our King is nearly at hand, and of course, our revenge for our murdered brother,' announced Romoli loudly, 'Let us commence tonight's ceremony. Doctor, would you like to place the tenth candle and prepare for our anointing?'

The member of the clan referred to as the Doctor stood and approached the master of ceremonies. He took the candle in one hand and then, after Romoli kissed the blade, took a long knife in the other.

He knelt before the altar, bowed his head, then stood and took two further steps to reach the bench. The candle was placed carefully on an intersecting point on the star — there were two more points still to be covered plus the very centre, marked with an X. The Doctor bowed again, kissed the bench and announced loudly...

'Dear Lord, Prince of Darkness and Ruler of the universe, we ask that you accept this, our tenth marker.'

The other members were now all standing with arms outstretched. They recited the response.

'Accept our souls!'

'Dear Lord, Prince of Darkness and Ruler of the universe, we ask that you bless the blood of this unbeliever,' continued the Doctor.

'Accept our offering!'

'Dear Lord, Prince of Darkness and Ruler of the universe, we humbly ask your guidance and protection for our church – the 13th Black Candle.'

'Accept our souls.'

The Doctor moved over to the crucifix. Romoli took hold of the winch handle. With every turn, the long end of the cross rose slightly. The winch creaked noisily for two minutes, then stopped. The cries of the man grew louder as his weight, being suspended vertically, caused the barbs to embed themselves deeper. He probably could have screamed louder had he not been so exhausted. Fresh streams of blood began weaving their tortuous course down his body. The Doctor stood in front of the crucifix and steadied the slight swinging motion. The naked man's navel was at eye level.

A bizarre recital commenced.

Joj Sookyun,
Eithod Enk,
Chey Yduta,
Og Gubtuon,
Enk Kyltady,
Eillua Eillua Eillua.

The group now formed a line. In turn they stepped forward, knelt, and rubbed their fingers over the bloodied chest. They marked an inverted crucifix on their foreheads and smeared blood over their lips.

As one cloaked figure approached and touched his chest the tortured man opened and shut his eyes quickly several times. He strained and grunted. For a moment, he could focus.

'Angela Help me. Don't let me die. Angela, please,' he begged. She looked down at his bloodied head, smiled, and gave a long, sinister laugh before turning her back on him and walking away.

'Don't worry!' shouted Romoli, 'You are not going to die, at least not tonight. You are not the main attraction.' He plunged his hand into his robe pocket and pulled out a small plastic bag containing a micro-cassette tape. 'No, Mr Devlin, you are but the prelude to an unbelievable event. It would be nice if you were still alive to bear witness. And I thank you for guiding us to this tape. I'm sure it is going to prove very helpful.'

Chapter 24

Don't Leave Me This Way

The night staff had completed their handover report to the oncoming nurses and were almost ready to leave. The rituals of checking all the keys and counting the restricted drugs were the only tasks remaining before their departure. Mike's joke asking them if there were any bodies hanging around or if they had issued out any more plastic bags had not gone over particularly well. Eddy had stood stone-faced throughout the report. In addition to the small dressing still mounted on his nose, he now carried another injury, well bandaged, on his right wrist.

The drugs were checked and the morning staff each selected a set of keys for the day, noting the number on the tag and signing in the corresponding column in the book provided. Without saying a word, Eddy snatched up set number three, attached them to his personal clip, signed his name and left the office. Kym repeated the procedure before making her way towards the ladies' dormitory. Her black, tapered, crepe wool pants, cream silk shirt and black patterned tapestry waistcoat complimented her dark features. She always looked nice, but today she was particularly stunning.

Four women, in the six-bed dormitory-style room, still lay under their blankets, having not bothered to make a move since being woken earlier by the night staff. Kym's pace quickened when she saw them through the thin blinds.

'Bitches. Lousy bitches!' she whispered harshly. 'As if I haven't got enough on my mind. Lazy, inadequate morons!' As she pushed her way roughly through the door and entered the room, she turned on the fake charm.

'Good morning, ladies,' she said brightly. 'And how are we all today? I trust you all slept well? Mrs Alcott, let me help you up. I know how stiff that knee of yours gets in the morning.'

'Thank you so much,' replied the sleepy woman. 'You know it makes the day so much more bearable knowing you're on duty.'

Within a few minutes she had the ladies up showering, dressing, and tidying up the room.

'Breakfast in fifteen minutes, ladies. See you then.' She left the room. She flicked her hair from her shoulders and forced a short, disinterested smile as she passed some patients sitting outside the nurses' station. They smiled back. 'Hello, Kym,' one said. She nodded her head but said nothing. Her eyes were fixed on room number eight. Simon was sitting on his bed reading a newspaper. There was no one in the nursing station.

'Where do you think you're going?' Eddy grabbed her upper arm tightly from behind and swung her around to face him. Kym gasped. Her body jolted. 'You've got some fast talking to do,' he added.

'Ouch! Let go, you're hurting me.' She tried to pry his fingers lose. 'Let go, you bastard. I've got nothing to say to you.'

'Oh, yes you have. Let's just step into the office here for a few minutes, shall we?' Eddy tipped his head in the direction of the nurses' station and marched her towards the door.

'No, we shall not,' she protested, while Eddy unlocked the deserted room. 'No I said! Do I have to scream?' Eddy pushed her into the room and down onto a chair.

'Sit there like a good girl while I tell you a short story about a small yellow pill.' She immediately stopped squirming. He lifted his hand off her shoulder and sat down. 'How absolutely radical, eh? The little *ching chong* is all ears now.'

'Make it quick, will you? The others will be wondering what we're up to,' said Kym. Eddy told her how he sustained the injury to his wrist last night. How he gave the pill to his dog and how this changed a sedate, fat Labrador into a crazy, wild animal, biting trees, running into fences, and eventually biting his arm. Kym sat motionless. All initial expressions of discomfort and surprise had been replaced by a fixed, cold stare. She breathed slowly and evenly through a small round hole between her lips.

'And what's more,' he continued. 'The reason I gave poor Cactus the pill was because I had an idea that you had been interfering with Stacey's medication. After all, you acted strangely when I sprung you in the drug room. I found Stacey's medicine bottle spilled after you left, and your behaviour about getting that pill back yesterday got me thinking.' Kym remained still. Her eyes were moist and a slight quiver had developed in her lower jaw.

'So, when Cactus went ape-shit I knew you must be playing some pretty stupid games. And what about old Hartley? I asked myself. Could dear, sweet Kym have anything to do with that? You know, I must admit I don't much care for that bastard Stacey, and old George was a bit of a prick, but for Christ's sake, I would never do anything...' Kym had a stream of tears running down her face. Her mascara had formed two black snaking lines down her cheeks.

'Don't start that crap with me. It just won't wash,' said Eddy. She began some quiet sobbing and wiped her nose with a tissue.

'It's just that...' She cried louder and covered her face with her hands for a moment.

'Just that what! Come on, I want to hear it. Stop that, please.' Despite his earlier decision that he would not be manipulated by this predictable antic, his resolve was already weakening.

'I can't help it. I've got a drug habit.' She blotted her eyes once more and then produced a small vial from her pocket containing several of the yellow pills.

'You're trying to tell me that you're addicted to those things? Hallucinogens? That doesn't seem likely. How would you ever function at work?'

'Eddy, you take these for two years and then you'll really know what they can do to a person.' She blew her nose again, then leaned forward and placed one hand on Eddy's knee. 'I know you're a good psych nurse, Eddy, and I've always been worried that someday you'd find out about me. That's why I've been so rude to you, to keep you away from me. I'm so sorry. It was so wrong.' She dropped her head and cried some more.

'Shit, I hate this. What am I supposed to do now? Look, Kym, I'm sorry I said some of those things, but you must admit it all seems very strange.' He placed his hand on her downcast head. Kym raised her head. His hand slid down her hair and brushed her cheek. She clasped it firmly with both her wet hands and held it close to her lips.

'I know we've had our differences, but I have always respected your judgement. You're a strong, sensitive man and I like that. I need your help. Please.'

'Okay,' he nodded. 'But I still have some questions for you.'

'Sure, that's fine. But right now, I need to go around to interview room one to take a moment and clean myself up. I can't walk around looking like this.' She gave a little smile and a sniff. 'Tell the others I have a migraine and needed to lie down.'

'Okay, Kym. I can do that, but what — '

'Eddy,' she interrupted. 'Please come and talk to me after breakfast. I'll wait there for you. I'll give you the whole story, beginning to end. And thank you for being so understanding.' She kissed his hand and left.

Eddy, much to everyone's surprise, was rather energetic during the breakfast sitting, helping patients carry meal trays, feeding some of the older residents, and even wiping down some of the tables. Once the cutlery count was correct, he promptly excused himself and left the dining area, not remaining for his usual bowl of porridge.

The interviewing room was located immediately to the left of the door which opened into the courtyard. It was at the opposite end of the building to the dining room and out of view from the central nursing station. Kym sat on one of the two straight-backed, armless chairs facing the door. Her Walkman was playing the Communards hit song 'Don't Leave Me This Way' through her earplugs. Her arms were folded, her eyes closed. The light was out. She swayed gently to the beat of the music.

A faint hum filtered through the air-conditioning vent. The small room, closed all night, was cold. Sunlight from the greenhouse had begun to nuzzle its way between the top few slits of the closed venetian blinds. In the partial light the floor, walls, furnishings, and even the white sheets of the examination bench appeared grey and sterile.

Kym opened her eyes and slid her left hand slowly into the deep pocket of her pants.

The blade of the knife was long and slender, cut away in a gentle arc that accentuated its sharpness and length. The polished blade and black ebony snake-shaped handle glistened as Kym held it up and rolled it over and over in front of her face. Her tongue protruded ever so slightly as she moistened her lips.

A minute later, Eddy knocked and entered.

'Gee, it's dark in here!' He reached for the light switch.

'No! No lights please.' She removed one earplug.

'It's bloody cold, too!' Eddy raised his shoulders and rubbed his hands together. 'Are you feeling any better now?'

'Oh yes, Eddy, much better. Much better indeed.' Her speech was faint, almost a whisper, and unhurried, as if she was savouring every moment. 'You haven't told anyone about my problem, have you?'

'Of course not, just that you had a migraine and were resting. But I do need to know more.' Eddy scratched his head as his eyes adjusted to the dim lighting. 'Why, may I ask, are you wearing a plastic apron?'

'I took a moment to quickly help old Maude in the shower before I came to rest in here.'

'Right.'

'Are you going to stand there staring at me all morning? Sit down.' Eddy sat across from her. Kym stood.

'So, tell me the story then? I'm sure I can help you,' said Eddy.

She took one step forward, extended her arms, and ran her fingers through his hair. 'Yes, I'm sure you can help me with my problem. I would like to get to know you more deeply, Eddy.' She pushed his head back and gently caressed his neck with her fingers. She felt the rasping stubble of his whiskers, the outline of his Adam's apple, the muscles at the sides of his neck, and finally her fingers came to rest over his carotid pulse just below the line of his jaw 'You have such a strong heartbeat.' She moved forward, straddled his legs and sat on them.

'Oh, my God! Are you for real?' Eddy was stunned. 'To be honest this was not quite the therapy I was thinking you were after. But I'm not one to argue the point. Carry on, please.'

Kym put the loose earpiece into his ear. 'Hey, cool. I like this song.'

Her right hand left his neck, replaced by her lips. She unbuttoned his shirt. He reached behind her and began tugging at the knots of the apron.

'No, no, not yet.' She pulled his hand back and lowered her face to his chest. 'I don't want to get undressed just yet, big boy. Don't get too frantic. The best is yet to come.' Her hand glided over his sparse chest hairs before coming to rest over his left nipple. Her excited panting became louder.

'Kym, you've blown me away completely. This is radical, absolutely radical!' Eddy made a few thrusting movements with his pelvis.

'Oh, I can tell you want me. And I'm so glad you agreed to help me. I just want to express my thanks in a very special way. Are you okay with that?'

'Oh yes, I am very much okay with that. Why have we waited so long?' Eddy seemed both excited at bewildered at the same time, but he was not one to look a gift horse in the mouth.

Kym stretched her left hand so her thumb remained on his nipple and her index finger rested on his sternum. She drew the two digits together to locate the centre between the two landmarks. Her right hand clutched the snake handle.

There was a brief glint of shining metal as the blade disappeared full length into Eddy's heart. His eyes widened in momentary surprise and horror. A rush of air and a loud grunt, and his breathing ceased. She removed the knife. A spurt of blood sprayed bright-red spots over Kym's apron. The spurt quickly changed to a fast gush, then just as quickly again to a steady ooze.

'Oh, Eddy, you do disappoint me. What a little spurt for such a big prick. You know, you really shouldn't use your penis for thinking. Now look at the trouble it's got you into. Really radical, eh? Tut, tut, tut.'

Chapter 25

The Departure

Simon sat back down on his bed and once again picked up yesterday's newspaper. It had been another strange night of vivid, emotive dreaming, and it was difficult to separate fact from fantasy. His room being left unlocked was reassuring; at least he couldn't have created too much havoc. After a disturbing thought that maybe he was losing his mind and really needed to be in this madhouse, Simon decided he should try as best he could to occupy his mind by concentrating on everything he was doing, however minor the task. It felt a little unusual attempting an in-depth study on eating breakfast, teeth cleaning, nose blowing, and dressing, but at least it helped provide the moment with some sense of reality. Despite the pain and bruising to his cheeks, chest, and abdomen from yesterday's encounter with the jigsaw juvenile, it was also important to make a special effort to look and act well — to avoid the empty, lifeless stare of the depressed, the irrational conclusions of the psychotic and the stiff, shuffling gait of the drugged.

How his clothes had ended up washed, ironed, and neatly folded on the end of his bed was both a mystery and a blessing. It had felt good to slip into his own clothing. The simple blue denim jeans and red velour collared sweatshirt provided a sense of individuality and personal freedom.

Simon directed his attention to page one of yesterday's news. He had already read the first three pages before breakfast, but had only partial recall of the main stories. He nodded as he remembered the main headline — it was the latest on the police drug scandal. Four police officers had been charged, but the ringleaders had neither been detained nor identified. The names were listed. Stacey took his pen and circled two whom he knew. He thought long and hard. He'd had dealings with them in the past. He remembered there was some conflict and disagreement. He nodded as he recalled they had provided some assistance in determining the outcome of some very beneficial horse races. 'Ah yes! The penny drops. Greedy bastards,' he mumbled, as he reflected on their demands for more of the action. It was a long time ago, and there had been times then when he'd had concerns for his continuing state of health. It was a good thing it was well behind him now.

He scanned over the front page, reminding himself of other stories he had read. At the bottom right-hand corner, some bold print caught his attention: POLICE APPEAL FOR HELP IN KIDNAP CASE page 4. Simon turned two pages and located the page-four story.

Police are appealing to the public for any information that may assist their enquiries into the kidnapping of Daniel Goldsmith, aged 23 months. Daniel is believed to have been abducted by his babysitter, known as Robyn Mortimer, over a week ago. The boy's father, Dr Harold Goldsmith, says no ransom demands have been received. Melissa, the mother, remains under heavy sedation. Police have issued the following descriptions...

Simon stopped again to collect his thoughts. Daniel and Melissa. Those names. I've seen them somewhere before. They were written down. Neat, bold printing. Not a newspaper. Not a magazine. Not a letter, or could it have been? No. Maybe a book?

'Shit, shit, shit! What the hell is going on? Why can't I remember?' Even the name Goldsmith had something vaguely familiar about it. He thumped himself on the leg with his fist and gazed into space. Some movement caught his eye. It was Kym. She was in a hurry.

'Simon!' She hotfooted it into his room.

'Kym, what's wrong?'

'This is dreadful. You're in danger, Simon. I'm so worried. It's Eddy.' She looked back over her shoulder and then sat on the bed next to Stacey.

'Eddy. I knew it.' Simon nodded. 'What the hell's he up to?'

'He's been tampering with your medication. Those yellow pills.'

'Arsehole! I knew it. I bloody knew it!'

'Listen, there isn't much time. They're transferring you to the security hospital this morning. Anything could happen to you there and you might never get out. They could be here at any time.'

'Jesus Carist! They've really got it in for me, haven't they? This is going from bad to worse,' said Stacey woefully. 'I've underestimated my opposition. I've lost my direction, and my mind is not far behind.'

'No, Simon. Don't say that, it's not true. Just pay attention, will you? Now, there's one more thing,' said Kym, glancing again over her shoulder. 'I found this in Eddy's work bag.' From her pocket, she removed an item partly wrapped in a handkerchief and placed it quickly under the newspaper that lay on the bed between them. Simon felt compelled to follow Kym's cautious lead, and he too scanned the immediate ward area. A nurse walked briskly past but paid no attention. A few patients were sitting quietly around the foyer, and a cleaner was mopping the floor. All of them were a reasonable distance from his room and seemed more concerned with their own activities than anything else. He gently raised the newspaper and carefully unfolded the handkerchief to reveal the knife. He ran his fingers lightly over the snake handle and moved his face closer to inspect the weapon.

'Romoli?'

'What did you say?'

'Oh, it's nothing. Just a strange association of ideas,' said Simon, somewhat surprised by his own remark. He tilted his head to one side and looked back at Kym. 'For some reason, it reminded me of someone who is not a very nice person.'

'Simon, please pay attention. You must get out of here. The sooner the better. Here, you take these.' She pulled a silver chain with attached keys from her pocket and dropped them in Simon's lap. He looked at them. There was something familiar about this key set also. He dismissed it as an aberration. There was too much else to think about.

'Oh, my God, I wish I could think straight.' He pushed his fingers hard into his forehead and massaged his scalp.

'Please, Simon, I don't want anything to happen to you. You must listen to me and do exactly as I say. I overheard Eddy on the phone, there is some sort of meeting on Friday night. You need to give me time to find out more, but you can't stay here. It's just as you said, a very dangerous place,' insisted Kym.

'Friday. Ras said Friday. "Friday, it's you," he said.' Stacey gritted his teeth and hit himself once on the forehead with his fist.

'Simon, please. There really isn't much time.'

'Okay, okay! You're right. I don't want to be carted off to some lock-up security joint. I'm listening. I really am.'

'The gold-coloured key opens the main doors. There will be a group meeting in...' She looked at her watch, '...in five minutes. Most of the staff and patients will attend. This will be your chance. I will signal the all clear from the office by wiping my nose with a tissue. Wait for me to enter the conference room. You then walk straight to the door and let yourself out. Don't hurry, and try to look relaxed.'

'Yes, I used to be able to do that once.'

'You must do it, Simon, and you must take that knife with you.'

'Jesus! Why? Is it going to be that difficult to get out?'

'Simon, I've taken a big risk doing this for you. I've put my faith in what you've told me. I've put my job in jeopardy.' Her chin began to tremble. 'The thought of that man with this knife scares me half to death.' A tear fell and she lowered her head.

'Right, Kym, I understand. Try not to worry. I'll take the knife. I'll wrap it in my paper rubbish bag. Now, don't you go taking any more unnecessary risks.'

'Thank you, Simon. I'll be very careful. One final thing. Take this.' She handed him a slip of folded paper. 'It's my address. I live alone. You'll be safe there. The door key is under the third pot-plant to the left of the steps. Now, is everything clear?'

'I understand the immediate plan, yes, but I must say that everything is far from being clear. What about these keys? How will you explain their disappearance? There's going to be questions about how I escaped. What will you tell them?'

'Everything is taken care of. Trust me, Simon, please. There's no time left. I must go. I'll see you tonight at my house.'

Simon watched Kym leave. She immediately started organising the patients for the morning meeting, directing some and assisting others to the conference room. Other staff soon joined in, and a procession of individuals ambled, strutted, shuffled, and even goose-stepped past Stacey's open door. He pulled the sheets from his bed, threw them on the floor, then began to slowly straighten them back out over the mattress.

'Come on, Stacey. Meeting time,' announced Mike.

'Sure. Won't be a minute. Just finishing this bed.'

'You've got three minutes. And what are you doing with that sheet? They normally go lengthways on the bed.'

'Shit! Just not thinking clearly today.' Simon swung the sheet the right way. 'Okay, I'll be there. You don't need to supervise my bed making,' said Simon. Mike shook his head and continued on his way.

Come on, Stacey, get a grip. Don't be an arse. You should relish this sort of thing. Come on, get with it, he told himself. He kept on fiddling with the bed linen and nervously glancing up at the central office and the clock. That lazy red second hand was, for the moment, the centre of his life.

At two minutes past eight, Kym signalled. Simon waited until she disappeared, then picked up the brown paper packet containing the knife and made for the main doors. He had rehearsed this several times in his mind. A casual thirty-metre morning stroll to the unlocked swinging doors. A quiet walk in the country admiring the scenery, what a lovely day. Once past this first barrier he would be out of sight of the nurses' station. He was doing well. He pushed on the double doors. They didn't move. They were locked.

'That's it. I'm stuffed now. My life is over,' he mumbled. Simon opened his right hand and examined the keys. There were four, all damp with sweat from his palm. The gold one for the main doors, he remembered that much. He tried another but it wouldn't even fit the slot. The next slid in nicely, it felt good. It didn't turn.

'This is it, Stacey,' he told himself. The third key slipped in comfortably.

'Please, God.' The lock slid back with a loud click that he was sure everyone must have heard. He dared not look back. A firm shove, and the doors parted. Now out of the foyer, he continued down the corridor between the conference room and the dining room. The two locked doors lay directly ahead. *A nice country walk. The birds chirping. So lovely and relaxing. How wonderful it is.* He glanced to his right.

'Oh, my God!' The blinds on one window of the conference room were open; he could see everyone sitting in a large circle. No one seemed to be talking. This was almost normal for these so-called therapeutic community meetings, but half of the group seemed to have their eyes fixed on him. He may as well have walked in through the conference room door, waved a red flag and announced here I am, I've got a set of keys and I'm running away. He saw Kym stand. She clapped her hands together and all heads turned like robots to face her.

Maybe there's still hope. Keep on walking through the woods. Sunlight not far away. What a calm, relaxing day it is. If it was any calmer my head would explode!

He unlocked the first door, entered the anteroom, and locked the door behind him. Through the narrow windows of the final door he could see the outside world. There was an ambulance and parking bay just beyond the exit. Just twenty metres further was a full-sized oval which separated the psychiatric section from the main medical area of the hospital. The gold key did its job. The last hurdle had been safely negotiated. *Out of the forest of darkness, I've done it. Now, home James, and don't spare the horses.*

As he turned to lock the door, a van pulled up in the ambulance bay. Two burly figures, dressed in well-ironed khaki with thick brown leather belts supporting holstered revolvers, jumped out of the paddy wagon and walked towards him. Simon finished locking the door, straightened up his shoulders and let the keys swing from the silver chain.

'Good morning,' said one of the men. It was a firm, strong voice, almost a shout.

'Good morning,' said Simon.

'Simon Stacey?' The man looked over at the document his partner was holding.

'Ah… yes,' replied Simon reticently.

'He is in here, isn't he?'

'Sure. Sure he is.'

'Well, we've come to take him to the Security Hospital. Get him out of your hair and put him where he belongs. Can you let us in please?' Simon looked back at the entrance to Ward 21. He couldn't possibly go back in — not now. Running was an option, but how far would he get? He suddenly realised he had that package under his arm. A warm sensation travelled from his neck to his ears. What a wonderful thing this is. A poker player with a red face. Red face. Red button. Stacey, you're a prize dickhead.

'You'll have to press the red button here and wait,' said Simon, indicating with his hand to the message written below the black panel. 'I'm in rather a hurry. Some nutcase playing up at intensive care. Excuse me.' He hurried away, brushing the men's arms as he passed between them. They turned and watched him walk through the parking bay and disappear around the corner of the Ward 21 building.

'What a strange bloke.'

'He's been working here too long by the looks.'

'Yeah, I guess. Anyway, I always thought the intensive care ward was across the oval in the main hospital building.'

'Yeah, I think you're right. Where's he going then?'

Chapter 26

The Great Pentacle

Dempsey, Hogan, Marshall, Briggs, and Johnson sat quietly. All eyes were on John Cochran, who stood behind the desk at the large whiteboard, armed with marking pen and eraser. It had been five minutes since the morning meeting commenced and no one had yet spoken. Despite their investigative efforts, no breakthrough had been forthcoming. Sergeant Carter had run a second, but fruitless, check on the list of known past offenders that resembled the body at Stacey's place. An air of solemnity and disappointment now pervaded the team.

The whiteboard was a conglomerate of black, blue, and red words, circles, and arrows. The most prominent feature was the name STACEY in large red letters in the centre. Taped on the wall to one side of the board were several sheets of paper. There were lists of names, various reports, computerised case data, and rough, handwritten notes. On the opposite side was the increasing collection of ghastly photographs — old George Hartley being the latest addition. The inspector drew an arrow next to the name GEORGE HARTLEY, then in red wrote: MURDERED. He ran one hand slowly over his head, pushing his fingers through his grey hair and then massaging the back of his neck.

'Okay. Attention you lot!' announced Cochran. He took one step back to admire his masterpiece before completing a rather ungainly pirouette to face his five charges.

'Well this is a change, I must say,' he said with some surprise. 'No idle chatter. No scribbling in notebooks. Not a smile. Not a sound. How depressing indeed.' Cochran strolled between the chairs like a schoolmaster.

'How sad it is for the future of justice in this country that we are producing crime fighters who give up thinking, discussing, and analysing when the criminal doesn't cooperate. Perhaps I can lodge a notice in the local rag, let me see.' He placed one hand to his unshaven chin as he brushed against Cathy Johnson's shoulder.

'Detective Inspector John Cochran hereby requests that local thieves, murderers, and other nasty individuals temporarily curtail their activities, as it is having a deleterious effect on the mental state of his colleagues. If the persons concerned could forward any evidence, or even give themselves up, this would be greatly appreciated. We would like to advise the public that we will resume normal duties following intensive psychotherapy.' He continued his walk, looking at the tops of heads, his fists clenched and his cheeks showing the tell-tale sign of discontent.

'This is not a difficult case. It is too complex to be difficult,' added Cochran loudly. 'It is said that the more featureless and commonplace a crime is, the more difficult it is to bring it home.' The walkabout ceased, and the big man half-sat on the front desk, supported by his arms. 'This case, my depressed colleagues, is far from commonplace, and therefore must be ready to crack wide open. Am I right?' Everyone looked. Johnson and Marshall almost nodded. No one spoke.

'Am I right!?' he shouted. Both his eyes were clearly visible — a rare sight indeed.

'Yes, sir,' all replied in staggered fashion.

'Yes, sir, yes, sir,' squeaked the inspector sarcastically. 'What are you lot? A bunch of bloody schoolgirls? Get with it, for Christ's sake!' The group stirred in their seats. Marshall and Johnson seemed to be studying Cochran's abdomen. Briggs and Hogan were examining the cracked paintwork on the ceiling while Dempsey flicked nervously through his notebook.

'Now, this preliminary autopsy report came through late last night.' Cochran held up the typed report. 'It is quite clear that Hartley was murdered. Sure, we wanted to talk to him, but don't despair; don't go slashing your wrists just yet. Hartley can still talk. He's told us that whoever killed him wanted it to look like suicide, and so it did initially. He did die of suffocation, but the level of tranquillisers in his blood were sufficient to render him unconscious at least an hour before the time of death. An unconscious man cannot place a bag over his head and tie pyjamas around his neck, can he, Johnson?' Cochran was staring at Briggs, who refused to engage in eye contact. Cathy stalled, expecting Briggs to answer for her.

'Can he, Johnson?' said Cochran again.

'No, sir. Not unless he did it in his sleep.'

'Johnson! I said unconscious, didn't I? Not asleep like you seem to be. Fuck!' The inspector was still fixed on Briggs. 'Our friend Hartley also told us that his killer has a good knowledge of drugs and access to them. Correct, Briggs?'

'Yes, sir. It would also have to be someone who could get their hands on a Ward 21 seclusion room key.' Briggs looked up briefly as he spoke, then focused on his fingernails and began picking at them with his thumb. An uneasy silence filled the room once more. John Cochran hadn't altered his gaze. Johnson turned slowly to look at Marshall. She gestured with a quick glance towards Cochran and Briggs and then looked back at him. Marshall shrugged his shoulders in response. The inspector's eyes slowly began to return to their more usual size and there was an almost indiscernible nodding of his head. Something was on his mind. Something he was so far keeping to himself.

'Hartley died around three in the morning,' continued Cochran, at last breaking his stare at Briggs. 'The night duty staff have so far come up clean, apart from their admission that they spent at least half of the shift sleeping. Of course, this makes finding out as much as we can about this club of Hartley's a priority. How many staff names on that suspect list, Dempsey?'

'Thirty-seven, sir. Twenty-one nursing staff, six doctors, four administrators, three paramedics, two social workers, and one occupational therapist. All these people either have their own key or have easy access to ward keys. In addition, there are many persons who have secondary access to all those staff keys. This could add another thirty or so to the list.'

'And let us not eliminate Stacey at this stage. It seems unlikely, considering the state he's been in, and one would think he might have some difficulty getting a key. But he's a devious bastard. Johnson, tell us all about the chessboard in Hartley's room.'

'Yes, sir. It took some checking. I talked to a fortune teller, who also claims to be a white witch. She showed me a book on black and white magic which proved helpful.' Cathy's words stirred everyone's interest, particularly Briggs, who sat well forward on his seat. 'The symbol roughly depicted on the chessboard is called The Great Pentacle,' continued the constable. 'The book says it is used to conjure up infernal demons and spirits. It can be used either for evil purposes or to control certain demons and thereby protect the user. The correct incantation must be used for it to be of any value at all.'

'Didn't afford Hartley much protection, did it?' declared Cochran. 'This, my friends, is Hartley talking to us. Telling us that he was in danger; in fear of his life. Thanks for that, Johnson. Was there anything else?'

'Only a warning from the lady not to meddle with things I don't understand,' added Cathy.

'Well, you just keep on meddling. We need answers and we need them yesterday.'

'Sir!' said Briggs eagerly. 'I saw a book in Madden's drawer about that sort of stuff. Sorcery and black magic it was. I'd forgotten all about it till now.'

'You forgot about it?' Cochran shook his head in disbelief.

'It didn't appear important at the time, sir.'

The inspector placed his hands on his hips, closed his eyes, and took a deep breath before continuing. 'Well then, as I said before, this case is ready to crack...' The door opened and Carter marched in. All heads turned. He stopped halfway across the room.

'Sorry, guys, but there's another one. Another murder. In Ward 21. It's one of the staff. And Stacey's escaped.'

'Jesus Christ! That bastard was supposed to be on the way to the security hospital!' roared Cochran.

'He passed the officers at the door. They thought he was one of the staff. He had a set of keys attached to a silver chain. A nurse there thinks the keys belonged to the dead guy.' The inspector walked back to the whiteboard and took pen in hand. He wrote 'STAFF MEMBER' above Hartley's name, bracketed the two, and drew a line directly to 'STACEY'.

'Sarge, do we have a good description of what Stacey was wearing?'

'We certainly do.'

'Let's get it circulated immediately. I also want a watch back on Devlin's flat and on the Bodytone Fitness Club. We're going to need more officers. I'll arrange that after we've been to the psych ward. All of you mark my words from before. This case is ripe for the taking. Now let's do it before anyone else gets killed. No more pussyfooting around. No more forgetting things.' Cochran glanced in Briggs' direction. 'And no more bloody fits of depression!'

Chapter 27

Devilish Creatures

It had taken Simon nearly a full hour of brisk walking to arrive at Kym's house. It had seemed that everyone he saw was staring right back at him, as if they knew he had escaped from a lunatic asylum. The snake-handled knife, now held in his jeans and concealed by his sweater, had only added to his anxiety and paranoia. His neck was feeling stiff from repeatedly checking his back. He felt sure the police car he had seen outside the hospital was close behind.

The red velour sweater, so nicely cleaned and ironed earlier, was soaked with perspiration. Perhaps that's why people stared, thought Simon, a man sweating like a pig on a warm morning, wearing a sweater, and almost running up the street while looking back over his shoulder. *You stupid oaf!* he told himself. *What a way to behave!*

Stacey felt a great sense of relief as he noted the number six on the letterbox and the row of pot-plants to each side of the three steps leading to the centre of the front veranda. He unfolded the small piece of paper and checked the address. This was certainly the right place, but not quite the modern brick home he had imagined Kym would live in.

'Of course, you meathead,' he said loudly. Kym's home was in an old part of town which Simon knew well. If he'd have stopped to think he would have realised an older-style house would have been more likely. He shook his head, dispirited at both his woolly thinking and fallible behaviour.

The old white chamferboard home was surrounded by a wide veranda closed in by a heavy latticework through which could be seen some cane furniture, an assortment of potted ferns, some garden utensils, and a watering can. There was a certain freshness and peacefulness about the dwelling. A pleasant feeling of déjà vu swept over Stacey as he placed his hand on the paling gate. His parents' old farmhouse was always covered in greenery. His mother was a strong-minded woman and at the same time caring and protective. Simon thought of Kym — yes, there definitely were some similarities between the two women. He lifted the latch. For the first time in many days he sensed that everything was going to be all right. As he entered the oasis, he failed to notice the metal sign attached to the gate: 'Beware of dog. Enter at own risk.'

The gate clicked shut and Simon ventured towards the plants to the left of the steps. Bending down, he lifted the third pot, revealing a set of house keys. Some movement caught his eye. He had no time to turn his head. The Rottweiler thumped heavily into his head and shoulder, knocking him to the ground. Simon instinctively drew his knees up, pulled his head onto his chest, and covered his face with his arms. He lay curled and motionless on his side, straddled by the snarling animal. The dog didn't bark but hovered above him, hackles raised, while snarling through a fierce display of teeth. Simon parted his fingers slightly to see the dog. The eyes looked like shiny black holes. There was a silver chain around the neck with a metal name tag swinging from it. As the dog continued growling but moving little, the tag slowed sufficiently and could be read. The name Satan sent a shudder through Simon's body.

'Satan, good doggy. There, boy. Good boy, Satan.' The dog maintained its position. Stacey began to slowly unwind and turn onto his back — the position of surrender.

'Satan's a good doggy. He doesn't want to eat poor Simon.' As he turned he felt the animal's heavy panting in his face.

'Oh, my God, Satan, what the hell did you eat for breakfast?' said Simon, keeping the tone as friendly as he possibly could. Satan moved backward. Stacey turned until flat on his back with his knees slightly bent. The dog pushed his moist nose into Simon's groin.

'Satan, please, not that!' He reached forward with his hand to discourage the personal invasion. The dog snapped at his fingers and barked twice.

'Okay, that then. Just no teeth, please.' Simon settled himself back down and let the animal proceed with its nuzzling. He prayed for two things: one, that his manhood be left intact, and two, that no one was watching. After a couple of minutes Satan sat down, seeming to have accepted the intruder's presence. Simon moved slowly. He collected the keys, stood, and unlocked the veranda door, never taking his eyes off the dog. Once on the veranda, he promptly closed the door, turned to face the house, and dropped to his haunches. The dog moved quietly to the top of the third step and poked its nose partly through the lattice on the door. Simon took a few deep breaths then turned his head slightly, catching a glimpse of a black, moist nose.

'Fuck off, Satan! Shit!' snapped Simon. With that the dog quietly moved away and disappeared. After taking a moment to compose himself, he pushed himself upright, stood, and entered the house.

The interior was a delight, with numerous scatter rugs strewn over the highly-polished floorboards, finely carved, high archways joining the lounge, dining room, and kitchen, and several vases of strategically placed freshly picked roses. Simon slipped off his shoes. The home was so neat and clean it seemed the right thing to do. Sliding his socks along the smooth floor, he noticed each join in the flooring. It felt nice. He breathed in deeply through his nose and took in the fragrance of roses — a personal favourite.

A picture of Alison with dirty knees tending her cuttings formed in his mind. His thoughts started to wander. Fleeting images of his wife and son began flicking through his mind, and now familiar sensations of discomfort began rising from his stomach to his chest and throat. While there remained some element of self-control, he forced himself to focus intently on his surroundings and began chatting with himself.

'Keep the brain in first gear, Stacey,' he said out loud. 'No more getting lulled into a false sense of security. It's not good for you. Be observant and objective, and watch out for the man-eating black cat. There'll be plenty of time for your emotions later, but you'll need to be alive if there is going to be a later.' His personal pep talk was sincere, but not sufficient to override his exhaustion. Now inside

Kym's house there seemed to be some comfort and security, a place to rest, and perhaps even a cold drink in the fridge.

The spacious kitchen was also spic and span. With the scalloped, lacy curtains, the fresh flower arrangement near the sink, and the variety of Weight Watchers cookbooks stacked on the microwave, it was definitely a woman's room, thought Simon. He opened the fridge. The large carafe of what looked like freshly squeezed orange juice sat up boldly on the top shelf. He reached out with his foot to the pedal waste bin. Sure enough, there were the skins of the bisected oranges.

'Kym, you are a honey, and maybe a bit of a mind reader, too.' Simon lifted the tumbler from the mouth of the carafe and quickly downed two full glasses of juice. It was most refreshing, but with a slight tang. He suspected there was possibly a grapefruit mixed in there somewhere.

It only took a moment for Simon to shuffle his way into the lounge and discover the sofa. He sank down into the olive-green duffel fabric and dropped his head onto a small cushion.

Across the room, mounted on a long, two-metre metal frame was a huge aquarium. Inside, the black tiger snake slowly uncoiled, stretched upward, and twisted itself around the thick grey branch under which it had been resting. The diamond-shaped black scales shone as it moved with an effortless grace. Finally, the tail became mobile as the reptile's head, tongue flickering, extended toward the top corner of the enclosure. The heavy glass lid was firmly in place. The snake casually returned to the rocky bottom of the aquarium. It glided into the cluster of greenery at the opposite end of the confine where it disappeared.

Simon breathed deeply. It started happening again. While he recognised the sensation, he was powerless to prevent it. His eyelids seemed to close by themselves and he was once more drifting into a land of vivid and frightful fantasy.

Through a slowly clearing smoky haze he could see Robbie dressed in a white bathrobe. He was smiling, arms outstretched and running towards his dad, yet not getting any closer. Alison was there, too. She was dressed the same. She stood still, with tears streaming down her cheeks. The tears fell to the ground where they formed shining pools of blood. Simon could neither move nor make a sound. His son began to cry. Robbie stopped running and threw his little arms tightly around his mother's legs. The ash covered swimming pool materialised between Simon and his family. The quagmire bubbled excitedly — almost expectantly. It seemed to be alive. Long arms from the water stretched out towards his family. The smoke closed in once more. Silence fell.

Chapter 28

Return of the Lust Busters

The first of the four Wednesday afternoon aerobics sessions was over and the sweaty bodies filed out of the room. Some were going home, but most headed toward the showers, sauna, or pool. It was Deborah's class and a record attendance, breaking the old one for the third time in as many weeks. Charlie Madden was delighted. There had been some concern that recent events and newspaper stories might have had a damaging effect on both the club's cash flow and reputation, but the reverse seemed to have been the case.

Charlie and Wendy stood behind the reception desk, checking through the members' book. The club manager had specifically timed this activity to coincide with the end of the aerobics class. He had not seen Deb since the debacle on Monday night and was eager to arrange another intimate evening. She had taken yesterday off to help look after her ailing mother, and for Madden her one-day absence had been a mental marathon.

'Five new members so far this week, Charlie,' said Wendy, pointing to the dates alongside the last few names. 'Membership renewals are up from 45 to 62 percent this year. It's marvellous. We're going from strength to strength.'

'We are indeed. I'd still like to see a further increase in renewals. Perhaps you might like to think about some incentive scheme. Good ideas are worth money.' Charlie was looking away. His mouth was on automatic as he focused his attention on the glass doors leading to the aerobics room.

'Are you saying you would pay me for my ideas, Charlie?' Wendy put her hands on her hips, noticing Madden's preoccupation. His neck was outstretched over the counter.

'If club profits are up, Deb, Stacey will certainly be agreeable to award a quarterly bonus.' Madden prattled on, oblivious of his error. Wendy restrained her laughter. 'It makes good business sense to encourage staff to become part of the affair with management.'

'So, I can expect a healthy bonus then?'

'Certainly,' said Charlie. Deborah was still out of sight.

'Could I expect, say, $20,000?'

'Certainly, my girl. Certainly,' continued Madden, much to Wendy's amusement. 'It's all about motivation and job satisfaction. Management needs to be flexible, and when they consult properly with all workers…' Charlie paused. Deborah finally appeared. 'It's such a beautiful, wonderful thing.' He shook himself to attention and turned quickly to Wendy.

'What I'm saying is… well, it's simply good for everyone you see. Excuse me.' Charlie skipped around the reception desk with a surprising degree of acrobatic elegance. Deb's hot-pink leotard with a stripe of white lightning down the centre clung like a second skin. There was a light glow on her cheeks. She smiled. Charlie took her hand in his.

'Hi, Charlie. Look, I'm really sorry about Monday. I feel terrible about it. I really had no control…'

'Hey, hey.' He placed a finger over her lips. Her mouth slowly opened. He drew his finger away sharply and looked around. Wendy was leaning on the counter, her chin cupped in her hands and head tilted to one side with a ridiculous grin. Madden scowled. She giggled and turned away.

'Deb, it turned out to be a bad night for both of us. Let's try again, shall we?'

'I'd like that, Charlie. Friday night is fine for me.'

'The night club will be open then. I'm barman until nine. We can go to Pluto's first. Then I'll take you out,' said Madden, quick as a flash, as if he already had everything planned. 'I have a special place in mind. A secluded, candlelit place. I know you're just going to love it. What do you say?'

'I say yes, but on two conditions.' Her mouth opened once more and the tip of her tongue rested on her top lip.

'Two conditions?'

'Yes, two, and no questions or debate. Do you agree?'

'Why do I feel I might regret this?' Madden paused as if considering the answer he already knew. 'Okay, yes I agree.'

'Firstly, there is something I want to show you on Friday night. There is a very special and secret part of my life that you are going to be privileged to see. And after that we will celebrate in fine style at whatever place you choose.'

'What secret part of your life? Is this some sort of elaborate joke?'

'Uh, uh! No questions, Charlie. But I will say that it's certainly no joke.'

'Sounds a bit mysterious. Okay, then, you've hooked me. I guess I'll have to suffer with the suspense till Friday. And what's number two?'

'You are to work out in my aerobics class tomorrow afternoon.'

'Hey! That's a bit tough. I don't know whether I can — '

'I'm a fair person, Charlie. You have a choice; either aerobics, or you can help my brother out tomorrow afternoon with his landscaping down at the Bribie Island beach house.'

'Now, I think we need to talk this over.'

'No,' said Deb, shaking her head. 'No debate. You've already agreed. The matter's settled.'

'Dear oh dear. I knew I was going to regret this. You do realise that I could end up with serious muscle fatigue and physical exhaustion, which could jeopardise my potential for Friday night.'

'If that's so,' whispered Deb, 'you will have to assume a passive role, won't you, and let me work my magic.' She quickly drew one finger up his inside leg, turned, and left the foyer for the staff room. Charlie lowered his red face, pushed at the carpet with his shoe as if studying some imperfection, then hurried into his office and closed the door. He dropped into the chair at his desk, stretched himself out and gave a long, manly groan through a smile. After completing a very satisfying stretch he grabbed a piece of foolscap from the desk, rolled it into a ball and tossed it over his shoulder. It ricocheted off the wall behind him and landed neatly in the waste paper basket.

'All right! A bit of gardening never held such huge rewards. What a manager you are, Charlie!' He raised his clenched fist. There was a short, sharp rap on the door. Schliemann entered, not waiting for the customary come in.

'Oscar!' announced Madden brightly. 'You shouldn't barge in like that. Who knows, I might have been in a delicate position with a young lady.'

'Yeah, and Joh Bjelke-Peterson will be our next prime minister,' replied Oscar, without cracking a smile.

'Now, now, behave.' Madden raised his index finger. 'My chances might not be as remote as you think. And I must say, it is comforting to know that you don't know everything that goes on around here.'

'You mean your lusting after Deborah's body? The whole club knows about that.'

'You bastard, Schliemann,' muttered Charlie light-heartedly. 'What's up, anyway?'

'You'll know soon. We can expect a knock on the door at any moment. The cops are here.'

'Shit, not again. What now?'

'They probably want to find out more about Stacey. I'd like to stay and hear what they've got to say. Any objections?'

'Certainly not. Would it matter if I had?'

'No. But it's polite to ask first.'

*   *   *

Both Dempsey and Hogan were wearing white shirts, ties, and dark trousers If they had been a little more particular about their ironing and adjustment of their ties, they may have passed for two Mormons doing the rounds. They sat across the desk from Madden. Dempsey was armed with pen and notebook and was sitting forward in his chair while Hogan reclined back, crossed his legs, and threw a piece of gum into his mouth. Oscar, hands in his pockets, remained on his feet, leaning casually against the wall near the door. Charlie wasn't the least bit impressed to see the same two faces that had deflated his plans for an endless night of passion only two days earlier. Glad that he agreed to let Oscar in on the meeting, he sat back in his seat and folded his arms in a mild gesture of defiance.

After a second apology on behalf of the inspector, Dempsey proceeded with what seemed like a predictable interview. Enquires seeking information about various Bodytone staff, other contacts of Stacey, and the whereabouts of Adrian Devlin, produced nothing more than short, sharp replies and a cocky smile from Charlie Madden, who seemed to be extracting some personal justice from the situation.

'It seems we're not making much progress,' continued Dempsey, fully aware of Charlie's passive-aggressive manner. 'Tell me, Mr Madden, has Stacey called you?'

'No, he hasn't. I wasn't aware they had access to telephones in those sorts of places.'

'What sort of places might that be?'

'You know what I mean. Mental institutions.'

'Oh, those sorts of places. I do believe they can use a phone. They seem to do silly things like that these days. What's the world coming to, eh?' said Dempsey tauntingly.

'Phone or no phone, he hasn't called I said.'

'Perhaps he's dropped in to see you then?'

'What on earth are you talking about?'

'Oh, you haven't heard. Stacey escaped today. A male nurse was stabbed to death and we need to talk to Stacey about it ASAP!' Dempsey's blunt admission did the trick. The brash grin fell away from Madden's face and he sat to attention. If Oscar was surprised it didn't show. He slowly turned his head and looked at Dempsey.

'And the rest of the story, detective?' he asked politely.

'There have been two murders in Ward 21. An old man was the first. You may have seen some mention of it in the paper.'

'No,' replied Madden.

'Yes,' said Oscar. 'George Hartley. It was reported as a suicide.'

'And it looked like one at first. We want to talk to Stacey about that one as well. Now, have you seen or heard from him?'

'We certainly have not,' said Madden.

'And of course, you'll let us know if you do?'

'Naturally.'

'It's reassuring to know that,' added Dempsey with a hint of sarcasm. 'The late Mr Hartley left a symbol set up on a chessboard. It had something to do with evoking spirits and demons. Which brings me to my next point. I would like to gather a little information on devil worship or witchcraft.'

'What particular aspects did you want to know about?' asked Oscar. 'Do you have a preference for the sexual, sacrificial, sadistic, or just the plain filthy?'

'Oscar, go easy. This is getting beyond a joke,' said Madden.

'I'm not joking, Charlie. This bloody cop knows you had a book on sorcery and magic in your drawer. He is wondering how you and this club tie in with everything that's happened. I would like to point out that such knowledge was gained through an illegal search. You are not obliged to answer.'

'Well, I haven't got anything to hide. I don't see any harm in telling the truth here, do you?'

'We will see,' said Schliemann.

'Do you guys really think I had something to do with all this?' continued Madden as he opened his drawer.

'How the hell do we know?' said Hogan sharply. It was the first words he'd had to say since the interview commenced. 'Bastards that fuck around with this sort of crap are so bloody secretive. Like wolves in sheep's clothing. Hartley was involved in some sort of club. Something to do with sex, black magic, or both. And there's someone here who knows about it. Maybe it's you, Madden.'

'Cut the crap, will you? Here's the bloody book. Take it. Keep it.' Charlie grabbed the book from the drawer and tossed it across the table towards Dempsey, who immediately reached forward, snatched it up, and flicked quickly through a few pages.

'Where did you get this?' asked Dempsey.

'Found it in the staff room. It's not mine.'

'Really. It's been in your desk drawer a while. Perhaps you have an interest in this sort of stuff?'

'I do not.'

'Whose book is it?' Dempsey looked at the two men expectantly. 'For Christ's sake, you're the manager, and you're the bloody security officer; one of you should know.'

'We don't know who owns the book,' said Oscar sharply. 'It hasn't been an issue of importance up till now, has it?'

'Well, it might pay you to find out. Consider this visit as a warning. The bodies are stacking up. And it's not over yet. I would suggest a little cooperation wouldn't go astray.' Dempsey flicked his calling card across the desk. The two detectives stood to leave. 'Think about it. Call me.'

Chapter 29

A Snake in the Grass

The uncomfortable bed and stinging sensation in his arm were all too familiar and for a moment, Simon thought he was back in Ward 21. He squirmed and stretched, opened and closed his eyes several times, then took two deep breaths. The musty smell of the small room filled his nostrils while his eyes strained to achieve focus and identify his surroundings. An attempt to lift and examine his aching right arm was inhibited by a firm restraint on his wrist. He rolled onto his side to investigate.

'Oh, my God. What the fuck,' he groaned. He rattled the handcuffs angrily against the metal bed frame to which they were secured. There was a bandage, also, neatly applied around his forearm. On the underside, a small plastic tube with a soft yellow rubber end protruded from between the layers of material. He touched it gently with his free hand.

'I would advise you to leave that alone, Simon.'

It was Kym. Her voice triggered some hazy memories. The slightly bitter orange juice; being dragged along the floor by two men; Kym one minute laughing, the next wiping his brow with a cold, soothing cloth; a shiny black snake. These events seemed so long ago. He had no idea how long he had been sleeping.

His attention strayed from the cannula in his arm. He sat up as best he could, supported by his elbows. The woman in whom he had placed so much trust stood, empty syringe in hand, at the end of the partly rusted bed end. Through the open door behind her, Simon could see the kitchen. He took some comfort in gaining orientation of the place, but none in the realisation that he was at Kym's house, for there was a sickening feeling developing in the pit of his stomach. A feeling of being comprehensively outwitted and deceived.

'Kym, help me. Get me out of here.' He thought it was rather a vain hope, but there was no harm in testing the water.

'I'd love to lend you a hand. You're quite an attractive man, Simon,' said Kym invitingly. She pursed her lips, tilted her head to one side and let her eyes travel over his body. 'Seeing you lying there helpless, in a light sweat, baring your chest and legs and filling out those black jocks so neatly sends wonderful messages to my groin.'

Simon grabbed the thin pillow from behind him and threw it quickly between his legs. He looked about for more protection, but there were no sheets or blankets on the old mattress and his clothes lay untidily in the corner, well out of reach.

'Who undressed me?' demanded Simon. 'These are not my jocks. I wasn't — '

'Wearing any? Oh, I know. I wondered what you were dreaming about. You had a huge erection. Was it me, Simon?'

'Cut with the bullshit. What the hell is going on? What day is it? What drugs have you been filling me with?' Simon quickly examined the bandage once more, found the taped end and started roughly pulling it free.

'I wouldn't do that if I were you. I have done you a favour and taken one set of cuffs off your left wrist.'

'It was you all the time, wasn't it? You were the reason that the Ward 21 phone number was on the newspaper clipping that *shit for brains* had in his pocket.' Simon pulled some more at the bandage. 'You murdered my family.'

'Ooh! Very harsh. I did no such thing,' said Kym. 'I would suggest you leave the bandage alone, but if you wish to pull it out go right ahead, we will simply secure you by both arms, shove in another one and give you more sedation.'

'And who the hell is we? Anyone I know?'

'Don't concern yourself with that, just know that if I asked them to remove your heart they would do it without a second thought.'

'How perfectly charming. Good friends are so hard to find these days.' Simon grunted his dissatisfaction and tucked the end of the bandage back into itself.

'Ah, it's good to hear the real Simon Stacey. A sarcastic, quick-witted, intelligent guy. And a nice, rather horny bloke as well. It's a shame, really.'

'What's a bloody shame? That you're going to kill me?'

'Oh, my goodness me,' said Kym. She placed her fingers over her mouth as if somewhat alarmed by the statement. 'Whatever gave you such an idea? No, that certainly won't happen, at least not unless you bring it upon yourself, of course. You know it is a shame we're not working towards the same goals. I think we'd have been a good team.'

'In your dreams, or should I say in your psychoses. What the hell have you been pumping into me?'

'You mean this?' Kym held up the empty syringe. 'Why do you think you're awake? Only because I was kind enough to give you a narcotic antidote. So, don't go doing anything silly or you will just have to go bye-byes again, won't you,' she said, waving her finger and looking down her nose like a schoolmistress warning a class of pre-schoolers.

'Gee thanks, teach. What day is it?'

'It's Thursday. Nearly midday.'

'The twelfth?'

'Yes.'

'It's on tomorrow, isn't it? Ras knew, didn't he? And you killed him. Murdering bitch!'

'A deluded old man of no value to society. Murder? No, I don't think so. I prefer to think of it as a positive form of euthanasia. Now, I'll go and prepare you some food.' Simon shook his head slowly as he watched her make for the kitchen. She stopped and turned.

'One more thing. When your bedroom door is closed the room is almost soundproof, so if you're well behaved and there's no calling out for help, we can leave the door open and your short stay with me can be quite civilised.'

Simon watched her preparing lunch in the kitchen. There was no doubt that she had gone to extraordinary lengths to find out as much as she could about him. Only Alison and his mother had ever prepared him sandwiches with meatloaf, pickles, and tomato sauce. It was a real delicacy, especially when served with freshly squeezed orange juice. Kym returned and placed the tray on the end of the bed.

'Is it drugged?' asked Simon sharply.

'Of course not. If I'm going to give you something I'll inject it, won't I?'

'Silly me.' Simon lifted the top slice off one sandwich. It looked lovely and he was certainly hungry. For some reason he found difficult to understand, he believed what she was saying. He raised the sandwich to his mouth and aggressively tore off a large piece. Outside his room a telephone rang.

'Eat up now. I'll be back soon.'

Stacey leaned over to the wall. He was just able to see Kym's bare feet near the cane telephone stand. She didn't answer the phone immediately. It rang a couple more times before the answering machine cut in.

'Hi, this is Kym. Sorry I'm not here to answer your call, but if you leave a message after the sound tone I'll get back to you as soon as I can. Thanks.' The tone sounded and a voice emanated from the machine's speaker.

'Kym, it's the Doctor.' She promptly lifted the receiver and switched off the answering machine.

'Yes, I'm here.'

Simon's eyes grew wider and his pulse quickened. From only those four words he recognised that voice; the English accent was quite pronounced. He strung together some recent thoughts. The news story about the kidnapped child; the birth of Robbie; the obstetrician who had been so good to Alison. Could it be the same man? It sounded just like him. He stretched his neck out as far as possible and cupped his free hand to his ear.

'All's well, but I do need some more ampoules,' said Kym. Her feet shuffled lightly on the smooth floor. 'Yes, that's fine. Six will do nicely.'

Simon felt reasonably sure that this guy was Doctor Goldsmith. Goldsmith had assisted in the birth of Robbie. And now Goldsmith's own son had disappeared. Stacey was both revolted and outraged. This wealthy and well-respected doctor who had influenced his family, particularly Alison, was a veritable Jekyll and Hyde.

'I'm pleased to hear that. Everything is running like clockwork. There will be no problems,' said Kym confidently.

Thanks to the antidote, it was first time in several days that Simon had been drug free and at last able to think clearly. The names Melissa and Danny, the wife and son of Doctor Goldsmith, he remembered from the kidnapping article in the paper. He clenched his left fist and gave a short jab into the air as he recalled where he had seen those names before. At the back of one of Teddy Duncan's photo albums there was a solitary photograph with the names Melissa and Danny printed beneath.

'In five minutes at the front gate then. See you soon.'

Kym hung up, switched the answering machine back on and returned to Stacey's room.

'Another friend of yours?' asked Simon pointedly.

'I have many friends, in many places. You'd be surprised.'

'I think I'm almost beyond any further surprises.'

'No, you're not. Believe me.'

'And what the hell is that supposed to mean?'

'Can't tell. It's a surprise. Wouldn't want to spoil it for you.'

Kym continued to be cheerfully evasive and tormenting until she heard Satan barking. After delivering yet another word of caution, she left the room. Simon heard the front door open then close. Something had to be done quickly; whatever surprise there was in store, it was certainly not going to be a pleasant one.

'Running like clockwork, eh. We'll see about that,' whispered Simon determinedly. He slid his legs over the right side of the bed and pushed it into the middle of the room. After placing his tray on the floor, he tossed the mattress against the back wall and tipped the metal bed onto its side. He was intent on getting to the phone, despite his involuntary affiliation with the bed. After a few frustrating moments getting the angles right, and with a minimum of noise, Simon finally succeeded in getting the bed through the door. Kym was still outside. Time was of the essence.

His cuffed hand held the upper section of the metal frame while his other had a firm grasp on the springs. He shuffled awkwardly but quickly across the polished floorboards. After setting his encumbrance down quietly on a small rug next to the cane stand, he grabbed the telephone and quickly punched out a set of numbers. He kept a close eye on the front door.

'Answer the bloody thing. Come on. Come... Wendy, shut up and listen. It's Stacey. Shut up I said. Tell Schliemann to check out Goldsmith. Got it? Doctor Goldsmith.'

Stacey heard a car door shut and a vehicle drive away.

'Got to go, bye.'

He grabbed the bed. Kym's voice could be heard just outside the door talking to the dog. Although only stepping a few inches at a time, Stacey's frantic jerky dash quickly had him at the bedroom door. With a slight change of direction, he negotiated the first bed end around the doorway with all the precision of a skilled removalist. There was a loud click. It was the front door latch. His foot caught the lip of his lunch tray, catapulting the tumbler of orange juice into his knee. A quick sidestep to avoid slipping in the mess resulted in the second bed end striking hard against the architrave. The sudden jolt, while slightly off balance, threw him to the floor. The bed tilted over and jammed tightly in the doorway. Simon's right arm extended vertically like a swimmer in distress. The handcuffs cut into his wrist. A trickle of blood ran down his arm.

'I turn my back for a minute and you start playing silly games.' Kym stood near the obstructed entrance shaking her head in a mild display of condemnation.

'You're a fool, Stacey. What are trying to do? Sneak out the back door? Get to the telephone? I've got it! This is an elaborate ploy to get some more narcotics. Now that I can help you with.' She opened her hand and displayed several small ampoules. A small twitch at the corners of her mouth developed into a broad grin and was soon followed by a long, hearty laugh.

Chapter 30

Goldsmith

Cochran, Johnson, and Dempsey had returned to the station to discuss their fortunes over lunch. Earlier in the day they had gone their separate ways to interview the long list of massage and escort girls provided by Briggs. They had compared notes on their return. Three of the girls had prior dealings with the mysterious club when it was strictly a sex get-together organised by Hartley. They all had left soon after an influential man, known only as Romoli, had insisted they spice up their acts by involving animals and animal blood. Two of the girls knew of one other who took particular delight in the new direction of the club. She was an attractive oriental girl who kept mostly to herself. Her name was Cherry Minx.

'This is really a sick book, Dempsey,' said Cochran. 'It's difficult to imagine who would want to read such stuff, let alone write it. Have you had a good look through this?' Cochran held up the book on sorcery and magic.

'Just flicked through it, sir,' replied Dempsey. 'It's pretty gross.'

'What about you, Johnson?'

'I've read the first few chapters.' She pulled an identical text from her handbag. 'There's a heavy emphasis on various rituals, human and animal sacrifices, drinking blood, that sort of stuff. Quite a few pictures of various scenarios. One that pops up regularly seems to be set in some sort of barn.' She opened at the *Consecration of the Feast* page. 'Like this here. Could be an old farmhouse or sawmill. Hard to be sure. In this picture, they are about to sacrifice a child. Friday the 13th is quite significant to these people; and that's tomorrow!'

'It is indeed. Thank you, Johnson. Keep reading. Is that from your own library?'

'Devlin's flat. It was with some other books in the bedside locker. I went for another look around there this morning after chatting to the girls.'

'Okay, so this was never noticed before on any of our visits?'

'I don't believe so, sir. Not that we were looking specifically at book titles. But it is the sort of thing that would stick in your mind if you saw it, and I think I would have remembered. Maybe it was planted there at the same time as Adrian Devlin's dental records.'

'Yes, Johnson,' nodded Cochran. 'Now you're thinking.'

'This is not a book you'll find in your library. It has no barcode, no ISBN, and no publishing information.'

*   *   *

Cathy Johnson arranged some plates and lunch on the desk in the debriefing room. She had brought along a range of healthy options. The inspector grunted as he prepared something for himself from the selection.

'Okay, Johnson, I'll eat it. Give us a break.' The inspector reluctantly bit into the filled pocket bread. Several alfalfa sprouts stuck out from one corner of his mouth as he chewed on the cottage cheese and salad. 'Tastes like grass,' he grumbled.

'Healthy grass. Now make sure you eat it all so you won't get hungry later,' replied Johnson. Richard Dempsey gave a secretive thumbs up to Cathy. He was amazed at her dealings with the cantankerous character. It was something of a miracle. His surprised expression didn't go unnoticed.

'And you can shuddup before you say anything, Dempsey. I am trying to lose a little weight. Is that so bad?' he snarled.

The phone on the wall of the debriefing room rang.

'Get that will you, Johnson?' She smiled as she got up from the small desk at which the trio was sitting.

'Johnson speaking.'

'Schliemann here. I want to talk with Cochran.'

'Hold on, Mr Schliemann.' The inspector needed no invitation. He dragged himself to his feet and with a little difficulty, managed to swallow the mouthful of sprouts and tomato.

'Schliemann, this is Cochran. Have you decided that you, or your newfound friends, might have something you want to tell us?'

'Listen. This information has just come to hand. And you might like to look into it. Stacey rang earlier. He was in a hurry. It was just a short message asking me to check out one Doctor Goldsmith. Do you know him?'

'His child was kidnapped recently.'

'That's right. I made a few enquires. Seems he was Alison Stacey's obstetrician. He delivered Stacey's child by caesarean section ten days early.'

'And what's so unusual about that?'

'According to one of the nurses in the labour ward, Goldsmith's claim of foetal distress as a reason for the operation was completely unfounded. She assures me that everything indicated mother and child were doing fine.'

'And what does all that mean? Plenty of doctors induce births for their own convenience. Maybe he had a game of golf on the due date?'

'The ball's in your court now, Cochran. You find out.'

'Where's Stacey?'

'No idea. Good-bye.'

'Hey. Schliemann. Hello?' The inspector glared angrily at the receiver. 'The bastard's hung up on me.'

John Cochran left Dempsey with instructions to find out what he could about Goldsmith, and to gather all the case notes on the kidnapping. He and Johnson would pay the doctor a visit. While there was no real evidence to indicate his involvement, it was clearly a coincidence worth checking out. If he was innocent, thought the inspector, there would be no harm done. If he had something to hide, then putting a little pressure to bear may force an error of judgement or perhaps put a slight hitch in any plans.

*　　*　　*

The magnificent modern-style home was towards the outskirts of Brisbane, at Bridgeman Downs. It needed to be; there was no way such a massive house would fit on a regular suburban block. The police vehicle proceeded through the open wrought-iron gates and stopped behind a late-model metallic-blue Volvo 760.

There were several long garden beds now in full bloom with carnations, daisies, and assorted marigolds. The gardens extended from the front white brick fence, alongside the circular driveway, and down both side fences to within a metre of the front porch.

Cochran ambled past the blue vehicle, taking enough time to have a brief look inside. Joined by Johnson, he continued to the porch. It was a spacious area, stylishly paved and sparsely furnished, with a high ceiling supported by four large white pillars.

'As a child, Johnson, I always tried to find the end of the rainbow and that elusive pot of gold.' Cochran nodded his head as he surveyed the dwelling. 'After all these years, I finally know where to find it.'

'Where? At a doctor's residence?' asked Cathy blankly.

'No, Johnson. The man's an obstetrician. Between a woman's legs, that's where the gold mine is.'

'Give me a break!'

'Hey, look at this place. It's worth a bloody fortune!'

The door opened before they had a chance to press the bell or continue their discussion. A middle-aged woman, wearing an apron, stood on the other side of the heavy security door that still separated them.

'Can I help you?'

'I hope so. I'm Inspector Cochran, and this is Constable Johnson. Would you be Melissa Goldsmith?'

'No, I would not. I'm the housekeeper. Do you have some identification?' she said bluntly. Cochran showed her. She unlocked and opened the next door. 'I'll see if Doctor Goldsmith can receive you now. Please wait.' The woman disappeared.

'You would have thought she'd invite us inside,' said Johnson crossly. 'After everything the department is doing looking for their child.'

A tall, stout-chested man dressed in a dark suit approached the doorway. A pair of thick glasses rested on the end of his nose.

'I'm Doctor Goldsmith. What seems to be the problem? Do you have news of my boy?' He spoke quickly and with a polished English accent as he peered over the top of his glasses.

'I'm Detective Inspector John Cochran. I am sorry about your son. We are here concerning another matter that may be related to the kidnapping. Just a minute of your time, doctor. May we come in?'

'You are not the investigating officer, are you?'

'No, sir, but there is some — '

'No, you may not come in,' interrupted Goldsmith coldly. 'I'm busy, and about to depart on business. If it is true that you just want one minute that will be in order. If you require any longer you will need to arrange an appointment with my housemaid or my receptionist at the surgery.'

'This is a very serious matter.'

'I'm sure it is, Inspector, but I have already spoken to the police handling my son's case. I suggest you do the same.'

'As you're very busy, doctor, perhaps we could talk with Mrs Goldsmith.'

'My wife is under sedation and is not receiving visitors. She is improving, but this entire ordeal has had a most damaging effect on her health. I would suggest you return in a couple of days and try again. Would you please leave now?' He placed his hand on the screen door.

'Was Alison Stacey a patient of yours?' Cochran took a step forward, blocking the security screen from closing.

'She was a patient of mine. Very unfortunate, her accident.'

'She was murdered, as was her son. It was no accident.'

'I am very sorry about that, but it is of no concern of mine. Would you please step aside?'

'Do you know anything about devil worship, black masses, or witchcraft?'

'You are a very rude man, Sergeant. Leave now or be reported to the commissioner.'

'It's, Inspector, thank you. Inspector John Cochran. Bye for now. No doubt we'll meet again.' He moved clear of the screen door. Goldsmith pushed it closed immediately, turned the lock and briskly walked away. The housekeeper appeared from behind the main door.

'Good day to you both.' She bowed her head politely. The main door closed.

Chapter 31

Lucy

Although it had been several hours since the capricious Asian had gently cleaned and dressed his cut wrist, Simon's arm still throbbed with pain. After a prolonged session of pleading to be spared any further drugs, he was not about to be requesting any analgesics. It was more good luck than good management that Kym seemed to believe that his accident had occurred trying to leave the room rather than return. It was a slight, but most welcome, change of fortune, thought Simon, and he hoped it was a sign that the dealer had at last opened a new deck.

He lay stretched out on his bed, still clad in a skimpy pair of black underwear. While he would have much preferred to have been more suitably clothed, he had deliberately not made any further reference to his near nakedness. He concluded that while she was enjoying looking at him this way she was less likely to be doing anything more diabolical. He was mistaken.

'Jesus!' screamed Stacey in horror as Kym entered the room. 'Please, no. Please!'

'I would strongly recommend you remain absolutely quiet and perfectly still,' said Kym calmly. The black snake stretched out from her hands and slowly wound its way through the metal struts at the end of the bed. 'It's a black tiger snake. If you look closely you'll notice a beautiful, deep blue on the underside. I can see you have a question for me, Simon. The answer is yes. It is venomous. It possesses a potent neurotoxic venom. Be careful. Be very careful. Don't startle her. Be still.'

On first sighting of the unholy reptile, Simon had drawn his feet up to his buttocks and pushed his body as far back up the bed as it would go. He now remained motionless, more through fear than obedience to instructions. A lifeless pallor displaced the last remnants of colour in his face as the snake glided onto the mattress.

Kym was ecstatic. She allowed her shiny blue silk bathrobe to fall open at the top and expose her neat, sallow breasts. One hand slid down her side, across the loosely tied sash, and then in towards her groin.

The snake slipped silently between Simon's legs and over his only clothing. Sweat oozed from his face. Kym kneaded the slippery material firmly into her crotch. The sinister pet paused on Stacey's sternum, and after seeming to study his terrified face, proceeded over his shoulder. He felt the last of the smooth, cool skin against his body as its tail passed over his neck. His eyes swung quickly from one side to the other, trying desperately to see the creature without moving his head.

'Don't move a muscle,' said Kym in a loud whisper.

Totally preoccupied with his own survival, Simon had not noticed Kym's antics until she spoke. He was instantly reminded of erotic dancers he had seen in Bangkok, and one in particular who also used a snake for stimulation. While it, too, disappeared at times, the audience always knew exactly where it had gone. Finally, the reptile came back into view. It skated past his left arm, across the mattress and onto the floor. Kym stepped forward and took hold of its tail with one hand. Her other hand slipped quickly up to its head. The one and a half metres of cold, black poison coiled itself around her arm.

'Isn't it just the cutest thing?' she said complacently. Simon was now breathing deeply and unable to speak. The snake charmer raised her arm and caressed the animal with her cheek before finishing up with a string of kisses up to its head.

'Aren't you talking to me, Simon?'

'Take it away,' he panted.

'You hear that, my pet? I don't think he likes you.'

'If you've finished your afterplay, I'd appreciate it if you'd just leave me alone.'

'Oh dear. Come on then. We're not wanted here. How would you like a nice white mouse?' Kym lifted the snake to her ear as if listening to it speak, then held it a few centimetres in front of her face. 'A live one! Why, of course.' She left the room.

*   *   *

It was thirty minutes later, when Simon's pulse had returned to something near normal, when Kym returned.

'Hello, Simon. Are you feeling better now? You were looking decidedly poorly before. I have such wonderful friends, don't you think?'

'No, I don't think. Not at all. A black dog called Satan and a black snake. What's its name? Devil I suppose?'

'No, no. It's a girl. Her name is Lucy. What else but Lucy for a girl and Lucifer for a boy.'

'I knew it. You're a very sick woman. You need help.'

'Don't condemn what you do not understand.'

'Well, perhaps you can give me some education. Purely a verbal education of course,' said Simon. He spoke almost casually. He knew his probe for further information was amateurish and transparent, but a probe nevertheless, and as such must be a trifle better than remaining putty in this woman's hands.

'Poor Simon,' laughed Kym 'I know you too well. You're like an open book.'

'Really.' Simon looked away briefly before resuming eye contact. There was a glimmer of hope in her words. A hint of overconfidence. He had seen and heard it many times before. Perhaps his unaccomplished display wasn't as bad as he had at first thought.

'I'll tell you something. Faith, loyalty, and absolute dedication to a cause are a rare combination to find in people these days. I have found them. Found them in myself and in others who follow the same mystical teachings of the 13th Black Candle. Teachings that give tremendous satisfaction in this life, and promises of great joy in the next. It's all about power, pleasure, and fulfilment of the hidden desires that lay deep within us all. You and many others may think it's sick or perverted; that's because you live in a world of denial. A world devoid of the ultimate in human experience and achievement. It's exhilarating, Simon. It's orgasmic in every sense, believe me.'

'You find murder so pleasurable. Women or children, it makes no difference to you. How can you believe such absolute crap? Pleasure and power. What sort of half-brained, feeble excuse is that for inflicting pain and suffering on other human beings?'

'You want to find out as much as you can, don't you? You're thinking about escape and about exposing us all. That's not going to happen. There's too much planning gone into tomorrow night, and all possible contingencies have been allowed for, even the unlikely event of your escape. How would you get those cuffs off? You could, of course, try again to take the whole bed with you, or maybe you could sever one hand and leave it behind just for me. I'd like that,' she said happily. Her face lit up at the thought. She stuck out her tongue an unusually long way, flicked it about in the air and groaned with pleasure, as if she could almost taste the warm blood.

'You know I used to do that as an adolescent,' said Simon. 'Standing in front of the mirror, trying to extend my tongue and perform oral gymnastics. I reckoned it would be a sure winner with the girls. But like you, all that happened was that I got a cold tongue and looked like the village idiot.' The desired result was achieved. Kym stopped fantasising and glared coldly at Stacey.

'Don't provoke me. If you think I'm a little unsavoury now, you should see me when I'm angry. Anyway, what do you think would happen if you got out of here? Presuming Satan didn't rip you to pieces first. The police maybe? Yes, they'd love that. They're looking for you now, and I think they'd be about ready to lock you up and throw away the key. You're responsible for more than you think.'

'I'm not stupid, Kym. I'm fully aware they suspect me for starting the fire, and they think I'm involved in Teddy Duncan's murder. I'll take my chances.'

'Oh, Simon, I must disagree with you. You are stupid.' Kym stood and headed for the door. 'There's a little something in my purse I'd like to share with you.'

Stacey's heart started to beat a little faster. What the hell was she going to produce this time? A funnel web spider called Nick? A scorpion called Mephistopheles? She soon returned, apparently free from any devilish creatures. There was a photograph in her hand.

'You're a man with an interest in photography. This is only a Polaroid shot, but I think you'll appreciate it.' She flicked it through the air. It landed on Stacey's chest. Tentatively he turned the print the right way up and brought it to his face.

'Oh God!' He tossed the picture away, leaned over the side of the bed and threw up.

'What's wrong? I really thought I got Eddy's best side.' She retrieved the photograph and looked at it more closely. 'Maybe you've got a point. Not that much blood, really. Perhaps another knife wound might have helped. You do realise, Simon, that you're suspected for his murder. More to the point, your fingerprints are all over the weapon, as well as his set of ward keys. You have been such a naughty boy, Simon Stacey. Tut, tut, tut.'

Chapter 32

Cherry Minx

'Well c'mon, Candy. Is she the one?'

'Why do Orientals look so much alike? No, I don't think so.' The woman's brow wrinkled as she moved her face closer to the car window. 'No, I'm sure that's not her.' She shook her head.

Cochran waved to Dempsey, who thanked the young occupational therapist and returned to the police vehicle.

'That's it for the hospital. The last two on the list aren't on duty today,' said the detective as he hopped into the driver's seat.

'Take us to the hospital canteen, will you, Dempsey? You can shout me a jam doughnut and this morning's paper. Then we can make a couple of home visits.' With his eyebrows raised in mild surprise, the detective glanced briefly at the inspector.

'Is that part of Johnson's plan, sir?' he said, unable to contain himself.

'Don't you start. Obviously, you haven't heard about the new filing system that's being introduced shortly. I'm looking for volunteers.'

'How many doughnuts was that, sir?' replied Dempsey instantly.

'I'll settle for just the paper. But let me tell you that's a decision I make purely because I choose, and not for any other reason. Is that clear?'

'Absolutely, sir.'

On the list of persons who had access to Ward 21 seclusion room keys were the names of five oriental women. Cochran was hopeful that one of these hospital employees might have once used the alias of Cherry Minx. He had recruited the services of Candy, a local escort girl who had past associations with Hartley's sex club, and a reasonable recollection of what Cherry looked like.

Cochran had turned to page six by the time they pulled up at the first address. Dempsey stopped the car and looked at the inspector.

'Well, man, what are you waiting for? Get out there and check it out.' Cochran never lifted his gaze from the newspaper.

'Yes, sir. Candy, you'd better get out. You'll never see a thing through all these trees.'

The streetwalker met the detective at the gate. He looked her up and down and rued his impromptu decision. She was clad in a skimpy, body-hugging skirt that partly revealed a bright red pair of lacy knickers that matched her high-heeled shoes and fishnet stockings. Her face entranced Dempsey.

'What are ya looking at, lover boy?' said Candy, chewing on gum.

'Some of your makeup seems to be cracking a little.' He pointed tentatively to the side of her eye. 'Just over there.'

'Well fuck, sweetheart. I've been working all fucking night. What'd ya expect?'

'Yeah, sorry.'

'Anyway, you don't root me eyes, do ya? Remember, I'm the whore with the strongest jaw. The best mouth in the south. You can easy find out for yourself, honey.'

'Good God! I'll pass, thank you,' said Dempsey.

'Your loss, sugar.'

'I'll get over it. You wait here at the gate.'

'It's a bloody myth, you know,' she announced coarsely, as the detective proceeded down the pathway. 'Those slant eyes are no better or tighter than the rest of us. And they can't handle big men. Maybe that's why you're so keen to see her, eh?'

John Cochran continued scanning the paper. It was with some surprise that he found the article he was looking for, tucked away on page six. Over the past few days the various reports on police corruption had progressively moved back through the paper. While steady progress was being made in identifying many who were associated with an alleged protection racket, there seemed to be no further developments pinpointing the ringleaders in the elaborate drug distribution network. Dempsey returned to the car.

'She's not the one either, sir.'

'Dempsey, what do you make of this?' Cochran folded the paper into a more manageable size and passed it over. 'It's a bloody cover-up. The minister says the police drug connection alleged earlier this month might not be as widespread as first thought. What bullshit.'

'Yes, sir, sounds like crap to me, too. Sir, she's not the one either,' repeated Dempsey.

'Okay,' said Cochran, still scanning the newspaper. 'Didn't expect she would be really. A bit too old I was thinking. Do you think they'll hang these blokes?' He pointed at an article in the paper.

'What blokes?'

'Barlow and Chambers; in prison in Malaysia. You been living under a rock or what?'

'Oh, those guys. Drug smugglers. Dead men walking. Bob Hawke may be a legend, but I don't think even he can save them now. We should press on,' said Dempsey. 'Candy, get in.'

'A please would be a nice courtesy. You've not paid me, ya know, so ya got no right to treat me harsh, lover boy.'

'Okay. Thanks for your assistance. Just one more to go, okay?' said Richard Dempsey, almost politely.

'Better be. I've gotta get cleaned up. I need to douche, you know.'

'Please, spare me the details. Will you just get in, please?' There was a hint of annoyance creeping into Dempsey's voice. He reefed out his notebook, scribbled a few quick details, and pushed it roughly back into his trouser pocket.

'Okay, don't hassle me. Bastard cops,' she muttered.

Within a few minutes, they were parked outside a low-set white timber home. Dempsey opened his door. Before getting out he turned to Candy.

'You can observe through the window this time.'

'Spoil sport.' She poked out her tongue.

'Dempsey,' said Cochran softly, while still fiddling with the paper.

'I'm sorry, but it's not something that particularly interests me at this moment. Perhaps the police corruption thing is a matter for a royal commission or some special enquiry, sir,' sighed Dempsey.

'It's not that. It's the sign on the fence. Good luck.' The inspector raised his eyebrows and gestured toward the gate.

'Shit,' cursed the detective on seeing the bold notice: 'Beware of the dog. Enter at own risk.'

He walked confidently through the gate and up to the veranda door. His loud knock accomplished two things; a close look at the gnashing teeth of a Rottweiler, and the arrival of a black-haired oriental lady. The lady opened the lattice door and patted her hand loudly against her hip. The dog stopped growling, moved up the three steps, and sat at her feet. She fed him a treat she had in her hand. The detective displayed his badge.

'Detective Richard Dempsey. I'm looking for a nurse from the hospital. Her name is Kym Sharma.'

'Yes, I'm Kym. I have already spoken with the police at the hospital. They have taken my statement. Eddy was a friend of mine. This is all very distressing.'

'I know my colleagues have already spoken with you, and I apologise for this intrusion. Would you be so kind as to show some form of identification, Miss Sharma?'

'I need identification in my own home? I do have a driving license. But is that really necessary?'

'I'm afraid so. If you wouldn't mind.'

'Just one moment, Detective.' She went inside. Dempsey looked down at the black dog; which now sat quietly just staring at him. He glanced back at the car. Candy held her fist at the car window with her little finger extended. The lady returned with license in one hand and a tissue in the other. She blotted her eyes.

'There you are. I hope that will be okay. It's an old photo and I have had my hair changed a little since then.' Dempsey quickly checked it over.

'Yes, I see. Thank you, Miss Sharma, that's fine.' He passed the license back. 'Now, if you wouldn't mind stepping forward a little, there's a lady in the car who thinks she may know you.'

Candy looked intently. She wound down the window just to be sure.

'That's not her, either. I've never seen that woman before.'

'Damn! Are you absolutely definite about that?' said Cochran.

'Of course I bloody well am. I don't know her. Now let's piss off, I've got things to do.' Cochran waved to Dempsey. The detective tipped his head politely, apologised once more, and backed up cautiously to the gate. Once outside he smiled and nodded again to the woman. She blotted her eyes and nodded back. Dempsey joined his companions and drove away.

The lady closed the doors, walked casually along the veranda and back inside.

'Thank you. You were wonderful. So composed, so confident,' said Kym proudly. 'And I think Satan has taken a liking to you. He's just a big softie when he wants a dog biscuit. That was a very special performance.'

'That's what you're paying me for, isn't it?'

'Oh, yes indeed. Here you are.' Kym counted out ten fifty-dollar bills.

Chapter 33

A Waiting Game

'Okay, that about sums it up. The whole sordid story,' said Cochran. 'It's Friday the 13th, sunset will be in two hours, and there's a gang of psychopathic devil worshippers out there somewhere. And if my guess is right, those bastards are planning to butcher an innocent young child sometime tonight, just like described in that damned book. We are not going to let that happen.'

Cochran, Johnson, Marshall, Briggs, six young constables, and four cadets had spent an hour going over many of the case details. The book on sorcery and magic appeared to be the cult's bible, and Cathy had read out several relevant passages. The most disturbing sections related to bloody sacrifices of young children whose bodies were described as being in synchronisation with Lucifer. References to massive surgical incisions, disembowelling, anointing sacrifices with urine, and the drinking of fresh blood had left everyone feeling uneasy and some of the new recruits quite ill.

Dempsey and Hogan were maintaining surveillance on the Bodytone Club. Police Operations had been informed of the probable satanic ritual, and all mobile and foot patrols had been placed on alert.

'Now let's not imagine for a moment that these people are your regular, run-of-the-mill crims,' continued the inspector. 'I suspect that many of these people are the so-called respectable *pillars of society* who hide their gross perversions behind suit and tie. Ordinary people? No, far from being ordinary. Crazy? Perhaps, but not insane in the true sense of the word. They are obsessed, not possessed. So I don't want any of that mystical and spiritual bullshit being used to explain some of the bizarre features of this case. We are dealing with real people and real murders, facts and figures, not phantoms, spirits, and demons. These people are cold, calculating, ruthless, and amoral. Let's distribute some justice tonight.' Cochran looked about the room. Six of the ten new recruits were standing against the back wall. The other four, all female, were sitting.

The inspector had not been backward in expressing his disapproval and disappointment to head office. He let them know that his request for additional officers had been rewarded with a wealth of inexperience — worse still, forty percent were female. The department had other, more serious investigations of a very high priority, he had been told. An attempt to discuss if this was the investigation into police corruption or the drug trafficking allegations met with silence and a hang up.

'I've divided you all into teams to cover several key areas.' The inspector distributed photocopies of the evening plan. 'You will all remain in radio contact at all times. If for any reason you need to leave your vehicle, you will have a two-way with you, so make sure it's charged and switched on. Stay alert, report anything unusual, and wait for instructions.'

Dempsey and Hogan worked well together; it was a shame to split them up. But with so many areas to cover and an absence of experience, there was little choice. Dempsey could remain close to the fitness club, accompanied by two of the new recruits. Hogan would have to go elsewhere. With no indication of the whereabouts of the meeting, Cochran was forced to allocate teams of two or three to various areas. It was possible that the cult may attach some spiritual significance to the murder scenes, so for the time being, while there was nothing more definite to go on, these areas would need to be watched, as would the Goldsmith's house. Devlin's flat was a central location, and it was from there that he and Johnson would base themselves. Even Briggs, much to the surprise of the regular team members, had been given some rein. He and a young male cadet were to watch over the burnt-out ruins of Stacey's house.

The meeting ended. All except Johnson and Cochran left. Cathy stood at the whiteboard studying the inspector's notes. There was certainly a lot of evidence against Stacey, and probably even enough for a conviction, but there were also some doubts. The old woman who thought that she might have seen a Mercedes at Duncan's house on the night he was murdered, and the alcoholic hardware storekeeper who couldn't pull Stacey's photo from a group of three others, were far from reliable witnesses. There were no fingerprints, no murder weapons, and excluding some loyalty to the satanic-type cult, there appeared to be no clear motive to pin on Stacey, either. Cathy picked up a handful of notes from the desk.

'Sir, mind if I take these with us?'

'Take what you like,' said Cochran. He stopped checking his revolver and grinned.

'What's wrong with you? What did I say?'

'Nothing, Johnson, nothing.'

'Well, why look at me like that then? I don't know what you might be thinking, do I?' said Cathy. There was just a slight hint in her voice to indicate that the big man might be thinking something a little unsavoury.

'I wasn't thinking anything of the sort, Johnson!' snapped Cochran. There was a tinge of colour in his cheeks, and for once it wasn't anger. 'If you must know I was admiring your application to your work. For someone who's a wizard with a shopping trolley you're not going to make a bad detective.'

'Well thank you very much, sir. That wasn't really that difficult to say, was it?' John Cochran grunted, looked away, and finished checking his weapon before securing it in the holster inside his jacket.

'You ready then?' he asked.

'As ready as I'll ever be.'

'Okay, first we go to interview Melissa and Doctor Goldsmith. His own child, although it seems totally incomprehensible, fits into the age group described in that book. And that, together with the frequent references to surgical techniques, leads me to think nasty thoughts about the doctor. Besides, sedation or not, I want to see Melissa. And if that upsets her posh pommie bastard of a husband it's just too fucking bad.'

*   *   *

After Cathy spent fifteen minutes head down going over documents she had already read several times, they arrived at the prestigious Goldsmith residence. She pressed the brass doorbell once while Cochran wandered about among the rows of gardens. Cathy stood patiently waiting at the entrance. After the third ring, the door opened.

'Perhaps you would like some flowers for your wife, Inspector!' called the housekeeper through the locked security door.

'No thank you.' Cochran walked slowly back to the door. 'Would the good doctor be in?'

'No, I'm afraid not. Out on business I believe. Don't know when he will be back.'

'Where's he gone?'

'He didn't say. Didn't leave a contact number, either.'

'Is that unusual?'

'A little,' replied the woman cautiously.

'I see. Would Mrs Goldsmith be available then?'

'She's still under sedation. Perhaps if you try tomorrow.'

'I'd rather see her now, if you don't mind,' said Cochran, almost politely.

'No. Doctor's orders. Sorry.'

Cochran turned his head away for a moment and stroked his chin. He swung back to face the woman once more.

'Oh, one more thing, if you wouldn't mind. I have a young child in my vehicle. He's not speaking. It could be young Daniel Goldsmith. Would you mind taking a quick look for me?'

'Oh, my God!' She unlocked and opened the door immediately.

Cochran pushed himself through the doorway.

'Apologies. There is no child. I just needed the door opened. Come on, Johnson.'

'How dare you!' squealed the woman indignantly. 'She is not to be disturbed. That's the doctor's orders!' Cochran turned sharply and moved close to the lady's face.

'Pardon me, madam, but I am expecting a murder to be committed tonight and there is a chance it may be Mrs Goldsmith's son. And your attitude makes me think you may know something about that.'

'I most certainly do not.' She took a step back to regain her personal space. 'The good doctor did say under no circumstances whatsoever — '

'A murder, I said. A child, I said. Tonight, I said!' shouted Cochran.

'There's no need to behave like that,' she stammered. Her eyes watered. 'Upstairs, second on the left.'

'I thank you.' The inspector tipped his head. 'C'mon Johnson.' Cathy followed him up the carpeted staircase.

'I might lose my job for this you know!' called the woman, blotting her eyes with a tissue. Cathy looked back with some concern for the sobbing housekeeper. John Cochran, with the help of the railing, moved his bulk surprisingly quickly to the upstairs hallway.

'Will you come on, Johnson!' he insisted. 'The doctor is out and about, and I don't like that. Don't like it at all. Time is of the essence.'

The two entered the bedroom. The king-size hand-carved four-poster bed took up little space in the huge room.

'Shit, this room is bigger than my entire unit,' announced Cathy.

'Remember what I said yesterday?'

'Yeah, the rainbow. How could I forget?' Cathy's attention turned to the patchwork continental quilt, where there was some movement. Melissa Goldsmith was almost indiscernible under the bulkiness of the bed cover. The duo approached the bed. Cochran drew an antique-looking chair alongside and sat down gingerly, a little unsure whether it was for use or display.

'Melissa. Melissa Goldsmith. I'm Inspector John Cochran. I need to talk with you about your son. It's most important.' He spoke quietly and clearly. The lady rolled onto her side. Her eyes and cheeks were sunken back into her pale face. Her shoulder-length auburn hair seemed thin and brittle. The prominent bones of her face and around her neck and shoulders reminded Cathy of famine victims she had seen on television.

'Oh, my God,' said Johnson in a loud whisper. 'She looks dreadful. Does anyone feed her?'

'Melissa, I'm Inspector Cochran. This is Constable Cathy Johnson. We're here to help you. Can you answer some questions? It's about your son. About Danny.' The mention of the boy's name caused her eyes to open slightly. She coughed. There was a deep rattle of thick mucus in her chest. Her cough was too weak to drag the secretions up to her throat.

'She's sick. She needs a doctor. A proper doctor,' said Cathy.

'Melissa. Devil worshippers, Satanists, witches. Is your son being held by these people?' John Cochran had moved closer to the poor woman's face. Her eyes opened a little wider.

'The doctor. The doctor,' she said feebly.

'Yes, we will get a doctor for you, I promise. What about the boy?'

'No, the doctor. My husband.' She coughed again. For a moment, she stopped breathing. Her lips turned slightly blue. She coughed again, dislodging a plug of mucus, then quickly sucked in more air.

'Johnson, go downstairs and call an ambulance. She's not staying here any longer.'

'Yes, sir,' replied Cathy, leaving the room without delay.

'Your husband is not home, Melissa. Do you know where he's gone?' She shook her head. 'Are you frightened of him?' She nodded. 'We are taking you to hospital. You will be safe there. Tell me why he scares you.'

'Danny, my son.' Melissa's brow was moist. Cochran gently pulled back the covers. She placed her hand over the inspector's forearm. 'My son.'

'Surely the doctor wouldn't harm his own child?'

'Not his, mine. My son. Danny. My boy,' panted Melissa.

'He's your son. I know Danny's your son. Doctor Goldsmith, he is the boy's father, isn't he?' She shook her head. 'Well who the hell is then?' said Cochran with surprise.

'Teddy,' she replied weakly.

'Teddy. You don't mean Teddy Duncan? Edward Duncan of Kingsview Terrace?' She nodded. The inspector patted her hand then massaged his brow with his fingers. 'Jesus Christ!'

*   *   *

The shiny black station wagon was parked in readiness at the rear of Kym's house. The back seat was lying flat, and there was ample room for a stretcher. Kym had everything carefully organised. Simon would not be given the narcotic antidote until after they had arrived at the ceremonial area. The plastic bag containing the snake-handled knife and keys, handled by Stacey, was in the glove box, and several hooded gowns had been packed into a suitcase.

Two stern-faced men dressed in black suits lifted the stretcher. They quickly and quietly positioned it in the back of the vehicle and removed the two supporting poles and separators. They returned to the house and soon emerged with a specially designed bottomless coffin. The glossy, dark wooden box with golden handles, crucifix, and trimmings was lowered slowly over the stretcher. Darkness engulfed the drugged Simon Stacey.

Looking the part of a bereaved widow, with black dress, wide-brimmed hat and black lacy veil, Kym took her seat in the car. The driver looked at her. She nodded, and the vehicle slowly departed.

*   *   *

'So you see, Johnson,' said Cochran. 'The good Doctor Goldsmith is not the boy's real father, even though his name appears on the birth certificate. Teddy Duncan was probably manipulated by Goldsmith with threats to harm the child if he didn't do as he was told. Keeping Stacey occupied on the night of the fire may have been one such task. It may have been his failure to do that which cost him his life. Although I think it would only have been a matter of time before he would have been silenced.'

They pulled up to the curb outside Devlin's flat. Cathy was driving.

'A little further down the road. Turn around and park away from the street lights on the other side. Let's not make our presence too obvious.'

'This whole thing sounds like it's been planned well in advance,' said Cathy. 'But why did they have to kill Alison and Robbie Stacey?' The car pulled up in the shadows.

'It seems they are keen to eliminate anyone with past connections to the cult who no longer aspire to their warped way of thinking,' said Cochran. 'The unknown male body may have been one such person, but I think that's unlikely. No, I think Stacey arrived just in time to find his family being incinerated, saw this jerk prancing around naked in the yard and blew him away next to the swimming pool.'

'You think this guy was one of those devil cult people?'

'Jesus, Johnson!' Cochran shook his head slowly and took a deep breath. He turned and whispered in Cathy's ear. 'I really think he's a streaker from Lang Park who lost his way, saw the fire, and thought he'd join the barbecue.' Johnson pulled herself away.

'Sometimes you're a real arsehole, you know? Just because you're pissed off with the department there's no need to make me look and feel like a bloody fool, J. C.,' retorted Cathy boldly. Cochran was momentarily silenced. Being called an arsehole was nothing particularly new, but very few people called him J. C.

'Why did you call me that?'

'Why is it necessary to humiliate people, particularly women? You're a man. You've got a dick. We all know that. There's no need to go slapping people around the face with it, is there?'

'Very succinctly stated. What I meant is, why did you call me J. C., not why did you call me an arsehole?' Cathy clenched her teeth and released a short, sharp squeal.

'There you go. You're doing it again. Making me look stupid!'

'Oh, my God.' Cochran threw his head back. 'You don't need my help to do that. Jesus Christ, you're starting to sound like my wife.'

'Well ha ha, bloody ha! Very funny,' said Cathy, as she huddled up against the car door, took a torch from the glove box, and began reading through the case documents once more.

*　　*　　*

It was nearly nine o'clock when Dempsey noticed Charlie Madden leaving the Bodytone Club with Deborah.

'Maybe something's happening at last,' remarked the detective. His two inexperienced companions, stretched out comfortably in the back seat of the vehicle, opened their eyes and looked at each other with some concern.

'Sir, this is Dempsey,' he announced into the radio as he rotated the volume control. 'Madden and Watson are leaving. They're just getting into his car now. Over.' The radio crackled loudly as he awaited instructions. After a few seconds, Cochran's harsh voice blurted forth.

'Follow them. Leave the pretty one there to keep an eye on things. I want to know every turn you make. Is that clear, Dempsey? Over.'

'Roger. All clear. Out.' He turned to the two in the back. 'Okay, pretty one. You heard the boss, off you go. Now you've got a two-way radio. Your job is just to observe and report, nothing more. Just hang around here near the car park and keep a low profile,' he said reassuringly. She tentatively left the security of the vehicle.

'And don't look so worried,' he added as he drove away, following Madden's car. They headed northward out of town and up the highway. After fifteen minutes the plain white sedan made a right turn and headed down the Bribie Island Road. Dempsey slowed near the turnoff to lengthen the following distance and avoid suspicion. After notifying Cochran he proceeded along the narrow, potted bitumen course.

'This is a most unwelcome development,' said the inspector with some dismay. 'Madden may have some involvement in all of this, and if he does, we can't let Dempsey and a newbie handle it on their own. On the other hand, if we commit ourselves to a Bribie Island beach party we may end with egg on our faces and a dead kid.'

'How do you make a decision like that? Perhaps if — ' Cathy was interrupted by the two-way.

'J. C. this is Snake at city base. You receiving me? Over.'

'Roger, Snake, and don't call me that. Over.' Cochran looked over at his partner and raised his finger. 'Don't you say a word.'

'A report just in says there are candle lights and chanting going on at Nudgee Cemetery. Thought you might like to check it out. Over.'

'Isn't there a patrol car in that area? It's a good thirty minutes from here!'

'Sorry, J. C., none available for at least an hour, maybe longer.'

'Okay, Snake, okay. Leave it with me. And don't call me that. Cheers.'

'Sorry, J. C., cheers.' John Cochran clenched his teeth and growled like a dog.

'One of these days, Snake,' he mumbled into his double chin before squeezing the radio hand piece once more. 'Marshall, are you awake?'

'Marshall awake and receiving.'

'Did you hear all that? Over.'

'Didn't miss a word, sir.'

'No need to be a smartarse, Marshall. Get on it right away, will you?'

'Will do. Out.'

Cathy put her fingers on the ignition keys and looked over at the inspector, who reclined back into his seat and closed his eyes.

'Well?'

'Well what?' grunted Cochran.

'Shouldn't we be going, too? Isn't that what we've been waiting for?'

'I doubt it. Our lot are unfortunately a bit more sophisticated than that. I'm sure they won't be on public view prancing around some gravestones. Anyway, Marshall will call if he thinks it's more than a bunch of wankers.'

Over the next quarter of an hour, Cochran received another two calls from town. In the Indooroopilly Shopping Centre car park, a naked man had been seen dancing inside a huge flaming circle of beheaded cane toads. He had attracted quite a crowd. On the other side of town, at Mt Gravatt, there had been several complaints about a well-dressed man and woman who were conducting a door knock appeal for human organs. While that was a little unusual, the householders became quite distressed when told the organs were needed to feed homeless youths. The man was then opening his suit coat to display an assortment of butcher's utensils.

Chapter 34

Stakeout

Detective Dempsey and his uninitiated partner sat in the dark, peering through the car windscreen. They had followed Madden and Watson to a secluded Bribie Island beach house without being spotted. Strategically positioned about thirty metres from the small house, they had driven the car off the road and a little way up a sandy path, parking amongst a small crop of acacia bushes. Madden and Watson were inside with at least two other people who were visible as silhouettes against the lightly coloured curtains. Dempsey had notified the inspector, who in turn had instructed Hogan to join his more regular companion. Cochran considered the beach location to be an ideal spot for some unsavoury satanic-type activities, and Charles Madden was still on his suspect list.

'You stay here and watch from the car. I'm going for a look around the other side of the house,' said Dempsey. 'You know we are on the lookout for a child aged about two years. And we are very concerned for the child's safety, right?'

'Yes, sir. I know that, sir,' said the recruit.

'I won't be long. So just relax and be observant. If there's an emergency, sound the horn three times. And by the way, how long have you been out?'

'Two weeks,' squeaked the young constable. He coughed and repeated himself. 'Two weeks.'

'That long, eh? What the hell are you doing here? This is unbelievable.' Dempsey shook his head. 'Departmental decision makers. As long as they protect their own arse, eh?'

'I volunteered, sir. There's a shortage of staff and I thought the experience would be useful. The police commissioner, Mr Lewis, has announced there will be one hundred new recruits starting this month.'

'Did he? Well fuck me, Junior!'

'I realise that's not much help right now, sir.'

'Your astuteness is astounding. And keep calling me sir. I like that,' said Dempsey. He opened the car door then turned back to his young partner. 'Oh, one more thing, Junior. If I hear that horn and find and there's no emergency...' he smiled and placed his hand over his revolver. 'I'll be forced to blow your balls off and then advise our Commissioner, Terry Lewis, of your shortcomings.' With that Dempsey disappeared into the darkness.

Junior sat well forward in his seat with his nose almost touching the windscreen. The glass fogged. He moved back slightly and polished it hurriedly with his handkerchief. Every few seconds his gaze would dart to the sides, probing into the darkness, searching anxiously for the remotest sign of movement. With the slightest turn of his head he found he could tune in to every sound like some form of acoustic radar.

*   *   *

John Cochran completed the fifth circuit of a walk to stretch his legs and then dropped heavily back into the front passenger's seat.

'Ah, that's a bit better,' he groaned, as he twisted himself into a comfortable position. 'Take a walk, Johnson. It'll do you the world of good. Help you think.'

'I hardly think five laps around the car is going to do that much for my circulation, sir. If you don't mind, I'll stay where I am.' She eyed the inspector up and down, rolled her eyes, and then continued studying the paperwork using a small pocket torch.

'I know what you think of me. Those silly little glances of yours. Let me warn you now, this is neither the time nor the place to be getting up my nose.'

'If you know so much, tell me,' said Cathy assertively, not put off by the threat. 'Come on, tell me what I think. You think you know me that well. Let's hear it then.'

'Oh dear, do we have to get into this, Johnson? Look, I know what you think about me, so let's just leave it at that. If you want to argue the point, perhaps some other time.'

'I knew you didn't know. That's a bluff answer and you know it. I was right. Thank you.' Cathy assumed a smug grin and looked back at the documents on her lap.

'Okay, Johnson, you want to hear it?' said Cochran defiantly. 'Well listen up, and then you tell me who's right. You think I'm a fat, lazy slob who wouldn't know what the word *healthy* meant even if he had it tattooed on his arse. You believe I have no personal strength to change my habits, and I treat any new recruits and all women like garbage. To round it all off you think I'm a rude, demanding, uncaring, sexist pig.' Cochran sat back in the car seat and crossed his arms. Johnson stared at him while rubbing her chin between thumb and forefinger.

'I guess there's no arguing with that, is there? You were right,' she replied nonchalantly. John Cochran sat motionless, looking straight ahead. Cathy leaned slightly to her left, trying to get a better look at his face for a clue to his reaction. There was a faint grinding sound. It was his teeth. She bit her bottom lip, unsure now as to whether she had overstepped the mark. The inspector turned to face her.

'You can be a real bitch sometimes. I think that's why I like you.' Cathy released the breath she had briefly held and smiled. 'Now if you're quite finished, we should make a move in the direction of that beach house.'

'Before we go. I just want to check on something. There's a name on this list that's been whirling around in my silly brain. It may be nothing, but I want to have a closer look.' She pulled a pen from her shirt pocket and scribbled down a string of letters on the sheet she had on her lap. Some letters were crossed out and others added with increasing haste.

'You're not doing what I think you're doing, are you? Next thing we'll be playing I spy.'

'That's it. Number 17!' squealed Cathy with excitement. 'Sons for Lucifer. I've done it, J. C. I'll bet that's the dead guy; the corpse at Stacey's!'

'Now hang on. Speak slowly, and explain exactly what in the hell you're talking about.'

'This is the list of persons who resemble the dead guy at Stacey's. All of them have supposedly been eliminated, twice! But this name,' she said, sticking the page in front of Cochran's nose and pointing at the spot with the torch. 'This name, Orson Ruscliffe, is an anagram for sons for Lucifer. Satanic sacrifices of young boys. It must be right. I'd like to run a check to see if he really has been accounted for.' John Cochran puffed up his cheeks with air and then blew it out slowly.

'Are you for real, Johnson?'

'Absolutely. I know I'm right. I just know,' she insisted. The inspector passed the two-way across.

'You call it, Johnson, and pray that you're wrong. If you're not, then we're gonna have some really heavy shit to deal with.'

Cathy called through to Senior Constable Blake and gave him the details to check. As she returned the hand piece to its clip, the penny dropped and she realised Cochran's concerns and the implications of her inquiry. No wonder he had hoped she was wrong. If this fellow turned out to be the unknown body at the fire, there was either some gross neglect of duty or a cover-up. Possibly a mole in the department. The excitement of her discovery was soon replaced with a lengthy five minutes of uneasiness while they waited for the return call.

'Constable Johnson, Blake here. Is J.C. with you?'

'Yes, he is. Go ahead, please.'

'Orson Ruscliffe comes from South Australia. There is no record of any inquiry into his whereabouts with the boys down there. His name used to be Oswald Madison. He changed it by deed poll four years ago. At present, he is thought to be holidaying in Queensland, location unknown. No past convictions but has been suspected of involvement in child pornography. Did you get that? Over.'

Cathy felt a rush of blood to her face and her heart beating in the back of her throat. She looked at Cochran.'

'Well answer the man, for Christ's sake! He might have more to tell us yet.' The inspector clenched his fists and pushed them hard into his knees. He broke eye contact with Johnson, looked at the floor, and shook his head slowly.

'Okay, okay. Don't get your knickers in a knot,' retorted Cathy.

'Johnson, are you receiving me? Over.'

'Yes, yes. We've got all that thanks, Senior. Do you have any dental records?'

'Shit, Johnson, I'm not a bloody magician, course I haven't. The only other thing I've got at the moment is that it has been reported that he operates some sort of group or club. It can go by two different names. Either the 13th Black Candle or Bodytune. Over.'

John Cochran snatched the hand piece from Johnson.

'Spell that second name, Snake.'

'Bodytune. B-O-D-Y-T-U-N-E. Hey, have I done good or what?'

'You've done well. Maybe a bit too well. Cheers and out.' He hung up the radio. 'Drive, Johnson, drive.'

Loose dirt and stones peppered the underside of the car as Cathy pulled out from the curb. The back of the vehicle slid to the left as she negotiated the 'T' junction into the main thoroughfare.

'Jesus Christ! You give a woman a big car to drive and she thinks she's got balls. Hasten slowly, Johnson, and we'll all live a little longer.'

'You know who it is, don't you?' asked Cathy, totally ignoring the previous remark. 'It's Briggs, isn't it? You've suspected him for a while, that's why you've been riding him.'

'Continue straight ahead and go down McPhail Road, then shoot down the highway.'

'Am I right? Is it Briggs?'

The inspector slammed both his hands hard on the dash. Johnson jumped.

'Shut up! For five minutes just shut the fuck up!' he bellowed. 'It's not a bloody competition for Christ's sake. I'm wrong, you're right! Who gives a shit? We've got the information and now we can act on it. And you can cut out all that girlie crap. I'm sick of it!'

Cathy's moistened eyes glistened in the headlights of the passing vehicles. She was determined not to give the fat man any indication of how he had made her feel. Her first inclination was to punch the rude blimp squarely between his podgy eyes, but as she drove and had time to think, she realised his behaviour since Snake's message was uncharacteristic. Sure, he was often loud, rude, and insulting, but this was different. There was a troubled tone behind his shouts and an agitation beneath his anger. They turned onto the highway. After a few more minutes of silence, Cochran spoke.

'Take the Anzac Avenue exit.' Cathy remained quiet and followed instructions.

'Now second on the right and pull up at number forty-two.'

It was a neat, low-set brick home. There seemed to be nothing to set it apart from the many other similar suburban dwellings in the area. A narrow cement path extended from a small metal gate and brick fence to the front porch. A light set into an amber glass shade illuminated the entrance with a peaceful yellow glow.

John Cochran stood at the door, fumbling with a set of keys pulled from his pocket. Cathy looked wide-eyed at the inspector. Her mouth opened as if to speak, then closed. He unlocked the door and marched in, flicking on the light as he entered. Cathy tagged along behind while Cochran briefly checked each room. He pushed open the main bedroom door.

'The bastard's not here. Shit!' A pillow from the double bed flew across the room, landing on top of a chest of drawers. A framed black and white photograph teetered on the edge for a moment before falling to the floor. Cathy knelt and picked up the cracked framed picture. It was a photo of three people; John Cochran, Emily Cochran in the middle, and Sergeant Alistair Carter. Both men had their arms over Emily's shoulders.

'Oh, my God. It's Carter! Fuck! I'm so sorry.'

'Damn you. Damn you, Carter. Why couldn't you be here? Why?' cursed Cochran. He dropped himself onto the bed, leaned back on his arms and threw his head back.

'Policeman's Ball?' said Cathy, still studying the picture.

'How is it possible? The guy's been a friend of mine for years. I've spent many nights here at this house. I've even got a key to his front door. We've been out together; shared good times; shared stories; shared problems. I never knew. Never had a fucking clue. What an idiot I am. He must have had many a laugh at my expense.'

'Why are you so sure it's Carter? I don't want to harp on about this who's right and who's wrong thing, but is it possible you could be mistaken?'

'I'm sorry about that. I was out of line. But when you find out something like this it just doesn't sit too well in the guts. And no, I'm not mistaken. Marshall and Carter worked on that list of names together. Carter said that he checked it through a second time. Who do you think prompted me to take the watch off Devlin's flat? And then, just by coincidence, some arsehole goes in and shoves dental files in the dunny and a book in the bedside locker. The other morning, he inadvertently says *Bodytune* instead of *Bodytone*. Finally tonight, all these fucking incidents all around the city. All a calculated ploy to keep us off the scent, of that you can be sure.'

'How could you know? These people are so secretive and devious.'

'I should know, I'm a bloody cop for Christ's sake. It's my job to know! Looking back now I was given a clue. Two years ago, I had very nearly saved a girl from jumping off the Story Bridge. She was prattling on about all this devil stuff. Sacrifices and shit. I was an arm's length away. Carter directed a squad car there with lights and sirens and that's what scared her. Made her jump.'

'So sorry. But you're not expected to be dissecting your friends,' replied Cathy.

'Perhaps not. But from now on it might not be a bad idea. You have no idea what this is like. No idea at all.'

'I think I might.'

'Oh no, not this again. Spare me, please.'

'It's like suddenly waking up and finding out that your right arm is missing. The worst thing is, you realise it never belonged to you in the first place. Someone with all the privileges of a friend has been revealed as an impostor after trespassing through your mind. Your psyche has been raped.'

John Cochran sat forward. Cathy stood, took a few short steps, and handed over the broken picture. He lightly ran his fingers over the cracked glass.

'You're an interesting woman, Johnson. Whoever caused you to experience such feelings? Obviously, someone who never deserved you in the first place.'

'What's our next step, J. C.?'

'First, you get on the radio and get everyone, except Dempsey and Hogan, back to their original positions. Then get back in here and help me search this place.'

*   *   *

Dempsey crept quietly back towards the parked vehicle. He stopped a few metres short, picked up a rock, and tossed it over the car. Like a flash the young constable's head spun round to the direction of the sound. He could see a few of the taller trees sway gently with the breeze. There was a multitude of darkened shapes out there. He slid slowly down in his seat, his eyes just peering over the top of the car door. Dempsey reached in through the other window and jabbed him on the shoulder with a small stick. He successfully scared the living daylights out of his young apprentice, who jerked into the door, causing his nose to strike against the lock button.

'Ah! Jesus!'

'Shut up, you bloody fool. Do you want to give away our position? What the hell are you doing? Junior, have you been sleeping on duty?'

He sat upright, squared himself up in his seat and hastily brushed a few creases in his shirt with his hand.

'No, sir. I haven't been sleeping. Honestly. There was a sound. I thought there was something…I mean someone out there.'

'Will you settle down,' interrupted Dempsey, dismissing the young man's concerns with a wave of his hand and sitting himself back in the car. 'Just tell me, are there any messages? And clean up your face, will you?'

Junior blotted a small cut on the end of his nose with a handkerchief and passed on the inspector's latest message, which Dempsey noted carefully in his diary.

'That's all?'

'Yes, sir. What does it mean?'

'It means, Junior, that you don't go to sleep,' said the detective, waving his finger.

'I won't, sir, and I wasn't before. I was just concerned there was someone — '

'Listen. This stakeout might be the real deal. The boss has said we need to stay put. Hogan is on his way. You just need to be concerned about doing a good job, sport.'

'I want to. I want to do a good job. It's important to me.'

'Well shit, that's just so lovely I might need to have a little puke. Now, I'm going back out there again. So, don't forget…' the detective tapped himself between the legs, formed a gun shape with his hand and pointed it at the constable's groin. 'Bang, bang.'

Dempsey returned to his strategic surveillance point, lying down behind the gardenia shrubs towards the rear of the small beach house. This location allowed him clear vision of front and rear entrances and a glimpse into the lounge area through a gap in the curtains. And besides, the bed of small wood chips offered more comfort than would the moist grass or gritty sand.

The young constable was again on his own, peering nervously out into the darkness and checking out any silhouetted movement in the house.

Someone near a half-lit window struck a match. The light flared brightly for a moment then settled as a candle took up the flame. Junior stared intensely. A woman placed the candle on some large rectangular object. The procedure was repeated. A second candle joined the first.

'Oh, my God,' whispered the constable. 'It's not happening. Do these devil people use candles? Oh, my God. Please tell me it's not happening.' He rested his sweaty palm lightly on the car horn and looked out the rear window, hoping to see the faintest glimmer of approaching car headlights. There was nothing.

*　　　*　　　*

Cochran and Johnson were back where they'd started, in the bedroom. If there had been any doubts about Carter's involvement before, finding the book Sorcery and Magic by Oswald Madison had dispelled them. It had been carefully tucked away beneath some old jumpers in the top of a tall linen closet. Cochran looked about the room. All drawers and cupboard doors were open, the bed was stripped, and clothing was strewn all over the carpet.

'You bastard, Carter. Always so neat and fucking tidy. Everything in its place.' Cochran backhanded the bedside lamp onto the floor. 'Well, I hope you like your room now, you prick.' The big man continued cursing incoherently through his teeth. 'First, we have to find him, don't we?' said Cochran, talking aloud to himself.

'What do you mean by first?'

'Sorry, just contemplating various forms of public execution.'

'Sounds like you're ready to string him up.'

'Ah! Hanging, beheading!. How perfectly delightful. Anyway, these pleasantries aren't getting us anywhere,' said Cochran, bringing himself back down to earth. 'We're still no closer to finding out where he and his cronies have gone.'

'Well, his car's still in the garage, so he's either got a lift or he's jogged to wherever he's going.'

'I would expect he's been driven. Of course, it depends how close the meeting place is. In either case, he'd wear his jogging shoes.

He wears them almost constantly.' Cochran walked over to the built-in wardrobe and squatted. Several pairs of assorted shoes sat neatly in pairs on the floor. He lifted them out two at a time and scrutinised the soles.

'His new pair of runners aren't here. No surprise there.' The inspector checked the last pair — a set of brown leather sandals. He tossed them over his shoulder.

'Johnson, chuck me over that box of tissues, will you?'

Using a fistful of them as a duster, he meticulously gathered all the debris from the bottom of the wardrobe into a small pile.

'Plastic bag. Quickly now,' said Cochran. His open hand shot out to one side like a surgeon waiting impatiently for the next instrument. Cathy slapped a bag into his palm. Carefully he pushed the sweepings into the packet with his finger and then ran his thumb along the press seal.

'Check it out, Johnson.' He tossed the bag over to her, then with the support of the wardrobe door, pulled himself to his feet. 'Well, what do you make of that then?'

'Looks like dirt to me.'

'Keep looking. What else?' asked the inspector. Cathy held the packet up to the light.

'Some small splinters of wood. And there appears to be sawdust in here, too.' She stared straight at Cochran, who appeared to be looking right through her. 'Goldsmith's house?' stated Cathy with some conviction. 'He does use sawdust in his gardens.'

'No, but you do know where, Johnson,' said Cochran. 'It was you that showed me the pictures.'

'Okay then, a barn or sawmill maybe, as per the book. But where?'

'Chuck me that sorcery book,' said Cochran with a hint of urgency. Johnson obliged. The paperback partly opened itself in the inspector's hands. 'A popular page, this one. This looks more like an old deserted sawmill than anything else. There's not many around; in fact, I only know of two. There's one near Caboolture, but it's a bit too close to the built-up area. The other is at Eaton's Crossing, which is about twenty-five minutes' drive from here. I'll bet that's where Goldsmith gets his fertiliser for his precious flowers, too. It's time to POQ.'

'POQ?'

'Piss off quick. Shit, where'd you go to school? A bloody convent?'

'As a matter of fact, I did.'

'Jesus.' The inspector shook his head. 'Out to the car and on that radio. I want everyone to drop what they're doing and get to the bloody sawmill. I'll be with you in a moment.' He flipped open his notepad and searched for a contact.

*   *   *

Hogan still hadn't arrived, and Junior had broken into a light sweat. He heard every sound and studied every smallest movement. But most of all, he focused on the house.

'Get with it now,' he whispered to reassure himself. 'I know you're a bit worried. But that's okay. Gets the adrenaline going. Ready for action. Just focus on the job. Who knows? There could be a career opportunity in store after this.'

The candles seemed to be glowing brighter. The silhouettes glided effortlessly and slowly past the curtained windows. Then, unexpectedly, his worst fears were realised. Another shadow appeared at the window. It was a struggling child being held in the air by another person. At another window a man held a long, slightly bent object with both hands. It looked for all the world like some sort of weapon. The recruit swallowed heavily and slapped himself lightly on the face.

'This is it. Time to act.' He sucked in a couple of deep breaths then quietly pushed the car door open, hopped out, and bolted for the front door of the beach house at full pace. Behind him he heard the crackle of the radio and the inspector's voice. He couldn't turn back now, there was too much at stake.

Dempsey stood and brushed a few adherent wood chips from his shirt and trousers. A glimpse of movement and the snapping sound of dry twigs drew his attention. He looked up in time to see Junior take one giant leap up three steps and lunge at the door while screaming *Dempsey!* in a long, loud roar as if charging into battle.

Bruce Watson, Deborah's brother, had been showing off his extensive collection of aboriginal artefacts. He and Charlie Madden had been fooling around with the nulla-nulla, making suggestions as to how they could keep their respective women in line. The handsomely decorated straight piece of heavy wood sat firmly in Charlie's hands. The door swung open with enough force for the interior handle to punch a neat, round hole in the plywood wall before rebounding back to almost close itself again. Junior stumbled, fell, and skidded along the floor on his shoulder, stopping at Madden's feet. It was an instinctive act of self-preservation. Charlie raised the club. The constable managed a brief view of some earthy coloured dots surrounding shapes of goannas and crocodiles before the fighting stick struck him sharply below his ear.

'Bloody hell, Charlie!' said Bruce Watson, both amazed and perplexed. 'What is going on? Who is that?'

Madden was stunned. He looked at Bruce, at the unconscious man on the floor, and then across the lounge room to Bruce's wife. Deborah stood near the candlelit piano holding her young son tightly against her chest. No one had any answers.

'Well,' continued Bruce, 'Whoever he is, he's not going to cause us any trouble for some time. That was a spot-on shot, mate. Six and out. What a beauty!'

Bruce was an unusual character. A tall man with a square jaw and a very thin top lip, he looked like something of an ogre. But for those who knew him he was an amusing, unflappable, gentle giant.

'He's not dead, is he?' said Madden, squatting down and checking the man's neck for a pulse with one hand while the other clung to the heavy stick, just in case.

The door flew open again.

'Freeze! Police!' Dempsey stood feet apart, knees partly bent and arms outstretched, holding his revolver. He pointed it menacingly at everyone in turn.

'You, drop that club. Move away from that man. Do it slowly.' He waved the gun nozzle, indicating which way Madden was to go. Charlie stalled in what appeared to be a defiant and courageous but rather silly act.

'Move it, Charlie,' said Bruce calmly. 'A nulla-nulla is a handy weapon but I'm afraid it rates poorly against a Smith and Wesson.'

He didn't hear what Bruce had said, but the deep voice helped to unlock Charlie's petrified body. He dropped the stick, sat on the floor, and slid himself backwards until he touched the wall.

'Now, everyone copy Madden and sit on the floor.' Richard Dempsey scanned the large room. Apart from Junior lying on the floor, everything appeared to be in order. 'Thank you. That's very good. Now you, Mr long streak of misery, slide over against the wall too.'

'My name is Bruce Watson. And you're an uninvited guest in my house. I'd be pleased if you'd pick up your friend and leave.'

'Just do as you're bloody well told until I find out what the fuck is going on here.' Bruce edged his way to the wall. Dempsey knelt next to the constable, grabbed his ear, and gave it a sharp twist. Junior stirred and groaned.

'Lady, whose child is that?'

'Mine!' snapped Deborah fiercely. She turned the boy away. 'He's mine, you keep away from him.'

'Okay, keep your shirt on. I'm Detective Dempsey, CIB. No one is going to come to any harm.'

'Don't you answer your radio, Dempsey?' The detective looked up. Hogan was standing at the door chewing gum.

'Jesus, it's the two of them again. Bloody stalkers. You guys need to cut me some slack,' grumbled Charlie.

'What took you so long? Been playing pocket billiards?' asked Dempsey.

'Nope,' replied Hogan, displaying his blackened hands. 'Flat tyre. What's the caper here?'

'Party games,' piped up Bruce. 'Seeing who has the hardest head. Like to be the next contestant?'

'Who's the galah?'

'That's Bruce Watson. It looks like this is his place. And I'm sorry to say it appears that Junior here has been a touch overzealous in pursuit of fame and justice.'

'Stuffed up, eh?' said Hogan. 'Cochran wants us out of here. We can drop shit for brains off at the hospital on the way back.'

Chapter 35

Let the Service Begin

Simon was on his knees. His arms were extended behind his back, and secured around a thick timber upright by a pair of overtightened handcuffs. His head faced the dusty ground and his limp body hung forward, causing the cuffs to make fresh cuts into his wrists. Particles of sawdust clung to his naked chest, arms, and the left side of his unshaven face.

Numerous cloaked figures, only differentiated from one another by body size and height, stood nearby, awaiting the effect of the antidote injected into the cannula in Stacey's forearm. The drug worked quickly. Simon's shoulders twisted. He raised his heavy head several times before it remained in a somewhat unstable, but vertical position.

'Excellent,' said Romoli as he looked at the wakening Simon Stacey. He placed his hand on the shorter figure next to him. 'You have done well, and you will be justly rewarded. Tonight, there is a vacancy in the inner circle, and you will become one of my chief ministers.'

'It is a pleasure to serve you and our Master,' said Kym. She tipped her head and took a couple of steps backwards.

Simon looked around the semi-lit room. He soon assimilated the available information and realised that the business end of his prolonged adversity had arrived. There was little doubt he was at an old sawmill; whether it was the deserted one only a few kilometres from his Samford property he was unsure. On the left side of the staged area there was a large, unrecognisable object lying horizontally. A long, heavy chain seemed to connect it to a wooden beam in the roof.

'Simon Stacey, hello, and welcome to our celebrations.' Romoli squatted in front of Simon. 'You will be remaining here in the rear stalls for the time being, but you will have a very good view of the proceedings going on directly in front of you and up there on the raised platform a little later.'

'If you don't mind, I'm feeling a touch off colour and I'd like to go home. Thanks for the invite, but maybe next time.'

'You awaken in fine spirits. That's good. You will be able to scream very loudly then? We would appreciate that. It adds enormously to the atmosphere.'

'Who the fuck are you? You're not that moron, Goldsmith, I know his voice. Why don't you take that cloak off?' Simon squirmed against the upright at his back to ease the pain in his wrists and the strain on his shoulders. He pushed his head back against the timber and bellowed out. 'Look at yourselves! You're a pack of chicken-livered, murdering sons of bitches, too scared to face up to the real world! You've all failed in aspiring to anything truly meaningful in your own lives, and for that you must maim, mistreat, and murder the innocent! Show me who you are, you gutless bastards. Take those hoods off!' A few heads turned momentarily. No one spoke. There was not even a murmur. Romoli broke the brief silence.

'A nice little speech. I'm impressed. You're certainly going to be good value tonight.'

'Whoever you are, you'll never get away with this. You're all going to be spending many years looking through steel bars.'

'On the contrary, we will continue to prosper and expand. Of course, it does present certain difficulties having bodies lying around. That's where you come in. Kym, the package, please.' Romoli held his hand out to one side. Kym handed over a paper bag. 'We had a little whip around and put together a present for you. Take a look.' He opened the top of the packet and held it in front of Simon's face. Simon initially pulled pack, unsure of what to expect, then, realising it was not another beast of terror, peered cautiously down into the bag.

'Bring that candle closer,' ordered Romoli. He looked at the expression changing on Stacey's face. 'Ah, now you see, don't you? The pistol, the knife, and the keys. Your fingerprints all over them, I'm afraid. A small cassette tape, too. The police will be most interested in that; after all, it is essentially a murder confession. A bit silly of you to make it in the first place, but it won't go unappreciated. And let's not forget the jerry can, which is in my car boot, but will reappear somewhere in the long grass near your garden shed. Sadly, it has only your prints on it. And you wish to know my name? I think you know that already. It's Romoli. Does that sound familiar?'

'Bullshit. He's dead, and a good thing, too,' said Simon. 'I didn't do the tongue thing and I didn't leave him naked. What's the story with that shit? You got your secret fetishes?' Simon peered at the cloaked head. Through the dim lighting and the loosely hanging material there was something vaguely familiar about the shadowy features.

'Ah, you think you killed him? Shot him dead? Not a nice thing to do at all. Romoli cannot die, Stacey. You can destroy a body, not a spirit. The spirit lives on in me. Through our special communion, his body becomes my body.'

'Really? Special communion? Excising someone's tongue? Fuck off!'

'Not just excising it. Devouring it.'

'You ate his tongue?' Simon half-laughed. 'You people are even more fucked-up than I first thought. There's no stupid spirit, he's just plain fucking dead and that's all about it. And you're next, dog breath.' Simon was trying his best to irritate the cool satanic sultan. Obviously, this shithead had been insulted by the best, he thought. It was time to try a new angle. 'You might like to know,' he continued, 'I have been praying like you wouldn't believe. Been praying that there is a God. Because if there is, you and your fellowship of fuckwits are in the deepest shit of all time, because you're all going to burn in hellfire for a thousand years, and I can't think of anyone more deserving.' Romoli stood and spat in Stacey's face. Simon didn't flinch. The white, bubbly saliva ran slowly down his cheek and past the corner of his mouth. 'Burn, Romoli! Fuckin' burn!' The leader slapped him hard across the face, then turned away and addressed his room of followers.

'It is time. The service will commence.'

The black-robed worshippers assumed their designated positions. Only the six chief ministers and Romoli were permitted to sit within the two large concentric rings. Each of them sat cross-legged, in the centre of one of seven interlocking circles, with their hands on their knees, head angled slightly upward and eyes closed. Romoli occupied the most central position. He held the two shining blades crossed above his cloaked head.

The other devotees had settled themselves around the outside of the canvas sheeting in preparation for the last event in the supreme ceremony: The Consecration of the Feast.

Romoli, it is you who will lead us.
Romoli, it is you that have the power.
Romoli, it is through you we will contact the King.
Lucifer, provide us with strength,
Provide us with pleasure.
Let out bodies feel the joy and the ecstasy.
Lucifer, we remain your loyal servants,
Now and forever ... Amen.

Chapter 36

The Sawmill

Cochran was confident he was on the right track. He had consequently issued instructions for all teams to proceed to areas within a few kilometres of the old sawmill at Eaton's Crossing, and then to wait in position until confirmation was given. The numerous false alarms had, for the moment, achieved their purpose, and dispersed his officers to all parts of Brisbane. It would be some time before they all would be close enough to lend assistance. Detective Briggs and his companion were closest and would be there first, followed by Cochran and Johnson. The Tactical Response Group had been placed on standby, awaiting further information.

*   *   *

Noel Briggs switched his headlights off as he turned into the gravel road. He proceeded slowly until he could see a dull, flickering light coming from the old building.

'We'll stop here,' he told the young cadet. 'You man the radio and keep your foot off the brake. I'm going for a little stroll.' He crept away quietly into the knee-high grass and ventured cautiously forward. His grassy cover came to an end near a dirt road only ten metres short of the sawmill. Briggs lay on his belly and surveyed the area. There were two dark-suited men near what looked like the entrance. One sat on a small, metal drum, smoking, while the other walked slowly back and forth, occasionally stopping to peer at proceedings through a gap between the old boards. A black station wagon was parked near the seated man. Several other vehicles were parked to the right of the building near a small cluster of bushy trees. Noel Briggs lay quietly, considering his options. After retreating a short distance, he began edging his way in a wide arc around the parked vehicles and towards the rear of the sawmill. He stood and popped his head up to recheck the scene. The two men hadn't changed their activities. All seemed well until, without warning, a large hand smothered his mouth and nose. Simultaneously a sweeping kick left him legless. A huge weight dropped onto his back and the soft ground seemed to fly upward to meet his face. With his arms pinned beneath him, there was no chance of reaching his shoulder holster.

'Don't move a muscle. Don't say a word,' a voice whispered. A hand grabbed his hair and twisted his face sideways. The greasy mud smeared over the detective's cheek. 'Who is this snake in the grass? Briggs! Well, well, we meet again.' It was Schliemann. He seemed to take some pleasure in his discovery. He released the pressure of his hand over Brigg's mouth.

'You bastar — ' blurted Briggs loudly. The hand quickly covered his face again. A beam of light flashed across the tops of the long grass. Both men froze. The light travelled slowly back once more, then disappeared.

'You'll get us both killed. Will you be quiet?' whispered Oscar firmly. Briggs' eyes opened wide. His head nodded vigorously. Once again, the grip was released.

'What's your caper, Schliemann? What the hell are you doing here?' snarled the detective softly.

'I hope we're both here for the same reason. Where's the backup? Or are you taking matters into your own hands again?'

'They're on their way. I'm just doing some surveillance. Get your backside off me.' Oscar shifted his weight onto one knee, allowing Briggs to slide free.

'I would suggest you be a bit more alert then. If I wasn't such a nice fellow I might have broken your neck first and asked questions later.'

'Fuck you! What's going on? Have you had a look? Is Stacey in there?' asked Briggs, while wiping his face with a handkerchief.

'You're a very rude man. I don't like you at all. The only thing I have to tell you is don't cross my path again.' Oscar turned to leave. There was a sharp click. He stopped and slowly turned. Briggs had his service revolver cocked and pointing at Oscar's head.

'Answers are required.'

'Briggs, you're a bigger fool than I thought.'

'Now! Tell me what you know.' Noel made a slight adjustment to his aim. 'Or your eyes will be parting company with your nose.'

'You're obviously not a career man. There's a lot at risk here. The lives of Stacey, an innocent child, yours, and mine, and who knows who else.'

'So, he's in there?'

'Yes, he's in there, and so are about thirty of them.'

'Is Stacey at this end or round the back?'

'This end, handcuffed to a post and probably drugged. Got a plan, super-sleuth?'

'Maybe I have. The first thing is for you to make tracks. Now piss off.'

Noel Briggs watched the tips of the long grass bend side to side as the large man slipped silently away and disappeared into the darkness. He sat motionless for a couple of minutes, just to be sure Schliemann wasn't doubling back. Confident he was now alone, he turned and continued his trek towards the rear of the sawmill.

*　　　*　　　*

'Briggs is out there checking things out. Oh shit, that sounds particularly bad. Let's hope we're not too late,' said John Cochran to the young cadet sitting in Briggs' vehicle. 'You set with that gun, Johnson?'

'It's not comfortable.' She tugged at the shoulder strap. 'It doesn't feel right.'

'It's like that. Eventually you'll only feel comfortable when you're wearing it. Let's go.'

'What about the others?' asked Cathy nervously. 'Aren't we going to wait for them?'

'If I thought we could spare the time, Johnson, I'd strike up a barby. Sorry to thrust this upon you, but the apron strings have now been cut. Marshall's got the drum and he'll sort out the details at this end.' The inspector paused, clenched his fist and held it near his chest. 'Think of those photos. Think of Melissa Goldsmith, and think of the innocent children this gang have been tormenting, torturing, and murdering for goodness knows how long. Now, let's end this thing. And by the way, I've got a secret weapon.'

'Really? What, a leopard tank?'

'Perhaps.' Cochran turned to the cadet, who immediately brought himself to attention from his semi-reclined position against the rear car door. 'Do you know how to operate the radio?'

'Oh, yes, sir. Detective Briggs showed me,' he said proudly.

'I take no comfort from that, let me assure you. If I call and confirm a siege situation you are to advise Detective Marshall immediately, assuming that he hasn't arrived by then. Is that clear?'

'Absolutely, sir.'

'I hope so.' Cochran looked at Johnson and nodded. They moved away towards their objective.

Chapter 37

Sacrifice

Simon had refrained from shouting abuse for several minutes. It seemed that such behaviour was only enhancing the perverse pleasure of the congregation. His last coarse remarks had been directed at a man whom Romoli had addressed as *the Doctor*, and who Simon felt sure was Goldsmith. This man occupied a position within the two concentric circles, giving him some seniority in the organisation.

Simon had been listening intently, and methodically scrutinising all the robed clan for any sign of familiarity. While there were many he didn't know, there were three that he had identified. There was Angela Philpott, Wayne, the gym instructor, both from Bodytone, and Howard Morgan. Somehow it all seemed to make sense. Angela's involvement helped explain two things: firstly, the disappearance of Adrian who may already be another addition to the body count, and secondly, the discovery of the micro-cassette tape. Howard's party on a Tuesday night for his so-called fortieth birthday was just too convenient. Simon had never thought much of Morgan, who had gate-crashed his way into the regular card-playing group via a painful encounter with Teddy Duncan's wisdom teeth. There were several others that Simon thought he should recognise, but as yet was unable to attach names to. Had he not been in such an unfavourable position, the realisation that a cult of devil worshippers had been constructing an evil empire right under his very nose would have caused him more than considerable anger and embarrassment.

Simon's focus of attention changed when the monotonous muttering and chanting that had persisted for several minutes ceased. Romoli stood.

'My brothers and sisters,' he announced with his arms outstretched. 'Tonight, we shall bear witness to a very special offering. It will be a divine and rare privilege for us all. We shall see a prepared earthly body attain synchronisation with our Lord Lucifer. Bodytune will be achieved. And through the most perfect of spiritual sacrifices, the two will become one. The power and desires of our Lord will be nourished, and our future of pleasure and eternal survival will be maintained. It is truly a joyous occasion, my friends. Hail, Satan!'

'Hail, Satan!' they replied in unison. Romoli touched the kneeling candle bearer on the head.

'Tonight, you will have the honour of placing our final marker — the 13th black candle'. You may proceed to the altar.' Kym's features assumed a lifeless yellow glow as she raised the candle in front of her face. She smiled, bowed her head slightly, and then moved forward to the platform area. After the ritual kneel and bow, she reached carefully across the other burning candles and placed the thirteenth marker in the centre of the star.

'Dear Lord, Prince of Darkness and Ruler of the universe, we ask that you accept this, our final marker.'

The congregation stood, their arms extended forward towards the altar, and recited the response.

'Accept our souls!'

'Dear Lord, Prince of Darkness and Ruler of the universe, please let us feel your presence at this divine service,' continued Kym.

'Accept our offering!'

'Dear Lord, Prince of Darkness and Ruler of the universe, we humbly ask for your continued guidance and influence in our lives.'

'Accept our souls.'

Kym returned to her central position. Romoli glanced to one side and gave an affirmative nod. A hooded man, whom Simon had recognised as Wayne from Bodytone, returned the gesture, walked to the left of the platform, and began turning the winch handle...

Cathy Johnson tugged nervously at John Cochran's sleeve.

'What's that noise?' she whispered.

'Not sure. Something mechanical. A little unusual coming from a supposedly deserted sawmill. You got the two-way?'

'Yes.'

'Okay, let's go.' They moved a little quicker through the grass.

Pausing at the dirt road, they surveyed the scene. There were two men sitting on the ground, leaning against each other with their backs supported by the rear wheel of the black station wagon.

'What are they doing?' asked Cathy.

'Hmmm. Let's find out.' Cochran selected a suitable sized stone and tossed it towards the two men. It fell just short of their feet. There was no movement.

'I thought as much,' said Cochran. 'Cover me.' He clutched his service revolver and in a semi-crouched position scurried, as best he could, across the open space to the front of the vehicle. The two men still hadn't moved. He signalled the all clear to Johnson and beckoned her over. She repeated her leader's example almost step for step. The two cautious investigators moved around the vehicle and squatted next to the two men. Cathy removed her penlight torch.

One man's head was twisted back over his own shoulder. His eyes were wide open in a startled expression. Cochran felt for a carotid pulse. There was none. The other man was unconscious. His irregular, stertorous breathing the result of extensive bruising and swelling around the front of his neck. Both men had empty shoulder holsters.

'Briggs?' asked Cathy.

'No chance.'

'Who then?'

'My secret weapon.'

'The leopard tank?'

'That's the one. Get on the two-way. Tell Marshall we want all the support he can get and we want it now.'

The clicking metallic sound stopped. Almost immediately it was followed by loud shouts. Cochran recognised Stacey's voice at once.

'You bastards! Take him down. Please take him down!' bellowed Simon. Cochran peered through a gap in the old boards.

'Jesus Christ! I think it's Devlin!'

Adrian Devlin was suspended on an inverted crucifix over a large circle of candles. He looked particularly unwell, and not aware of what was going on. His bare white body appeared much leaner than Cochran had imagined. A good deal of the blood that trickled down his legs and arms dripped from his hair into an old wooden bucket positioned beneath his head. The inspector traced the heavy supporting chain along the timber beam and back to the noisy winch. He scanned the room. There were a lot of people. It could be risky to barge in too soon.

'We've got to do something,' said Cathy uneasily. 'We can't just watch that poor man being tortured.'

'You've called Marshall?'

'Yes, yes.'

'Okay, then we wait.'

'And he dies?'

'Maybe he does. I see no child in there. If we rush in now we might lose more than Devlin.' The sound of Stacey's voice quickly returned their eyes to the old wall.

'Don't do this,' he pleaded, having received no attention from his shouting. 'Anything you want you can have. Money, a flight to Brazil. You can have the Bodytone Club, it's all yours. I'll sign it over, no strings attached.'

Romoli spoke quietly to Kym.

'Follow me. We should talk with Stacey now.' They turned and slowly left the circle. Romoli held one of the ceremonial knives in his hand.

'Continue with the service,' he announced. 'I'll be returning shortly. Doctor, you may proceed with the first stage of our communion when you are ready.' The worshippers once more broke out into monotonous chanting.

Romoli knelt again in front of Simon.

'Stacey, you are sounding in a very generous mood, but there is nothing you can give us that we do not have or cannot attain if we wish.'

'Please, put Adrian down. I beg you.'

'He will be put down shortly, I assure you,' said Romoli calmly.

'Don't kill him, please don't.' Simon's gaze darted between Kym, the suspended Devlin, and the cult leader.

'I must tell you he is not in the best of health at present, and while he may die, we have no plans to kill him. At least not tonight.'

'I think I'm pleased to hear that. What about that knife in your hand? I suppose that's for me?'

'Oh this.' He turned the blade around slowly in front of Simon's eyes. 'It certainly will be used, but not on you. Kym, can you explain the finer points of this special occasion to this confused man? I am returning to receive communion.' Romoli stood to leave. 'Remember to scream. Scream very loudly. Being in such a generous mood, I'm sure you won't disappoint us.' He proceeded around the kneeling group to the altar.

'Dear Simon,' said Kym. She gently stroked his face. He pulled away. 'I do wish we had spent more time together. It's a shame it has to end. Let me explain. Bodytune is a very special form of worship. We, like in many Christian churches, accept communion in the form of the body and blood. As you can see, your friend's blood has been collected for that very purpose.'

The Doctor held the bucket in one hand. Following Romoli, the other worshippers filed up one by one. They knelt in turn with head back and open mouth. The Doctor smeared a bloodied finger over each tongue while uttering the words: 'Blood for pleasure. Power for Lucifer.'

'Oh, my God.' Simon shook his head in disgust. 'Okay, is that it then? Is it over?'

'No, no, no, that's the blood. The body will be arriving to the right of the altar at any moment.' Simon's thoughts started racing. What body? There are so many; Alison, Robbie, Teddy, Ras, Eddy. He looked at the Doctor. He recalled the photo of Melissa and Danny in Teddy's album, and there was the kidnapping.

'You wouldn't. Not little Danny Goldsmith. No, not a child!'

'Simon, think a little harder. It cannot be just any child. It must be a child whose body is tuned to this special day. This is Friday the thirteenth, a very significant day in our church. A child who attains the age of 666 days at this time is indeed very special.'

There was some movement to one side of the altar. A side door opened. A shadowy figure moved in the darkened corner. There was something in his arms. Simon's head began to pound with the rush of blood that now hammered against his temples.

'It's not possible. It couldn't be.'

'Oh yes, indeed it is,' said Kym joyfully. The figure moved into the light. The young child, asleep in his arms, squirmed lightly. 'It's your son. It's Robbie.'

Simon screamed his son's name repeatedly. He pulled hard against the handcuffs. His wrists bled. Tears ran down his distorted face as he desperately strained every muscle in his body to free himself.

'He cannot hear you, Simon. He is drugged. Just like you were.'

'You fucking bitch! What do you want of my son? Take me. Use me. Kill me if you must. Let him live!'

'He will provide us with the body for our communion. Romoli will remove the beating heart from his chest.'

'No! No! No!' Simon gave a prolonged, shrill scream. Kym left Simon in his agony and presented herself before the Doctor — the last to receive the sacred blood.

*　　　*　　　*

'Where the hell are they? Johnson, give me the two-way.' Cathy quickly obliged and Cochran pushed the button.

'Some vehicles are approaching now, sir. Could be them.'

'Listen, Marshall, I don't think we can wait. Put your foot down, man. We're desperate. You'll hear us if we go in.'

'J. C, they've placed the child on the altar,' said Cathy, keeping a close eye on the evil proceedings. 'You've got to go now.'

'Me!? We both go, Johnson.' He paused and gave Cathy a reassuring pat on the shoulder. 'Okay, let's go. And don't wave that gun around so much. I'd be really pissed if I got shot by friendly fire.'

Dressed only in a small pair of boxer shorts, Robbie lay on his back, with his head near the flaming star. His sleeping body was clean, well-nourished, and apart from a small dressing on one arm, was free from any obvious signs of abuse. Romoli took a step up onto the platform, bowed at the altar, walked around it, and faced the gathering. He lay the long-bladed knife on the boy's chest and opened his arms wide. The recital commenced.

Chil Luxty Ona Goid,
Zado Tyo Ona Lux,
Zado Lux,
Zado Lux Nuna,
Eillua Eillua Eillua,
Jus Yokjet,
Jus Doo,
Jus Soenne,
Jus Kunso.

Simon struggled, shouted, and pleaded. Romoli took the knife in both hands, extended his arms above the boy's chest and spoke loudly.

'Lord Lucifer, master of our destiny, join with us now as we offer you this soul.'

'Carter!' shouted Cochran. 'Freeze. Nobody move!' A loud nervous mumbling spread through the kneeling assembly. Romoli responded quickly.

'My old friend. I'm most impressed. Come and join me at the altar. Guarantee yourself everlasting power and pleasure.'

'Walk away, Carter. Back right off. Now!'

'The service continues, my good people. The inspector is outnumbered and he will not shoot a friend.' His eyes shifted back to the child. The knife reflected the yellow candlelight as it moved in Romoli's hands. Cochran fired. The shot struck Carter at the base of his throat and threw him backward against the rear wall. He slid slowly to the floor, leaving a thick trail of blood over the old boards before slumping into a motionless heap.

'Quite right, Carter. I would never shoot a friend.'

'Run, everybody. Run!' shouted the Doctor.

Simon watched as the room burst into life with people scurrying in all directions. He saw many head for the exit to the right of the altar from where Robbie had been brought in, and he noticed others pushing against weak boards in a search for escape. A few charged for the main entrance near Cochran and Johnson. Simon jumped with fright as the inspector let off a volley of shots into the roof. It did little more than cause a few women to squeal. The big man positioned himself between the exit and the runaways and managed to use his bulk to good effect in knocking two to the ground.

Kym remained calm amid all the commotion and crept off quietly towards the rear wall. She felt around near the slumped body of Romoli and found the knife. After lying the body flat, she opened his mouth, grabbed his tongue with her fingers, and pulled it forward. She sliced three times with the blade, pulled the bloody tongue free, and shoved the entire piece of flesh into her own mouth. Meanwhile, the chaos continued in front of her.

Simon was trying to look everywhere at once. He noticed some movement near the dark back wall but could not identify anything clearly. His attention turned to a cloaked worshipper who stood too long near the inverted crucifix looking around for a way out. His robe touched some candles and lit up. The man ran forward and dove onto the dusty ground and began rolling over and over. The flames withstood the smothering attempt. He ran forward again, this time towards Simon, who pushed his leg out. The man tripped. Cathy Johnson ran over and began throwing dirt over the flames.

'Let him burn! Please, let him burn!' shouted Stacey. 'I know the bastard. He deserves nothing less!'

'I can't do that.' The flames went out. While Cathy cuffed the man, Simon used his feet to push the hood away and reveal the face of Howard Morgan.

'You lowlife, depraved son of a bitch!' He managed to deliver two firm foot jabs to the mouth and nose before Johnson moved the trembling man away and pushed him to the ground.

Kym finished chewing and swallowed the last of the tongue. She stood, knife in hand, and moved to the altar.

Simon continued scanning the scene. The blue lights of police vehicles now beamed through the dusty room. Most of the evil clan had left the immediate vicinity. The sounds of gunshots, shouting, and car engines indicated the battle was now on in earnest outside. As the dust began to settle, Simon noticed someone moving near the altar. Despite all the commotion, Simon could see that Robbie was still sleeping on the sacrificial bench.

'Cochran, my boy!' The fat man was near the door facing the other way. 'Johnson, my boy!' screamed Simon. Kym stood at the altar and raised the dripping knife.

'Lucifer, the child is yours.'

'Nooooo!' screamed Simon, finally managing to attract the attention he wanted. Cochran and Johnson both turned. A gun discharged. The right side of Kym's face exploded into a pulpy mess. She fell to the floor. Her body extremities jerked and twitched.

'Nice shooting, Johnson,' said Cochran.

'I thought it was you.'

'No, not me.'

'Briggs?'

'No chance.'

'The leopard tank?'

'I guess,' said Cochran. They looked about the room. 'An evasive bastard, isn't he? Go and rescue the child, will you?'

Cathy Johnson soon had Robbie safely in her arms. Marshall made an appearance through the top door.

'Johnson, this way. Ambulances at the ready. Is he okay?'

'Seems to be.' She turned and shouted back to Stacey. 'He's all right! We've got to get him out of here.'

'Thank you, God,' panted Stacey, looking up at the roof. Tears streamed down his face in an intense emotional catharsis. There was a rattle of keys behind him. He felt other hands touching his, but was unable to turn his head far enough to see who was there. Suddenly the cuffs released and he fell face-first onto the powdery ground. His arms dropped like two lead weights at his sides. The relief was enormous. With his head on its side, he puffed away the sawdust from around his mouth and lay there motionless.

His respite was short-lived. Someone's arms wrapped tightly around his legs and began dragging him backward through the dirt and dust. He had no energy to resist, and insufficient strength to raise an alarm above the noise that was continuing outside the sawmill. Stacey's head bounced about like a rag doll as his abductor took a sharp right turn and jumped down two steps. His body slid to one side and came to rest when his shoulder struck a large, immovable metal object protruding from the floor. The grip on his ankles was released.

They were now in a long, narrow, dilapidated room and away from the main arena. Car and torchlights danced excitedly around the walls as they found the many gaps and holes between the timber boards. In the corner, a thick coat of cobwebs covering a pile of dusty timber glistened like silver threads as the beams of light struck them. Simon's shoulder was pushed up hard against a large rusted lathe.

'Hello, Stacey. Long time no see.' Simon couldn't see anything. His face was covered with sawdust, but he recognised the voice.

'Briggs?'

'I was hoping you'd be dead by now, but I can see I'm going to have to handle that myself.' He pulled his revolver from his shoulder holster.

'Briggs, what? Why? What's going on?' moaned Simon. He had managed to partly clean one eye and could see the blurry silhouette of his old business partner.

'It's only a matter of time before Internal Affairs will want a word with you. It seems that you're the only one still in the country who could dig up any evidence against me.'

'That's ages ago. Who cares about that? I know we didn't part very amicably, but I won't dob you in, Briggs. That's not my style. You know that.' Keeping his arm tucked in close to his body, Simon carefully gathered a large handful of sawdust.

'Sorry, old chum. It's just taking care of business. A shrewd devil like you should understand that. This fucking enquiry crap has already claimed a few scalps. I can't afford to have any loose ends around.' He raised the weapon.

'Just one thing, Briggs...' Stacey tossed the sawdust high and hard then rolled over and over, hoping to fall in a hole or find some cover.

'Shit!' The detective threw his head to one side to protect his eyes. He squeezed the trigger. A shot rang out, almost instantly followed by another.

Simon felt something strike hard against his face. He stopped rolling. With the handcuffs still dangling from his wrist, he felt his cheek then examined his fingers. They were smeared with blood.

'Jesus, I've been hit.'

'No, you haven't, but he has.' Simon's eyes darted about, searching for the person belonging to the other voice. A large-framed man emerged from behind the lathe.

'Schliemann! Thank God. I love you!' Stacey sat up and checked himself over. 'You sure I'm not bleeding?'

'Look between your feet.'

'Is that what I think it is?' He leaned forward. 'It's his finger. You shot it off.' The finger was intact from the nail to the second joint. The base was shredded and generously sprinkled with bone fragments.

'Only one? Too bad,' said Oscar nonchalantly.

Briggs dragged himself up from the pile of discarded timber. He was covered in cobwebs and blood was pouring from his right hand. He squeezed his wrist hard to stem the blood loss.

'Help me!' wailed Briggs. 'My finger and half my hand have been blown off!'

'What the hell's going on here?' John Cochran marched boldly into the room, accompanied by another officer. 'Shit, you're a mess, Stacey. Don't you own any clothes these days? Schliemann, what have you done to Briggs this time?'

'He shot my fucking finger off. That's what the bastard did!' hollered the detective. He crouched down and began sifting through the sawdust. 'Help me find it, you lot. Come on, help me for Christ's sake!' Stacey stood and walked over to the lathe.

'Is this what you're looking for?' He held up the finger, then placed it over a narrow slit near the rusted blade. With a block of hardwood, he belted it twice. The finger disappeared through the space and into the corroded interior of the machine.

'You fool! Get it out. Get it out now!' Briggs hurried over to Stacey, only to be greeted by a swift kick to the groin. He collapsed in a heap on the ground.

'Perhaps that'll get his mind off his finger,' said Simon, with some satisfaction. 'Cochran, where's my boy?'

'He's on the way to the hospital. He's going to be fine. I didn't want him hanging about here while some of these psychos were still on the loose.'

'Is he really okay?'

'Physically he appeared to be in good shape. Mentally?' He shrugged his shoulders. 'Who knows?'

'What about Adrian?'

'Should be on the way too, by now. Touch and go I'd say. They really gave him a hiding. You'll get to see them both soon enough, but right now we need to talk. Grab a blanket from the boys outside and I'll see you shortly.' Simon left, escorted by a uniformed policeman.

Cochran looked down at the detective still squirming on the ground.

'Your arse is mine now, Briggs.' He turned to Oscar and extended his hand.

'Thanks, Schliemann. It's good to have you on our side. If you're ever thinking of coming back to the force, call me.' The two big men shook hands and smiled broadly. Cathy joined her colleague.

'Things settling down out there, Johnson?'

'Seems to be. What's going on here?'

'My secret weapon.'

'Mr Leopard Tank, I presume?' She looked him up and down with admiration and extended her hand.

Chapter 38

Confessions and Apologies

With a grey blanket draped over his shoulders, a forlorn Simon Stacey stood silently next to the police vehicle. Two uniformed policemen flanked him. Other plain-clothed detectives wandered among the other parked vehicles, opening doors and boots, taking photographs, and jotting notes in diaries. John Cochran soon joined the quiet trio. He gestured to one side with his head and the two custodians left.

'It's all over,' said Cochran plainly. 'It's time to come clean, and I would suggest it's in your best interest to do so.'

'I suppose it is. Where do I start?'

'Tell me exactly what happened after you left Duncan's place.'

'Okay, but let me say that up to that point I had no idea what was going on, and I had nothing to do with any of this 13th Black Candle bullshit.'

'I'm listening,' replied the inspector, not conceding the point.

Simon went through the story of the confrontation with Romoli when his house exploded and he shot the cult leader in the head — by accident.

'I dropped the gun there and then. I wanted to get to the house but it was impossible — the heat was too intense. The house began collapsing within minutes. I never moved the guy from the pool and that's the truth,' said Stacey openly. Cochran nodded. 'I couldn't get near the house. It was engulfed in flames within seconds. I knew anyone inside had no chance. I tried telling myself that maybe Alison and Robbie were not even in the house. I was stunned and shocked. I just couldn't comprehend the whole thing. And I still don't know if I ever will. What would you have done? A gun in your hand, a dead man in the pool, and your family incinerated in front of your eyes? I got in the car and bolted. I needed time to think. It wasn't until I came back later that I really started to believe that Alison and Robbie had really been murdered.' Simon lowered his head. 'Well, thank God I was half-wrong.'

'Little Danny Goldsmith was used as a substitute for your son. Roughly the same age, height, and weight, and burnt so badly that no one would ever know the difference.'

'Yeah, I know all that now. That's why they could blackmail Ted. I've been putting all the pieces together, but the bastards were always one step ahead of me. And I know now why Goldsmith induced Alison's pregnancy ten days early. All so this Bodytune, six hundred and sixty-six-day crap could fall into place. They murdered Alison because she would have known all that.' Stacey paused, took a couple of deep breaths and had a big swallow. 'Jesus, Cochran, we need to bring back the death penalty.'

'Yeah, I know. At least we've been able to accommodate a couple of the pricks in that regard. Tell me. The psych ward. A lucky guess or what?'

'Lucky? Perhaps. There were several phone numbers on those newspaper clippings. Mine, yours, Duncan's, Angela Philpot's, and one other, which I rang.'

'Ward 21?'

'Sure was. It sounded like the perfect opportunity to do a little research and to get away from you guys. In retrospect, I wouldn't recommend it. That old guy there called Ras — '

'Otherwise known as George Hartley.'

'Yeah. He knew. I'm sure he thought I was involved. He goes to hospital around every Friday the 13th for protection and look what happens. Fuck!'

'That little hospital stunt of yours may have saved your life. I sent Briggs to your club to do a little quiet surveillance.'

'Briggs? Quiet surveillance?' said Simon, raising his eyebrows.

'Yeah, I know. It was calculated to get you two to provoke one another and blow open two investigations at once.'

'He wanted to kill me!'

'Yeah. I didn't figure he would go that far. Sorry,' smiled Cochran.

'How did you know that he and I…well, that we used to…you know what I mean. How did you know?' asked Simon.

'Carter, my ex-friend. He knew someone who knew someone. And Schliemann found drugs on Briggs when he busted him at your fitness club.'

'Clearly Briggs never left the business,' nodded Simon. 'So, Carter ends up being Romoli number two then? Tell me, who dragged his predecessor from the pool?'

'Carter did it himself. Possibly with help from some of the others. One thing I'm sure of is that Carter was in the pool, boots and all. Shoes that smell that bad you don't forget easily.'

'I remember the shoes. Propped in front of the heater, stinking the place out. It seems so long ago,' recalled Simon.

'It's partly due to those shoes that your son is still alive.' Cochran related the salient details of his search of Carter's home. He leaned casually against the car door as he spoke. Everything was now in hand; it was time to take a moment to relax and reflect. Both his sense of relief and achievement were tempered by feelings of loss and deceit. Cochran continued talking, bringing up numerous aspects of the case that had proved most frustrating. The two men spoke about their recent ordeals. For the first time since he had met Stacey, John Cochran found some pleasure being in his company. It was quite a turnaround for two men that seemed to have had so little in common to be agreeing on so much now.

'Perhaps if we had been a little more tolerant of each other in the beginning we could have put these morons to rest sooner,' conceded Cochran.

'I know I can be a bit of an arsehole sometimes,' admitted Simon. 'I have a problem with authority figures. I like to be the one calling the shots. I haven't been able to do much of that lately, and I can assure you it's been a most sobering experience.'

'We can afford to be less formal. Call me...' He paused in a moment of ambivalence. 'Call me J. C.'

'Okay, Cochran, and you can call me Simon.'

'Glad we sorted that out. Now, Stacey, we must get back to the business at hand. I happen to have a few trinkets with me.' Cochran reached in through the window of the police car. What he displayed in three plastic bags came as no surprise to Simon. There was a gun, a snake-handled knife, a set of keys, and a micro-cassette tape.

'Oh crap,' said Simon submissively.

'These items are of course important court evidence. This evil-looking knife,' said Cochran, pausing to display the appropriate bag. 'And this .38 calibre Berretta semi-auto will both be identified as the murder weapons of Eddy Anstey, the male nurse, and Orson Ruscliffe, otherwise known as Oswald Madison. Or if you like, Romoli number one. It would be reasonable for a jury to conclude that the fingerprints on these, and the confession on this tape, belong to a brutal killer. Now, I would like to point out that there will be another inquest into police corruption. Your fingerless ex-racing colleague will be making an appearance. I want to nail him, Stacey. Do you get my drift?'

'Well yes. I think I'm beginning to.' The inspector upturned one bag. The tape fell to the ground. Using his handkerchief, he bent down and picked it up. The tape had caught on his shoe. He pulled hard repeatedly. The tape spools spun rapidly until the tape snapped and the small cartridge was empty. His shoe ground the thin plastic ribbon into the dirt.

'You are a very persuasive man,' said Simon, looking down at the remains of the tape. 'However, there's still some other things worrying me.' Cochran emptied the other three bags.

'Would you look at that? You just can't trust people to seal up evidence properly these days. Now they're all dusty.' The inspector retrieved the two weapons and the keys and thoroughly wiped them with his hanky and shirttail. 'That's much better.' He dropped them back into the plastic bags and returned them to the car.

'There is another item. I believe it's in Carter's car boot,' said Simon.

'Okay, his car is still back at his house, and I do have his house key.'

'It's a jerry can. It has my fingerprints on it. The bastards left it strategically placed in my driveway so I'd have to move it."

'Shit, Stacey. They weren't leaving anything to chance. I can attend to that as well. Now, is there anything else?'

'I hope not,' replied Simon. 'I have thought it over, and I would be quite delighted to have a long chat about Briggs. He was always trying to squeeze more out of a deal than he deserved. I never did like him. I like him less now.'

'Excellent,' cackled Cochran. 'Stick that up your arse, Commissioner.' He did a little uncoordinated jig and then slapped a high five with Stacey. Both men smiled.

'You two all good mates now?' It was Cathy Johnson.

'Hello, Johnson,' said Cochran. 'We have been discussing a few matters and we have come to an understanding.'

'Hi there,' said Simon sheepishly. 'I think I owe you an apology.'

'No. Not at all. You were under enormous stress. It's okay.' She looked at Cochran. 'We identified the bitch that tried to stab Stacey's boy.'

'Yes!' interrupted Simon. 'Kym Sharma. Cold, calculating. An absolute psychopath. She had me hook, line, and sinker.'

'That's her. A nurse at Ward 21.'

'Very clever,' added Cochran. 'She knew we were coming to her house to identify her. She put someone else in her place. No doubt Carter gave her the heads up.'

'She is still alive. And I think she ate Carter's tongue.'

'Bloody hell,' said Cochran. 'What's with the tongue removing and eating?'

'Not absolutely sure. I think it's all — '

'Romoli,' interrupted Simon again. 'That's how they supposedly keep his stupid spirit alive, or some such shit.'

'Sick and twisted fucks!' Cochran shook his head.

'One more thing,' announced Johnson. 'There's a car down there.' She pointed along a row of parked vehicles. 'The fifth one along.'

'That Mercedes?' said Simon. 'Not mine. Same colour; different model.'

'What if I told you it used to be white?'

'My old car! Which of those bastards — '

'Goldsmith, who else?' said Johnson.

'They nearly had you, Stacey,' nodded the inspector. 'Nearly had you crucified! As for you, Johnson… I… well, let's say…well…never mind. Just come over here.' She took a step towards her boss. He grabbed her in a big bear hug. 'Good to have you on board, Johnson. And thank you.'

Chapter 39

Sex on the Beach

Charlie rolled onto his back and gazed wide-eyed at the stars.

'Wow! That was magic, Deb. Beautiful. Everything and more than I imagined it would be.' The brunette turned on her side and snuggled up close to Charlie. She positioned one leg over his waist and kissed him gently on the cheek.

'It surely was. You're a wonderful man. I'm so lucky.' She squeezed him tightly. 'I just want to eat you all up.'

'Well, the night is still young, and I think I'm getting my second wind.' The two chuckled and kissed. For several minutes they lay in a quiet embrace on a blanket on the beach, enjoying the peaceful afterglow and listening to the gentle sound of the waves.

'Been quite an evening,' said Charlie softly.

'You were so brave, Charlie.'

'I don't know about that. I was bloody angry, though.'

'You're a big hit with Bruce. Anyone who helps him with his gardening, especially when they organise a free delivery of woodchips and sawdust, is a friend for life.'

'Yes, and I'm still a bit sore.' Charlie twisted himself slightly. 'That full body massage you were talking about sounds like just what I need.'

'That's guaranteed, and very soon,' said Deb with a warm whisper in Madden's ear. 'What did you think about my little surprise?

'Your son? What a wonderful boy. You should be very proud.'

'Oh, I am. But I do prefer to keep my personal life separate from my work. I'll share everything, though, with the right person.'

'Sounds like an invitation.'

'Might be.'

'I like kids. He's about eighteen months, right?'

'Just on.'

'A lovely age.'

'What about that secluded, candlelit place you were going to take me to tonight?' asked Deb.

'We might take a rain check on that. I believe there's going to be a larger crowd there than I expected, and that would spoil the intimate atmosphere. Besides, a blanket on the beach with a gorgeous aerobics instructor is something else, and I'm not about to give that up easily.' Madden faced Deborah and ran his fingers lightly over her face. Her mouth sought out his wandering hand. She sucked and licked his fingers hungrily. 'Let me tell you,' said Charlie. 'That goes straight down to my groin.'

'Good. That's exactly what I want.'

Chapter 40

Unfinished Business

The strengthening sunlight creeping through the slits around the heavy curtains and the sound of a dog barking in the distance caused Simon to stir and wake. He yawned and stretched. It was the best night's sleep he'd had for months. Insomnia, coupled with horrific nightmares, had plagued him since the traumatic events of last winter. In recent weeks, thanks to his regular sessions with Dr Hutchinson, the disturbing dreams had begun to decrease in frequency and intensity. He turned onto his right side. Robbie was facing him, still sound asleep, with his head neatly cupped in the feather pillow. Simon wasn't the only one having a protracted recovery time. It was around ten o'clock last night when Robbie had stirred and was bedded down yet again with his father. The young boy's story of seeing an ugly witch was consistent with the many others that had often caused him to become frightened. Simon had reassured his son, locked the bedroom door, and both had gone to sleep.

Simon studied his Robbie's face. The smooth, flawless skin, the full, pink cheeks and his long, dark eyelashes he'd inherited from his mother. Yes indeed, a good-looking young man, thought Simon, as he leaned across and kissed him gently on the forehead.

'If only your mother could see you now,' he whispered. Simon, dressed only in a pair of red jocks, rose, ventured slowly to the window and opened the curtains. Outside there was a light breeze blowing, causing a steady ripple across the surface of the pool. The rose gardens were in bloom. All the garden plots were just as Alison had planned. Simon, never a keen gardener, had worked especially hard to present the garden exactly as she had wanted it. The house, too, a near duplicate of the original, reflected much of Alison's taste.

Simon followed the cobblestone path with his eyes, past the rose gardens, the swimming enclosure, the two pergolas, and the multitude of native trees and shrubs. Between some overhanging branches, he could just discern the end of the pathway near the green garden shed. He moved his face closer to the glass. There was an animal there. He unlatched the window, opened it, and peered out. It was a dog; a large, mostly black dog, just sitting quietly on the last few cobblestones, with its mouth open. Simon felt a little uneasy. He shrugged his shoulders, closed the window and drew the curtains. Black dogs are common. Must have got lost. He could call the pound later if it was still there, he thought.

After slipping into his Japanese robe and attending to his needs in the ensuite, he gathered up the small collection of coffee cups, unlocked the bedroom door, and headed for the kitchen. Partway down the hallway he felt a small, firm object between his foot and the low-pile carpet. He hooked the mugs onto one hand, crossed his left leg across his right knee, and plucked off the item that had secured itself to the bottom of his foot. It was a small, yellow tablet. Simon rolled it slowly between his fingers, then crushed it and let the powder fall. An uncomfortable sensation below his sternum had become more prominent. He lifted the keys from the pocket of his robe and pressed a button on a small key ring remote control. He swallowed hard before continuing on his way.

Back in the bedroom, an alarm near the bed began chiming the tune of "Incey Wincey Spider." Robbie stirred and opened his sleepy eyes. In a moment, he recognised the tune and got out of bed. He immediately reached behind the bedside table and pushed at something with his hand. A panel in the wall next to the wardrobe quietly slid open revealing a small, cosy chamber decorated with brightly coloured fire engines and trains. There was a small mattress on the floor, and several soft toys scattered about. Everything was illuminated by a Donald Duck night-light. Robbie picked up a teddy bear, lay down, and cuddled up like a ball. The panel slid closed.

There was something different about the house this morning. Simon looked about the hallway and then the kitchen. Nothing seemed out of place. There was a freshness in the air that triggered memories, both pleasant and harrowing.

'Roses!' he announced reassuringly to himself. 'They're certainly extra strong this morning.' Simon opened the fridge. A carafe of freshly squeezed orange juice sat prominently on the top shelf.

'Oh, my God! She's back!' He began a frantic dash through the house, opening doors and checking rooms. The lounge and dining area were decorated with several vases of roses that were not there when he went to bed.

'Holy shit!' He paused for only a second to think.

'The back door!' A fast sprint down the hall came to an abrupt halt as his foot caught the stainless-steel plant stand. Three large pots crashed to the floor, spewing rich, black soil over the cream-coloured carpet. Stacey bounced off the wall and landed face-first on the floor. Despite his soiled gown and blood flowing from a cut above his eyebrow, he sprang back to his feet and continued to the door that opened into the garage. It was locked.

'Shit, shit, shit!' He tried the library. No sooner in the door, he stopped dead in his tracks. An inverted crucifix made of red roses hung on the wall. 'Oh, Jesus!'

After sucking in a huge breath, he moved with some determination over to the bookcase and ran his fingers along some heavy, old books before settling on the one titled *Great Chess Games of the 20th Century*. He opened it, revealing a concealed cavity containing a Colt semi-automatic pistol.

Back in the hall near the soiled carpet, he noticed a trail of footprints leading towards the lounge. While they were small, they were far too big for his young son. Stacey's pace slowed. With his gun raised he followed the trail through the kitchen, and then slowly turned the corner into the dining area and lounge. The lacy, white curtains that hung in front of the sliding glass doors were drawn back. The doors were open. He moved to the centre of the lounge where he had a full view of the back landing. To one side, near the brick wall, he could see the dark outline of someone.

Simon stretched his right arm, sighted the gun, and moved forward slowly. The lace curtains were moving about, not giving him a clear view of the figure on the landing. As he eased closer he reached with his free hand and sharply pulled them to one side.

'Oh, shit!' He was staring at a hooded cape dangling from a small wall-mounted hanging plant. There was no one there; at least not in front of him, anyway. It may have been the faint sound of her breath or the gleam from the snake-handled knife that made him give a short, sharp shout and begin to swing his body around, but the handle of the knife struck hard against his temple and he dropped like a stone to the floor.

*   *   *

The right side of Kym's face was a mass of scar tissue. What used to be her right eye was now just a scarred, empty hole. Much of her black hair had disappeared. Her mouth drooped to the left, and saliva dangled precariously from her chin. The sleeves on her black, hooded robe were rolled up, and long cuts and trails of dried blood decorated both arms.

Simon's eyesight was somewhat blurred as he woke, but he knew immediately who it was. His position was also one that was all too familiar; he was handcuffed by one wrist to the end of the sofa lounge. Kym opened her distorted mouth wide. Her tongue protruded like a snake. She licked some of the dried blood from her arms.

'You sick, demented bitch.'

'Dear Simon, I'm delighted that you recognise me. Take a long, hard look. See what you've done to your precious Kym? But it doesn't matter now, because I am here at last, and all the unfinished business will be attended to. I'm sure you know what I mean.' Her voice had changed also. It was slower, and had taken on a harsh, moist, throaty sound. There was no doubt though, that she was just as determined and evil as ever. The Colt pistol was on the floor near the balcony and about four metres away. Kym noticed Simon looking at the gun. She reached behind her back and produced the shiny, long-bladed knife.

'No, no,' said Kym, 'I wouldn't even consider that if I were you.' She moved forward and crouched near him. The knife rested against his cheek. She turned the blade and began giving him a rough shave.

'Where is the boy?'

'Go to hell!'

'I know he is in the house. I will find him. The question is, will I find him while you are alive, or after you have bled to death?'

Simon swung at her with his free hand. He succeeded in pushing her off balance, but the blade dragged across his forearm as Kym staggered and fell. She lay on the floor and gave a twisted smile and chuckle before getting back to her feet.

'You choose the latter,' she laughed.

Simon pulled the tie from his robe and with the help of his teeth, tied it around the wound.

'Poor Simon. You look such a mess.'

'Really. Look who's talking.'

'You think I care? You think Romoli cares? I operate on a different level now. I work for my Lord Lucifer, and I am under his instruction. I am his disciple.'

'So now it's your turn to be Romoli. A fatal occupation indeed. You guys really need to look at your health and safety issues.'

'Romoli will always exist. I am the anointed one.'

'Something like the pope, is it then?' quipped Simon angrily.

'No! Nothing like that! You like to taunt me, don't you? I might just slice your ear clean off.' She held up the blade and took a step toward him.

He tried moving away, but the heavy sofa lounge only granted him about a metre.

'I am here to complete the sacrificial mass. The Bodytune,' she continued. 'You will be the audience. No one will prevent it happening this time. Of that you can be sure. Now where is the boy?'

Simon said nothing.

'That's okay. I have plenty of time. I like hide and seek. Let's see, where should I start looking? Let's say — the main bedroom!'

'Kym, don't be stupid!' shouted Simon. 'Okay. You want me? Then you can have me.'

'Oh, I will have you. Just be patient.'

Kym gave a droopy smile that made her facial features look more deformed than they already were. She moved backwards through the dining area and towards the kitchen. Simon pulled harder but was gaining little against the furniture.

'I'll be back in a minute with your son. Don't go anywhere now.'

'No. For God's sake!' Just as Kym was turning to leave, two large hands appeared like a shot from the kitchen entrance. One went under Kym's chin, the other on the back of her head. In one swift motion they twisted sharply backward and sideways. There was an enormous crack. Her arms fell to her sides. She collapsed limply to the floor.

'Good morning, Simon.' Oscar Schliemann emerged into the dining area. He kicked the knife away from near Kym's body. 'What a piece of work.'

Simon was on his knees, looking with both amazement and a huge sense of relief at the tall man. Oscar squatted near him and released the handcuffs.

'You okay?'

'Sure, I'll need a few stitches, but I'll be fine,' replied Simon. He got to his feet and promptly went and picked up the Colt semi-automatic. 'Anymore of them around?'

'No, she's a loner. The place is clear.'

'How did you know the bitch was here? How did she get in?' asked Stacey, quite bewildered and still somewhat stunned.

'Cochran called me. He figured I'd be in the area. She escaped from the nuthouse last night, but no one was notified until early this morning. An inside job I would think. And somehow, she knew your security codes. I'll be paying the security company a visit later.'

'Those pricks are everywhere. What the fuck!?'

'How's Robbie?'

Suddenly Simon raised the Colt, pointed it in Oscar's direction, and squeezed the trigger twice in rapid succession. Two shots rang out. The Rottweiler fell at Schliemann's feet. Oscar calmly squatted and examined the dog's head.

'Nice shooting. It looks like all that practice has paid off.'

'Let's get upstairs.'

Once inside the main bedroom, Simon reached behind the bedside table and flicked a switch. The secret panel slid open and Robbie came running into his father's arms.

'You'll be all right now. Daddy's got you, and Mr Schliemann has taken care of that terrible witch. Everything is okay.'

__The End__

ABOUT THE AUTHOR

Bob Goodwin has been writing for many years. He is a registered nurse with psychiatric and counselling qualifications and has a background of over thirty-five years working in mental health settings, and this experience has been a major influence on his work.

He has written novels, screenplays, short stories, short theatrical plays, and one-act plays. Several of his shorter works are available on his website for free, as is a free self-help eBook for managing anxiety and stress.

While Bob writes drama and comedy, most of his work is of the suspense thriller genre. He has written eight novels, the most recent being – "The Semblant." For Bob, this latest book is a switch from his regular genre, and his first venture into Erotic Horror.

There are numerous excellent reviews of his novels on Amazon.com. & the Readers' Favorite site. Bob has managed the website StoriesAndPlays.com and the Facebook group Writers and Readers for over ten years.

Novels by Bob Goodwin:

- Strike Me Dead (2014)
- The 13th Black Candle (2015)
- Max Justice (2016) Book 1 in the Max Judd series
- Max Justice: Turmoil (2017) Book 2 in the Max Judd series
- Max Justice: Vengeance (2019) Book 3 in the Max Judd series
- The Tree of Thorns (2020)
- Ezekiel: Madman, Mastermind or Messiah? (2021)
- The Semblant (2022)

Catch up with Bob at:

http://storiesandplays.com/ ,or
https://www.amazon.com/-/e/B00JC3SHIS
https://www.instagram.com/goodonebob/
https://twitter.com/GoodOneBob
https://www.facebook.com/groups/140516869352008/
https://www.facebook.com/Bob-Goodwin-Author-989354194414457/
https://www.tiktok.com/@bob_goodwin_author?lang=en

ACKNOWLEDGEMENTS

Some *Secret* codes are hidden in this book – can you find them?

Sara Endacott – Edit or Die – Editing and Writing Services.

My Sunshine Coast Literary Association (SCLA) friends for their inspiration, support and encouragement.

To my son, Luke for checking the proof.

To my wife, Jenny for her read and review.